CHALLENGING
DESTINY

CHALLENGING
DESTINY

The Untold Story of Anastasia

MARK JAY GANG

Challenging Destiny
The Untold Story of Anastasia

iUniverse books may be ordered through booksellers or by contacting:

iUniverse
1663 Liberty Drive
Bloomington, IN 47403
www.iuniverse.com
1-800-Authors (1-800-288-4677)

ISBN: 978-1-4917-4810-7 (sc)
ISBN: 978-1-4917-4806-0 (e)

Library of Congress Control Number: 2014917802

Printed in the United States of America.

iUniverse rev. date: 10/28/2014

To my family

FAMILY TREE

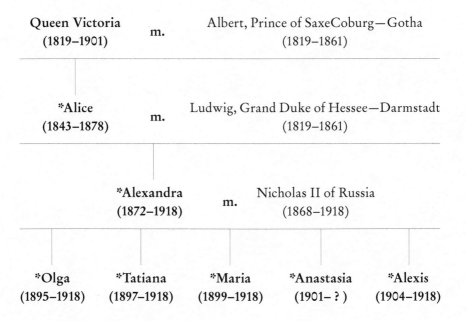

| Queen Victoria (1819–1901) | m. | Albert, Prince of SaxeCoburg—Gotha (1819–1861) |

*Alice (1843–1878)   m.   Ludwig, Grand Duke of Hessee—Darmstadt (1819–1861)

*Alexandra (1872–1918)   m.   Nicholas II of Russia (1868–1918)

| *Olga (1895–1918) | *Tatiana (1897–1918) | *Maria (1899–1918) | *Anastasia (1901– ?) | *Alexis (1904–1918) |

* Denotes Direct Descendent of Queen Victoria

PROLOGUE

The late nineteenth century was characterized by the triumph of imperialism. Industrial and technological advances were emerging. Germany and the United States were leading the way. London was the financial and shipping capital of the world. Imperial trade practices, escalating arms races, and numerous alliances began to threaten the tranquility of the globe. There was turmoil and upheaval on the horizon.

The economic and social issues of the poor were mounting, and radical political groups were forming and gathering momentum. Monarchies were being threatened, and the planet was at a place of tenuous transition. The years that would follow would be characterized by revolution, assassination, and a world war. Behind this backdrop of uncertainty was the Russian Empire, which was ruled by the Romanovs, Tsar Nicholas II and Alexandra. Their time to be eradicated had come, and with their deaths, an era would be gone forever.

The empress of the British Empire had a far-reaching effect upon the events that unfolded. Her own connection to the tsarina, along with her son's and grandson's relationships with the tsarina's family, provided the framework for a complicated and often intriguing series of events that had a profound effect upon the outcome of history.

There were a multitude of unanswered and conflicting questions and stories. The one most telling was that of Queen Victoria's great-granddaughter, a vivacious, outspoken, and determined child who grew to be as audacious an adult as she was a child. Although Queen Victoria never met this heir, Mother, the last tsarina of Russia, was one of her majesty's favorite grandchildren. It is not surprising how powerful and far reaching the queen's influence would be even years after her death. How this ultimately unfolded has been kept beneath a blanket of mystery; it has remained hidden from a world that has taken the mystique and created a labyrinth of speculation and doubt.

What has led us to question the scientists' conclusions about the Romanov family? Is it the body remains that were buried in a mineshaft one dark evening in 1918 that have been reexamined or removed from their original destination? Has vital evidence been destroyed during the process of discovery? Is it the scores of women who have asserted that the Romanovs are their family of origin? Is it the diaries that remain—or did the truth lie in what was destroyed?

Conjecture is the enemy of truth. Can we have any faith in the "scientific" findings of those who were responsible for such a horror-struck crime against humanity or others with special interests regarding the outcome? How does the truth override the tremendous odds against it?

Truth is but the unraveling of fact from fiction; it is mankind's attempt to unscramble reality from the feigned and is the essence of this historical novel about Anastasia, the grand duchess of Russia. Spanning a century fraught with despair, destruction, intrigue, espionage, and steamy, romantic entanglements, the story takes place on three continents. Royalty is portrayed in its most fragile state. Ultimately, the human spirit's unique ability to overcome obstacles forms the basis for this tale.

CHAPTER ONE

Decoding the Truth

David gazed outside the large picture window of his apartment as he propped his legs upon his wooden computer desk. His terrycloth robe hung loosely around his stalwart body. In the distance, he set his eyes on the colorful vista of the sunrise on the horizon through an array of evergreen trees that dotted the sparse yard. Several Canadian geese bobbed their heads into a placid lily pad-covered pond as they sounded their morning call. The peaceful collage of color captured his imagination.

Even though it had been decades since David's grandmother had departed this life, he felt an inner spiritual force that he could not explain driving him. He knew he had to commit his story of this great woman to writing. He stared at his computer, placed it on his lap, took a sip of freshly brewed coffee, and began his account of reflection and intrigue.

The untold story of this remarkable woman began some years before. It was an outgrowth of an innocent question from a precocious grandchild while he was playing at his grandmother's secluded apartment. From an early age, and through the years that followed, there were frequent visits where the two spent quality time alone together. These were special encounters. Love, admiration, and care characterized their relationship.

The purity and innocence of childhood have a way of cutting through to the truth. How the uncluttered mind assimilates the information is a wonder that only the child can know. An adult may become too influenced by experiences and memories, and the clarity could soon begin to fade.

On this particular day in May 1954, David and his mother drove to Brooklyn for a visit. He had awakened early that morning and rushed to the window of his house in Long Island, New York. It was a typical house, built during the post-World War II housing boom, on a tree-lined street with white and black shutters and a white picket fence. The lawn, which his father took much pride in maintaining, was perfectly manicured and appeared as a lush, green carpet. A birdhouse that David and his father had constructed out of pine was affixed to a branch of a massive maple tree that majestically stood just beyond David's bedroom window.

David heard the melody of the birds chirping outside his window as they welcomed the day. The neighbor's dog was barking, probably at a passing cat. A gentle breeze blew through his room. The Venetian blinds rocked against the window frame.

David felt a refreshing flurry of cool air against his face as it traveled through his curly, blond hair. He jumped out of bed, ran over to the window, and pulled the half-twisted cord that elevated the blind. He looked up toward the blue sky and the white clouds above. He felt a sense of excitement and delight. He knew that the day would be a special one. He was going to visit Grandma Sabrina in Brooklyn.

David's mother quietly entered his room. "David, up already?" she said. She walked over to him, wrapped her arms tightly around him, and gave him a loving kiss.

David melted into his mother's arms. He felt comforted by her nurturing embrace and soothing voice.

David's mother was in her late thirties. A robust and compassionate woman, she was dedicated to her husband, children, and family. Her anxious condition was usually masked by her outward personality and lively spirit. Her love for children was evident by her very approachable and playful manner around them. She knew how to satisfy their desires and usually placed their needs in front of her own. A very devoted child herself, she visited with Mother often and understood David's close relationship with his grandmother.

"It is time to get dressed," she said. His mother took an assortment of colorful clothes from the dresser drawer and gently placed them on his bed. "David, please get dressed. I will prepare your breakfast."

"Okay, Mom," he replied in an upbeat voice.

His mother smiled and returned downstairs to the sunlit kitchen.

David looked around his room, centering his attention on the toys in the corner. Speaking to one of his toy soldiers as if his words could be understood, he said, "I will get dressed quicker than you." Soon he was dressed and brushing his teeth in the bathroom. The tube of toothpaste fell off the vanity. David reached for it and managed to catch it with one hand. Some of the toothpaste squirted onto the tile floor. He glanced at his smiling face in the mirror. He thought for a moment. *I wonder what Grandma Sabrina has planned for me today?* He loved her and enjoyed visiting with her. Was she going to amuse him with a story? Teach him a new game? Take him for a special treat? Ice cream, perhaps?

"David, are you almost ready?" his mother called from the kitchen.

"Yes, Mom," he quickly responded. David hurled himself down the stairs. He glanced at the melted butter mixed with the warm maple syrup as it slid slowly down the pile of pancakes on his plate. "Pancakes! My favorite," he shouted with a look of sheer pleasure. He began to devour his breakfast.

"David, slow down. You will have plenty of time to play. Finish your milk and then go to the bathroom. You are doing a good job listening this morning. I am so proud of you!"

David and his mother walked out of the front door and down the paved sidewalk to the street. He stepped over the grooved lines in the pavement as they made their way to the street. His mother's first automobile was a black 1939 Plymouth with running boards.

David opened the slightly rusted door and positioned himself in the front seat where he would be able to watch his mother drive. David was amazed by how his mother was able to shift and maneuver the clutch with her foot. At times, it would stick, and the car would shake and buck back and forth. The car had a faint musty odor. The upholstery was worn and torn in several places, and the driver's window did not always open.

His mother hurried to the car and opened the squeaky door. She sat down, repositioned the mirror, turned the key in the ignition, pushed in the cigarette lighter, and shifted the car into first gear. They were on their way.

As they drove to Brooklyn, David enjoyed watching the people walking in all different directions. At times, the speed of the cars and their movements mesmerized him. David played a silent game by counting the cars and establishing sequences out of the numbers on the license plates.

His mother fumbled to open her large, black, leather pocketbook and reached for a pack of cigarettes. She took out a cigarette, placed it between her lips, and blindly searched for the lighter with one hand as the other held on to the steering wheel. As she removed the lighter, David noticed a red glow to its surface.

His mother inhaled, and the cigarette tip emitted a fiery glow. Thick smoke filled the car as his mother exhaled, and David began to cough. "Sorry, David. You can open the window," she said.

David studied a fly on the windshield as it carefully explored the surface. He opened his window, and the piercing creak startled the fly. It quickly ascended and flew out the window.

David looked at the line of cars waiting for the signal to change and announced that it would after he said the magic words. "Change light! Change!" he shouted.

The light turned green, and David beamed a broad smile in his mother's direction.

Several miles down the road, David and his mother came upon another traffic light. He shouted his magic words once again, but nothing happened. After trying several times, he went back to counting cars.

"Mom," David said proudly. "I am up to thirty-one."

"Terrific!" his mother replied.

David felt a sense of pride.

David's mother asked, "What do you think Grandma Sabrina has planned for you today?"

"I hope it is something really good," he replied.

"Grandma always has something special for you. David, I am going to stop at the florist to buy some flowers for Grandma. I think she will like that."

"Okay, Mom."

His mother parked in front of the flower shop. "David, do you want to go in with me or sit in the car?"

"I will go in with you, Mom."

"When we enter the shop, please do not touch anything without asking me first."

David looked down and replied in a soft voice, "Yes, Mom."

The florist shop was a bouquet of color and aroma. David loved to look at the assortment of flowers, each with its own unique mixture of textures. His curiosity piqued, David wanted to know the name of each assortment. He pointed to each and asked, "Mom, what is this flower called … and that one … and this?"

"That is an orchid, a carnation, a daffodil." She rattled off the names so fast that David had a hard time processing it all.

The clerk walked up to David's mother and said, "Good morning, Nicole. Can I assist you with anything this morning?"

"Yes, could you please give me one dozen roses?"

"What color would you like?" the clerk asked.

"David, what color do you think Grandma would like?"

David turned around and walked over to his mother. "I think she would like the yellow roses." He turned to the store clerk, stood tall and proud, and he announced in the deepest voice he could muster, "Yes, we would like the yellow roses." David followed the clerk to the counter. He stepped behind the counter to watch the man prepare the roses.

His mother said, "Is it all right for my son to go behind the counter with you?"

"Of course it is. So your name is David?" the clerk asked.

"Yes sir," David replied.

"I have a son by that name. How old are you?"

"I am six years old, and I am on my way to my grandmother's apartment in Brooklyn. What is your name?"

"My name is Harvey Ross."

"Where do you live?"

"I live in Queens, a place that is not too far from here."

"David, could you help me? Please place your finger on this ribbon so I can tie a bow."

David hesitated, glanced at his mother for acknowledgment, and then walked over to Mr. Ross. David placed his finger on the spot Mr. Ross pointed to.

"There we go. You are a great little helper and a very friendly boy. You have a nice son," he remarked to David's mother.

"Thank you, Mr. Ross. David, it is time to go."

"Good-bye, Mr. Ross, and thank you for letting me watch you," David said.

"Good-bye. Have a nice visit at your grandmother's. I hope she likes the roses."

David and his mother returned to the car. "Mom, that was fun."

His mother smiled at him and said, "Thank you for all of your help."

When they arrived at his grandmother's apartment, his mother said, "David, we are very lucky today. There is a parking place right in front of Grandmother's building."

It was an older, pre-World War I building. A black wrought-iron fence guarded its entrance. Large evergreen trees rose up beyond the top of the post caps. Two large cement planters were positioned on either side of the door. They were filled with green flowering succulents. A large black wrought-iron framed door with a brass handle guarded the entrance.

Once the car was parked and the engine turned off, David opened the door, took a breath of fresh air, and ran as fast as he could into the apartment building. He strained as he pushed open the entry door and bounded up the flight of stairs to his Grandmother Sabrina's apartment.

His mother followed him and was somewhat breathless as she approached the apartment. "David, you are too fast for me." She coughed as she lifted him up to reach the doorbell, which was positioned under the peephole high on the door.

After hearing the characteristic buzz, he heard his grandmother's footsteps in the distance.

"David, David, just a minute," she shouted from the other side of the door. First he heard the sound of the upper lock being opened and then the chain being unfastened. As he waited, his anticipation grew. Seconds felt like an eternity.

"David," his mother whispered in his ear, "give these to Grandma." She handed David the bouquet of freshly cut, yellow roses.

When his grandmother opened the door, David handed her the flowers and gave her a big hug. "There's my favorite little boy," she said as she stepped back to gaze at him. "Flowers? What a wonderful surprise!"

David and his grandmother spontaneously embraced. David gave her the biggest hug he could.

David's mother turned to David and said, "David, not too tight— you will break your grandmother's ribs."

His grandmother winked and smiled. "Nicole, I love David's hugs. There could never be enough of them. Do not worry; he is not hurting me. I am tough." She turned to David and smiled.

Grandma Sabrina was an attractive woman with short, silver-white curly hair. She wore a dark-gray dress and a handmade apron. Her shoes were large and cumbersome; they were prescribed for her painful bunions. A cheerful, relaxed, and pleasant woman, she always made those in her presence feel comfortable. She had a regal quality and carried herself with distinction. Sabrina loved her grandchildren and looked forward to their visits. She would lavish them with her most cherished gifts, love, and affection.

David smelled the sweet aromas he knew so well. His eyes lit up, knowing she had baked some of his favorite chocolate chip cookies.

Nicole asked, "How are you feeling today, Mom?"

Sabrina turned to David's mother and said, "Not bad."

"How is your sciatica? Are your legs and feet swollen?"

"A little better today. The weather is so beautiful today. There is not even a cloud in the sky. The low humidity really helps my condition."

Sabrina gazed at Nicole and said, "You are out of breath. Those cigarettes are not good for you. Perhaps you should stop smoking."

"Mom, don't worry about me. It was just the two flights of stairs. They seem to multiply with each passing year. How you manage them each day with your legs and feet is remarkable. Perhaps you should move."

Sabrina looked Nicole directly in her eyes and said, "My dear, I have been here a long time, and the exercise is good for me. At your age, the stairs should not be such a major ordeal for you. You should do something about your smoking. You do not want your health to be compromised."

"Yes, Mother. I guess you are right, but you know it is so hard for me to quit."

David, more concerned about the delightful aroma coming from the other room, interrupted his grandmother and mother's conversation and said, "I am hungry."

They walked to the kitchen. "I bet there is a little boy who would like to taste one of those cookies."

"Oh, yes, Grandma," David said.

"You can have one now and some more after your lunch."

"Would it be all right if I went out for a while? I should be back in an hour or two," David's mother asked.

"Of course. I would love to spend time alone with David." His grandmother winked at him. Her eyes glistened as she looked at him and smiled. "We will go outside for a little while and then come back and have lunch, and then there is a special dessert waiting for him."

"No, no," David's mother said. "We can go out for lunch."

"I already made something," his grandmother replied.

"All right. I will see you later," she said.

Sabrina turned to Nicole and said, "Have a good time. We will see you later."

"David, come give Mother a hug. I will be back soon."

David obligingly walked over to his mother. She knelt down, and he gave her a kiss and said, "Good-bye. See you later."

"Wait. We will go downstairs with you. I have a surprise for David," his grandmother said.

"What, Grandma? What is it? Tell me. Please tell me. Please."

His grandmother smiled. "You will see, David. If I tell you, it will not be a surprise."

As they walked down the stairs, David's grandmother moaned.

"Grandma, are you all right?" David asked.

"Are you sure you can take care of him today?" David's mother said. "Maybe you should stay in."

"I am fine. The fresh air and the walking will do me a world of good. Now off to do your chores, Nicole. David and I want to have some fun." She reached for his hand, and they walked down the street and around the corner.

"Wow," David exclaimed. "Look at that." He pointed to a carnival. In the distance, he could hear the music from the carousel. The Ferris wheel appeared to reach the sky. Multicolored canopies of the booths that housed various games spotted the area. It was a bounty of excitement and joy waiting to be explored.

"Yes, David. That is my surprise."

"Can I go on the rides?" David asked.

"Of course you can, but I need to buy some tickets first."

As they drew closer to the amusements, his grandmother said, "David, look. There is a penny toss. Let's try it. Here are some pennies. Try to get one in the plate."

David took the pennies and tossed them one at a time. "Grandma, look. That one went into the bowl," David shouted with delight.

A tall, muscular man with a green-and-red cap and a mustache exclaimed, "We have winner. Little boy, here is your prize." He handed David an orange glass bank that was shaped like an owl.

David was so proud of his accomplishment. He looked at his grandmother, and she gestured toward the man.

Oh yes, David thought. He turned back to the man, and with a beaming smile, he shouted, "Hey, mister. Thank you for the owl."

"David, that is so nice," his grandmother said.

"Here, Grandma. You take it. I won it for you."

"You are so thoughtful, but I would like you to have it. It is a bank, and you can save your coins. Saving money is a good thing." She gave David a hug as big as the one they shared when David first arrived.

She slid a shiny copper penny through the opening of the bank. David heard it drop into the bank as it made contact with the glass and looked up at his grandmother. "I will hold the owl while you go on the rides," she announced as she smiled at him.

David went on several rides, exclaiming his delight after each one.

"I bet you are ready for some of Grandma's chicken soup."

"Grandma, just one more ride."

"That will be fine, David. Which one?"

"The carousel. I want to go on the carousel. Will you please go with me, Grandma?"

"I am a little too old for the carousel."

"No, you are not. Please, Grandma, you can sit on one of the seats they have while I ride a horse. You can bring me luck when I reach for the brass ring."

Seeing the excitement in his eyes—and not wanting to disappoint him—she agreed.

David and his grandmother waited in line and then stepped up to the platform of the carousel. David extended his hand to help his grandmother climb up on the platform. He ran over to the horse he had eyed and waited for the attendant to assist him. His grandmother took a seat several feet away.

The music started. The carousel began to spin. They were playing a selection from Rachmaninoff.

His grandmother closed her eyes. As the carousel moved along, she became lost in her memories of days long gone when she and Jacob, her husband, spent sunny days and cool summer nights together at Coney Island. It was a wonderful time—a time she longed for and wished had never ended.

Life with Jacob had been so full of fun and laughter. They used to ride the train to the seaside amusement park. When they had arrived, they crossed the street, took off their shoes, and ran barefoot on the white, powdered sand to the water's edge. The water was crystal clear. It was bluer than any ocean or sky she had seen since she was a young child. It sparkled and shimmered in the sunlight. Sabrina became lost in her thoughts and began to drift further into the past.

"Let's go," Jacob called out to Sabrina they as made their way to the water's edge. "See if you can catch me."

"Come on, Jacob. You run like an old man," she teased.

"Old man? I am going to catch you," Jacob called out.

"No, you are not," Sabrina retorted.

Sabrina dropped a shoe and turned to pick it up.

"There, I caught you," Jacob yelled.

"Not fair. You do not play fair, Jacob." Sabrina pushed him, and he fell into the sand. Sabrina stood there and laughed.

Jacob reached over and grabbed her leg, pulling her down. They were both laughing as he crawled closer to her, bent over, and gave her a tender kiss.

Sabrina pushed him away. "In public, you do this?" She giggled. "This is no way to treat a woman with a child."

Jacob's face turned ashen. It was not that this news brought him anything but joy—only that it was so unexpected.

Before he could reply to this welcome pronouncement, Sabrina said, "I wanted to surprise you—and this is the perfect place."

"Oh, oh … I am so happy and thrilled," Jacob said. He drew her closer for another sweet kiss and an even tighter hug.

"Grandma? The ride is over. Did you fall asleep?"

"No, David. I was just resting my eyes and thinking about the time when your grandfather and I went to Coney Island."

"Grandma, I am hungry now. How about lunch and some of that delicious chicken soup you promised?"

David and his grandmother strolled hand-in-hand back to her apartment. It had been a wonderful morning for them both. David's insistence that she ride the carousel had given her untold pleasure, and she knew by the expression on his face that he loved spending the time with her.

"David, I just want to finish some things in the kitchen before lunch. Why don't you sit by the window in my bedroom?"

David enjoyed spending time in his grandmother's bedroom. The bedroom was filled with interesting objects that were yet to be discovered. Each visit was more of an adventure than the previous visit.

There was a large bed in the center of the room that protruded from the wall. Two dressers lined the other two walls. The fourth had a large picture window that overlooked a park. Behind one of the dressers, a mirror reflected a silver tray that rested on the dresser. It was this dresser that caught David's eye. On top were perfumes and a comb and brush set with silver handles. The handles reflected the light from the sun that shone brightly through the window. The mirror further enhanced their luminosity, but that would not be the object of David's interest on this particular day.

David was more intrigued with what was beneath the tray in the dresser. The drawer was partially opened, and he caught a glimpse. He wondered what treasures were within the enclosed space. Grabbing the brass handle, he slowly opened the wooden drawer and heard a rattling sound. Curious, he placed both of his hands inside. David felt the delicate weave of the fabrics as they passed over his small hands and up his arms.

David soon came in contact with something hard hidden beneath the garments. Whatever this was, it was purposefully placed in the back of the drawer. His curiosity compelled him to pull the item out of the drawer. David leaned on the drawer, and the drawer squeaked. Not realizing what was happening, David was frightened by the sudden noise and jumped back. He looked down at his hand. He was holding a brush made from something he did not recognize.

Why isn't this brush on the tray with the other brush and comb?

A voice calling him went unanswered, and when his grandmother entered the room, she was not noticed because David was so preoccupied. Eventually, as his grandmother came nearer, David was startled. His whole body trembled.

"I am sorry that I scared you, but what are you doing?"

"Just looking," David replied.

His grandmother had a sparkle to her eyes and a partial smile. "For anything in particular?"

Focused on what he was holding, David asked, "What is this brush made of?"

"That is ivory."

"What is that?" David asked.

"It is a very special material that can come from an elephant, hippopotamus, walrus, or mammoth. See this?" She pointed to her teeth.

"Yes, those are your teeth."

She smiled and said, "Elephants have tusks."

"Those are the long pointed objects on either side of their head," David responded.

"Yes, exactly." His grandmother smiled.

David said, "I saw elephants at the zoo."

"Those tusks are made of ivory. Things are made from ivory, like this brush."

"Why was it in the drawer and not on your dresser with the other?" Before his grandmother could answer, David asked how she received the ivory brush.

"It was a gift from my mother. She was born in Russia. It is very old and very, very precious to me."

"This is so soft," David remarked.

"Those are bristles," his grandmother explained.

David looked down. On the handle of the brush, he noticed something engraved. It look liked something he had seen on one of his toys. David thought for a moment and then remembered it was a mark he had seen on the shield his knight carried. David did not understand why it would be on a brush. "What is this?" Before this grandmother could answer, David said, "My toy knight has a shield with the same design. Why would there be one on the brush?"

David's grandmother quickly took the brush, placed it in her apron, and began to brush David's hair with the other brush.

"Did your mother make that mark on the handle?"

His grandmother closed the drawer. "That mark identifies who owns the brush. In the olden days, some families had what they called a crest that they placed on objects they owned to identify them as their own." She removed the ivory brush from David's sight; David would not see it again for many years.

Over time, David never forgot what he saw on the brush. Sometime he daydreamed about the engraving; later in life, he recognized the markings on a brush in a museum. It was the Royal Coat of Arms of the imperial family of Russia.

Long Island, New York 1976

David would have one other opportunity to ask his grandmother about the ivory brush. Many years had passed, and his grandmother's health was failing.

David's fragile grandmother looked at him and whispered, "My love, I am a very old woman now. I had a good life, and I am fortunate enough to have had the opportunity to be here today with you."

David cherished his grandmother. She had taken care of him after his mother died an untimely death. David's grandmother often told him that her own grandmother had died when she was young, and her great-grandmother had taken care of her. She was never very specific about Mother, Grandmother, or Great-grandmother, but she spoke of them with great reverence.

David always wanted to know about the ivory brush. He thought it would provide him with additional information about his grandmother's life. He wanted to know more about her family, especially after he had a high school homework assignment where he was instructed to construct a family tree. Although he knew his grandfather's family extremely well, he knew very little about his grandmother's family. She rarely spoke about them, and they never visited with her in his presence. There was also some doubt about her birthday. It was celebrated on a specific Jewish holiday that did not always correspond with the same date on the calendar.

"Grandma, many years ago I came upon your hairbrush, the one hidden in your drawer."

"Tell me more," she asked as she looked up into his eyes.

"Mother had left me in your care, and I was going through your drawer. I found a brush with an ivory handle."

Her eyes lit up. "David, it had a silver handle." Before David could speak, she winked at him. She then moaned.

"Grandmother, what is wrong?"

"David, it is the pain in my back and in my leg."

"Can I get you anything?"

"No, no, I will be all right."

"Grandmother?" David's eyes began to well up with tears; he understood how ill she really was.

"David, you must promise me that what I am about to share with you, you will keep in confidence. You will be the only one I have confided about the truth behind the ivory brush. Your grandfather and I did not even discuss its origin. It was best that no one knew because it might have placed the family in considerable peril. You will now be the keeper of the truth, the untold story of how it came to pass."

"Grandmother, what are you saying?" David thought the brush had been a gift to her. However, whenever she spoke of it, she became extremely emotional. Even after all these years, she was still quite attached to it. He wondered what it could be.

"I know that I can trust you, my darling. I know in my heart that you will never betray me. Who I am is not what is important; it is your heritage that is the key. No one can ever take that away from you. The truth is in my heart, and it must remain in your heart now. It is up to you to make the choice of what you want to do."

David was startled by his grandmother's words. He knew that she trusted him more than anyone else—more than even her own son.

"Yes, Grandmother. I can assure you that your secret will be held in my strictest confidence." He bent down and gave his grandmother a kiss. She smiled as she shed a tear.

"The brush was my mother's. It is the only thing I have left from her other than the memories." She began to cry.

"Grandmother, you are so distraught. Maybe we should not discuss the brush if it is going to upset you this way. I do not want to make you cry."

"It is not you," she replied. "It is just that I will soon be able to be with the family I have so badly missed over these many years. I feel I need to speak to you, and it would mean so much to me if you could be here for me."

"Grandma, you know I would do anything for you."

She looked into his eyes and said, "I know you would, and that is why I have chosen you."

He placed his hand over hers. A tear ran down his cheek as he softly said, "I am—and I always will be—here for you." David gazed into her eyes and was mesmerized by what she was saying. It was apparent to him that this was not going to be any ordinary account; it would have a major impact on his life.

CHAPTER TWO

England 1861

P rince Albert heard her footsteps approaching his room from down the hall. He could not mistake her characteristic walk as her steps echoed off the walls of the palace. Queen Victoria hurriedly entered the room. She looked at him. After twenty years of marriage, she still felt the tenderness, care, and affection she did the first time she met him. The queen's love and devotion for Albert was stronger than ever.

"You appear so upset, my dear Albert." The queen's eyes said it all. She was noticeably concerned and did not want him to be distressed. She knew his encounter with their eldest son was the source of his anguish. "You shouldn't worry about our son. He is just not going to listen to us."

Albert gazed back at her with a raised brow and reddened face, and in a stern voice he said, "But do you realize what a scandal to the monarchy will do, especially if it involves the heir to the throne?

"When I visited with him in Cambridge, the prince was set in his conviction to do as he pleases. Bertie's reckless desires foil any reasoning. He just does not want to consider his position in life. I am very disheartened," Albert stated. "His priorities have run afoul."

Victoria gazed out the window and then back at Albert. "Your health and well-being are most important to me. You must consider that," Victoria replied as her eyes met his.

He stared at her and observed how upset she was becoming. Albert, with great care not to offend her, said, "Yes, my dearest, but just as his grandfather before him, Bertie does what he wants. You have worked so hard and have given so much dignity back to the throne. I will not let him destroy that."

Always a pillar of strength, the queen was now vulnerable, and her eyes began to fill with tears. "I know how you feel, my love, but this has had a major impact on you and us."

Albert felt the tension in the room escalating. He knew better than to express his anger in front of his wife. Albert knew continuing this interaction would be counterproductive. "I need to go out," he said.

The queen immediately responded, "The weather is not supposed to be—"

"Enough with that. I need to go," Albert said.

"Albert, can't Mr. Brown assume your duties?"

Albert exclaimed, "These responsibilities are mine and mine alone." He had never spoken so harshly to his beloved. He was stressed, and his son was a burden he could no longer bear.

"Albert, do you realize that Bertie is causing us to argue? We cannot let him drive a wedge between us."

Albert loved and cared about Victoria. He knew that she felt partly responsible for their son's behavior, but it was getting late, and this conversation was likely to continue for some time. It was not the first time they had spoken about this matter, and it would not be the last. He knew that leaving the situation would be best at the time. It would give him the opportunity to reflect about Bertie and perhaps generate a favorable outcome.

Albert was tired and began to cough. He knew they had to do something soon. Their son must realize that he had an obligation to the monarchy and not himself. They had overindulged him, and he was stubborn and obstinate.

Albert stated, "I will try to speak to the prince again later in the week. I am sorry, my dear, but I cannot let you put yourself in the way of his wrath. He will fight you, and you deserve better. I must take my leave now or I will be late. We will speak later."

Albert was fatigued, he had not slept for several nights, and his cough was getting worse. Tired, emotionally distraught, and extremely frustrated, the prince consort left Windsor Castle for Sandhurst.

It was a damp, bitter cold, and dismal day when Albert left the queen. The wet mist blew against his face, and the wintry air pierced his fragile body. He was going to spend many hours outside. It would not prove to be a good decision. His clothes, specially chosen for him, would not shield him from the damp, penetrating elements of the day and would further contribute to the infection within his body.

The queen busied herself that day, but she often gazed out the window. She thought often about their last conversation. Her beloved Albert was so upset. She wished she could do something, but she knew it was futile to try to speak to Bertie. His need for sexual satisfaction was stronger than his will to refrain from wanton behavior.

The mist turned into a cold, steady, heavy rain that saturated the countryside. The wind howled, and its force swirled the copious beads of water against the panes of glass of the palace. The queen had a foreboding and was extremely anxious. She often worried about her husband, children, and affairs of state, but today was different. There was something that was not right. Albert looked so dreadful when he left. That sparkle and resilience so common to him were not there. She awaited his return, often pacing back and forth along the palace floors. Nothing and no one were able to comfort her.

The queen's official duties, the children, and attending to the staff did not inwardly distract her from her worst fears. When Albert arrived back at Windsor Castle, he was chilled and pale. His clothes were damp, and he was sweating profusely. It was difficult to ascertain how he was feeling because he rarely complained. He did not want to worry his cherished possession. He knew the queen had enough to worry about and did not want to be a source of her distress.

Victoria called for his staff and ordered a hot bath and tea.

Albert asked, "What are you doing? I am just fine. You need not worry. I will take care of it."

The queen said, "But Albert, you are chilled to the bone."

"I am going to my chambers and will return," Albert replied.

However, Albert did not return, and all would not be better. In fact, nothing from that point on would ever be the same.

In the days that followed, his condition did not improve. He developed a high fever. The congestion in his chest and his stomach pains became worse. The doctor was summoned. Albert had developed typhoid fever.

The queen kept a vigil at his bedside.

Several of the children tried to intervene, especially Princess Alice, but the queen would not leave his side.

"Mum," Alice said, "you need to rest. Let me sit here for a while so you can retire to your chambers."

The queen looked up at her daughter. "Thank you, Alice, but Albert needs me. I want to be at his side until he improves." Alice sat down beside Mother and requested that the staff bring tea and biscuits. She also attended to Father's needs, following the doctor's directives.

The queen turned when she heard Albert speak.

He said, "My dear, I am very tired, and I don't believe that I am getting better."

"Albert, you must not speak that way." She felt a sudden twinge to her heart and clutched her chest.

"My love, you need to believe that our years together have been the best for me," Albert replied.

"I know, Albert, but you will improve, and we will have many more years together. I need you. I order it."

"No, my dearest, that is something that is divine—and something that not even you can bring to pass," Albert exclaimed.

"I need you. I will not be able to go on." She reached out to him.

He placed his hand upon hers and said, "You will. The people need you. You have a duty to your country. You will be the best monarch England will ever have. Please have the children come to my chamber."

Albert's eyelids were heavy. He was exhausted. He nodded and fell asleep as his hand fell to the side of the bed. The queen could not believe what was happening. *It is just a nightmare. I will wake up, and he will be all right.* Tired and without many defenses left, she clasped her hands, placed them on his bed, lowered her head, and cried. That vibrant light within her was beginning to dim. She knew how sick he was. The end was near, and the children needed to be summoned. She raised her head, wiped her face with a white lace handkerchief, called to her staff, and impressed upon them the importance of having the children assemble immediately.

Albert's breathing was becoming increasingly more labored. The children had been there to visit, but Albert had requested an audience with all who were at the palace.

The children started to assemble in their father's room. Wooden chairs were placed alongside the bed. They were all present except Bertie. He had traveled from Cambridge through the night to be there. The queen was furious. "Where is the prince of Wales?" she demanded.

Alice, realizing the seriousness of the situation, stepped outside the room for a moment and spoke to one of the staff. He hurried off, and shortly thereafter, Bertie entered the room slowly, buttoning his shirt.

Albert opened his eyes. The faintly lit room did not distract from his fragile state. His face was thin and pale, and his eyes were sunken deep into their sockets. His lips were dry, and there were compresses on his forehead.

The queen stared at him, holding his thin, fragile, limp hand. Her eyes were tearing, and an occasional teardrop made its way down onto her dress.

Alice positioned herself next to Mother, but her presence did not appear to be noticed by the distraught sovereign.

Albert said, "My children, thank you all for coming so quickly. I am not doing too well, but I wanted to share with you some of my strong feelings about the monarchy." Albert began to cough, and the nurse offered some water.

The children were all young adults, and they were stunned at their father's choice of words.

"Albert, please conserve your energy," Victoria said.

Albert looked into the eyes of his beloved wife and continued in a soft voice that was intermittently interrupted by a dry cough. He said, "You all have been born into this world and have a responsibility to the monarchy and one another. In spite of the differences amongst one another, you must always think of preserving the monarchy for all generations that follow. It is a sacred duty. Do not let your self-interests take precedence over what is best for your country. Some of you have married—others will marry and will have other obligations—but you must never forget your allegiance to England. It is your country of birth. The people of England need you. You did not choose this for yourself; it has been destined for you."

The sick prince coughed. He looked at Victoria, and his eyes closed. His head turned to the side, and a drop of blood trickled down the side of his mouth onto the white, silk linens.

The doctor took his hand and searched for his pulse. He looked at the queen and said, "I am deeply sorry."

The children looked at their mother.

The queen crossed her heart with her hand and said, "My dearest Albert, may you rest in peace." She reached down and kissed him.

Victoria placed her head on his chest and cried inconsolably.

Alice placed her arm around her grief-stricken mother's shoulders.

The queen's beloved prince was gone. A part of her had died with him. She would never be the same. The queen would wear black for the rest of her long life.

CHAPTER THREE

Her Royal Highness

England, 1878

The fog blanketed the countryside with its dense mist. Alix of Hesse, the granddaughter of Queen Victoria and the daughter of Alice, could hardly see beyond the large oak tree outside the window of her palace bedroom.

In the distance, the church bell rang, and its discordant sound echoed through the passageways of the palace. She knew it would only be a few moments before Grandmamma, the queen, would enter her chambers. Her Royal Highness always made the rounds of the children's quarters before breakfast.

Mornings were not Alix's favorite time. The chill in the air penetrated her body and sent a shiver down her spine. At the queen's direct order, the footmen had not replenished the firewood in the fireplaces. Grandmamma felt that the brisk morning air awakened them; they would be ready for her early morning tour of duty, as Alix referred to it. It was easy for Alix to recognize her footsteps. The stone floors clamored and bellowed beneath her Grandmamma's boots as she walked through the palace halls.

As her pace quickened, there was a flurry of movement. It had been a long time since the queen felt so energized, and her gait told the waiting children so. For a number of years following Prince Albert's death, Victoria had ruled in virtual seclusion. Of late, however, there were signs that she was beginning to move past her self-imposed social exile. It was time to move forward—time to give back to her people and reestablish her role as the strong and imperative queen of England she had once been. Her blood was well represented across Europe. Her children married well, and her strength as a sovereign was a necessary condition if her dominance as a supreme ruler was to continue. Much time had been lost during her lengthy period of mourning; although it was impossible to recapture those lost years, she had much to do moving forward.

Alice, the second daughter of Queen Victoria, was the duchess of Hesse. Mourning the death of her own son, the duchess sent several of her children to visit their grandmother in England. Alix's visit would be short, but she was determined to make the most of it—even if it meant being subjected to wee-hour visits that made her tremble from the cold.

"Alix, are we up and ready?" the queen asked as she hurried into the room. A surge of air followed her. The petticoats beneath her full-skirted black dress made a loud rustling sound that was unmistakable as she came toward Alix.

Alix always wondered why a few more hours of sleep were not permissible, but she dared not challenge her grandmother. No one ever tried to. The queen was a formidable figure; she ruled her household like she ruled her country. Alix knew she was a favored grandchild, perhaps because her grandmother saw much of herself in Alix.

Grandmamma was forthright and outspoken. She demanded honesty and believed in hard work. She expected no less from others than she was willing to give of herself.

"Yes, Mum, I am," Alix declared with a curtsy.

"Well, then, let's begin our day with a smile," Victoria commanded.

"Yes, Mum," Alix repeated with a broad smile and another curtsy.

Since Albert's passing, any form of gaiety or laughter was out of character for Victoria.

Alix, although enormously surprised, was especially pleased to see the grandmother she loved shed her melancholy exterior. The queen's transformation was uplifting, and Alix was anxious to write Mother, the duchess, to alert her to the fact that the once again and as before, Queen Victoria was both willing and able to return to her duties as Head of State.

Victoria sat beside Alix on the sofa and tapped her palm on the pillow between them. "Now, Alix, tell your grandmamma what is your most favorite thing to do?"

"Grandmamma, I like to read."

"That's my girl. Just like your mother. Knowledge is strength. It makes you view the world from many dimensions." The queen smiled and looked into her granddaughter's eyes. "You look so much like your mother. I can remember as though it were yesterday when your grandfather played with your mother at Osborne. Those were such joyful days." The queen's voice began to fade as tears again welled in her eyes.

Alix glanced at her and, feeling her grandmother's despair, moved a little closer to her. However, within moments, the queen caught herself and abruptly rose from the sofa, ordering Alix to be down to breakfast in ten minutes. "I expect your lessons to be impressive today!"

Ever dutiful and anxious to please, Alix finished getting ready and was seated at the breakfast table several minutes prior to her Grandmamma's appointed time, something that did not go unnoticed.

"We will visit London this weekend. There are several important events that I have neglected and where our appearance is not only warranted but much desired. Since you are always cold, I will have one of the handmaidens pack an extra sweater for our travel," the queen said sarcastically. "We will have time to talk again after my morning ride."

Queen Victoria was an equestrian. With her beloved Albert, she had ridden every morning and was fond of the ride and the private time it offered. This unexpected return to riding brought a floodgate of fond memories the queen could savor as she jostled along the dirt paths.

The duchess had already informed her daughter, Alix, that Prince Albert was "a most likeable fellow." Although his non-English lineage initially presented a problem for some of the British subjects, Victoria was highly dependent upon him. Queen Victoria adored Albert. His children revered him as well. Alix never knew her grandfather. He had died before she was born.

New Palace in Darmstadt, part of the German Empire, 1878

"How was your trip to England, Alix?" the duchess of Hesse asked. "I am so proud of you. Traveling all that way at so young an age is, indeed, something to feel pleased about."

Before Alix could utter a word, the duchess said, "She can be so hard on you children, but from the look on your face, it is obvious that you recognize that my mother only has your best interests at heart."

Even my mom is under the queen's control, Alix thought. *Here we are so far away from her homeland because Grandmamma thought it best for her daughter to marry royalty for the alliances and the preservation of the bloodline.* Alix was increasingly aware that Father seldom embraced Mother. She often wondered if her parents were in love the way she was certain Victoria and Albert had been. *Is it just a marriage of convenience?*

Alix knew Mother missed her homeland. The duchess showed signs that she was growing tired of the duke. Their growing dislike for one another was apparent to all who knew them. *They were different in so many ways,* Alix thought.

"Why must my mother's deepest desires always take a backseat to the duties we must carry on as a part of the monarchy?" the duchess asked.

Alix knew her grandparents were so fortunate. The love they shared was still burning brightly in the queen's heart even after his death so many years before. *Will my children have the same good fortune as Grandmother and Grandfather, or will duty to their station in life take precedence over passion and desire?*

Not long after Alix's return from England, the duchess warned of a diphtheria epidemic. Many people had succumbed to the dreaded malady. While the duchess would have preferred to cloister her offspring in the safety of England, the duke was adamant about wanting his children with him, and his demands could not be ignored. It was not practical for Alix and her siblings to return to the English countryside anyway, having just returned home.

The duchess explained to Alix that she would not be able to leave the royal compound or invite guests to play. All contact with anyone outside the immediate family was strictly forbidden. Furthermore, it did not go unnoticed that Mary, Alix's sister, appeared paler and fatigued earlier in the day.

"Your father knows that I cared for your grandfather, and if sickness strikes us, he is keenly aware that I will be able to assist in caring for the ill if need be."

"Grandmamma will be furious with my father," Alix said. "There are more than enough people we could summon to care for the family. You are too precious to us to sacrifice your own health and safety."

The duchess was shocked that Alix would have been so presumptuous as to say anything that defiant in her presence.

Alix, on the other hand, was not intimidated by Mother's rebuke and thought it more than ridiculous for her to have been allowed to return to an epidemic-ridden country when there had been the opportunity for Alix and her siblings to remain in the sheltered bosom of England. What could father have been thinking?

The duchess looked at her daughter and then placed her hand on Alix's hand. "You should not be cross with him. He loves you and thought your place was here rather than away in England," Mother said in a more tender tone than Alix had expected.

Alix looked away and focused her attention on a bird outside on the windowsill. Mother stood up, walked slowly to the door, glanced at her daughter, smiled, and left the room.

It was not long before diphtheria descended upon the royal house; many within the family became ill, and Mary was among those most affected.

Alix was frightened for her sister. She appeared so ill. Her fever raged, and despite the duchess's unyielding efforts, Mary succumbed to the plague that ravished the royals and other subjects throughout the land. Not long after Mary's demise, Mother became gravely ill.

Alix's worst fears were soon realized when Mother died. As if in a twist of fate, the duchess died on the anniversary of Grandfather's death.

At the moment of her passing Alice called out Albert's name as if responding to his summoning. Like Victoria, Alix was bereaved; she wept for weeks. She was angry, and her grief drained her youthful energy. Alix would spend many hours alone in the seclusion of her room. She had no one to comfort her and blamed Father for not allowing his children to remain in England. Her feelings of emptiness and abandonment were almost too much for her to bear.

The duke was saddened by his loss, and in private, he did lament her death.

Alix heard him one night as she passed his room. In some ways, Alix felt fortunate to be at home so she could be at Mother's side to comfort her as best she could when the sickness destroyed her mind and body. Mother was a good woman who came to the aid of many. Alix could only wonder why the Lord had chosen to take her from their midst. *She must have been needed elsewhere,* Alix thought.

The duke was incapable of consoling his children. It was too much to endure, but Grandmamma took the news the hardest. Alix heard that the queen, once again, withdrew to her quarters, adamantly refusing to reply to correspondence—even messages sent from them. Alix did not think Grandmamma Victoria would ever truly recover from this most recent loss—and she didn't.

Growing up was never the same. Alix missed Mother. During the brief time Alix and the duchess shared, the duchess exuded special warmth, understanding, and affection that could not be replaced. The duchess would no longer be there to comfort Alix; she would not be there to explain things Alix had yet to experience. Without the nurturing love and guidance of her beloved mother, the world would remain a scary place. Alix thought of Mother daily until her own death.

In her sadness and grief, Alix overlooked the fact that she had gained something from Mother's death. Alix developed empathy. She understood how Grandmamma Victoria felt after losing her beloved Prince Albert. While losing one's spouse and losing a parent are two very different matters of the heart, Alix grew up in ways she did not even recognize.

Alix remained deeply depressed, at times despondent. Few could raise her spirits. She would not be fortunate enough to have a man enter her life until years later. Alix had heard of John Brown and his relationship with the queen after Albert's death, but Alix had never met him.

The queen had a special friendship with this man, and he revered her. People were aware of her affection for Mr. Brown, but it was mostly unspoken. No one would dare question the queen's relationship. Alix was aware that Uncle Bertie, the Prince of Wales, detested him.

Grandmamma was Alix's savior. Alix visited with her, and the queen was always so welcoming. It lifted Alix's spirits and made her feel good. The queen became a second mother to her. They laughed, told each other stories, and read poems. They both loved the outdoors; they would sit by the gardens peacefully.

One day, Alix slipped and fell into a pond filled with lily pads. The queen's guard, without hesitation, entered the pond to retrieve Alix, but he too slipped and fell in. When a frog jumped on his head, the queen laughed so hard she began to cry. Alix was thankful it was a warm day as she sat in the pond, awaiting her gallant rescue.

In 1887, Grandmamma celebrated her Golden Jubilee. The queen had ruled her subjects for fifty years. It was an exciting time. The British people came out in thousands to honor Queen Victoria. Alix was bursting with pride. She had come to love Victoria as much as she had loved Mother, and their special relationship served them both well.

Victoria had regained the trust of her subjects. She was a strong, respected, and much-loved monarch. Alix knew how proud Mother would have been to witness the adulation being bestowed upon the queen. Alice would have joyously participated in the celebrations that abounded to mark the height of Queen Victoria's greatness. Alix loved her, but as destiny would have it, everything would change.

Alix was older than was customary for her station in life when she married. She had first met Tsarevich Nicholas (Nicky) in 1884. Grandmamma Victoria and the English Court preferred Alix to have wed her first cousin, Eddy, Prince Albert Victor, Duke of Clarence, the son of Prince Edward (Bertie), Prince of Wales.

As fate would have it, Alix despised Cousin Eddy, thinking him a bit of a buffoon and mentally deranged. She knew she would never be happy. Alix did not want to be pressured into an arranged marriage with someone she did not love—especially Uncle Bertie's son. She had witnessed her parents' marriage and did not want to enter into a relationship based on duty alone.

Long Island, 1974

"David, you look at me so strangely. In those days, it was not unusual for people to marry first cousins."

David turned to his grandmother, and although he was puzzled by the revelation, he continued to listen to her untold tale.

England 1889

The queen wanted her favorite granddaughter near her. She realized that Eddy was rather unique and that his behavior was unusual for an adult, especially one who was in direct line to the throne. He was quite eccentric, and at times, he was outright inappropriate and bizarre.

Alix felt that she would not be happy with him, but she would never disobey a direct order from her grandmother. Alix would have to convince her grandmother about how she felt. Alix knew in her heart that her grandmother would want the best for her. There would be other women at court who would jump at the opportunity to be married to a man who someday would be king—even if he were a little strange.

After Alix met Nicky, she knew she would not desire anyone else but him. This handsome soft-spoken man was smitten with Alix. A warm sensation permeated her body whenever Alix came into contact with or thought about him. She had never felt that way about any other man. She was thankful that her grandmamma let her speak her mind.

At first, Alix thought the queen would command her to marry Eddy. However, when she confided that she had met the man of her dreams, the queen knew there would be no changing her mind. Alix believed her grandmother knew Alix's heart would always be in Russia—and not in England. The queen loved Alix, and although she wanted her granddaughter nearby, she yielded to her request.

Alix never understood why her grandmother did not pressure her to marry Eddy's brother. There was a remarkable resemblance between George and Nicholas, and they were cousins. Perhaps Grandmamma realized that Alix had fallen deeply in love with Nicholas and wanted her granddaughter to be as happy with her husband as the queen was with hers. Anyway, politically, Russia would make a good ally for England.

Alix was in major conflict for a number of years because of the religious difference. In addition, the empress of Russia was against their marriage. Several influential people tried unsuccessfully to match Nicholas with other women. All attempts failed. Being a spiritual woman, Alix had to choose between religious beliefs and the man she loved. She thought of what her grandpapa would have done, but she decided to become engaged in 1894. She found out later that her grandmother respected Alix for being forthright with her, and there were only a few who could do that successfully. The queen told Alix in confidence that the love she sensed from Alix was akin to what she had felt for Albert.

It was bittersweet for Alix to leave her homeland to be with the man she loved. Russia was a much different country. She would soon be Alexandra Feodorovna, the empress consort of Russia. The queen of England now had a presence in Russia.

Alexandra would miss her beloved grandmother. She had learned so much from her and depended on her no-nonsense approach to solving problems. Alexandra's official duties would not allow many visits to England.

Victoria would write regularly, and Alexandra looked forward to her correspondence. Many of those letters would be destroyed prior to the imperial family being placed on house arrest. Alexandra's last official visit to England was in 1896.

Nicholas and Alexandra returned to England with their firstborn to visit the queen at Balmoral in the Scottish Highlands. They were well received. Many English people turned out to welcome the imperial couple and their child, Olga. A sea of people greeted them. It would be her last visit with the queen, and when Alexandra said good-bye to her beloved grandmamma, that would be the last time she would see her. They embraced, and each shed a tear. The queen, a wise and insightful woman, must have had a sense of what was yet to come!

Russia was in marked contrast from what Alexandra was used to in England. Alexandra was now tsarina to a group of people who, for the most part, were impoverished. There were a few associated with the court who were wealthy, but the majority of people were haplessly poor and destitute.

Her husband had some empathy for his subjects. Nicholas was far removed from the general population growing up. He had private tutors and was not allowed to associate with commoners. His father, the emperor, also kept him uninvolved with political intrigue.

Nicholas knew the hatred some had for his family. He was present during the brutal assassination of his grandfather. Nicholas felt it was important to keep the military close to him.

Alexandra believed his association with the military helped him stay somewhat in touch, but the growing resentment from the poor was beyond her husband's grasp.

Nicholas knew little about how to lead his country when his father died prematurely. Nicholas was thrust into the position of emperor not too long after his marriage to Alexandra, and she was held in contempt because of her German heritage.

England 1898

"What does the queen want that she summoned me to her chambers? Isn't it time? Haven't we all waited long enough?" Bertie mumbled as he approached his mother's chambers.

Victoria was seated near the window. The sunlight beamed in, and every wrinkle and blemish on her face was visible. She wore her usual black garments. Her body was frail, and the once robust voice was now moderately audible. However, she still maintained her presence and control.

The door guard announced, "Your Majesty, Edward the Prince of Wales is here to see you."

"See him in. I was expecting him. Thank you for joining me, Bertie. Your promptness is appreciated."

He heard the sarcasm in her voice but chose not to respond.

Edward thought, *Bertie can't get out of his way and is usually late. He has really been a disappointment and perhaps is why our mom has not stepped down to let him rule.*

Bertie wondered if the queen was going to make the announcement that she was giving up the crown.

"There is something that I wish to share with you."

"Your Majesty?" The footman entered the room once again.

Prince Edward thought, *What now?*

"Prince George is here to see you."

My son? What could she want with him? Is she going to bypass me in favor of him?

"Oh, yes, send him in. Guard, we are not to be disturbed until I call," Queen Victoria ordered.

"Yes, Your Majesty," the guard replied.

George was also wondering what was happening. It was rare that his grandmother summoned both of them without the rest of the family.

"Enter, George. It is always nice to see you. I hope I did not interrupt your day."

"No, Mum," the prince commented. "The sun shines so bright; shall I pull the drape?"

"No, George, the warmth feels good. It limbers this aging body. I appreciate your concern. You have both been called because there is a delicate matter that I wish to share with you. It has to do with my granddaughter, Alexandra, and her family."

Bertie was puzzled by the queen's interest with his cousin. *Aren't there enough issues in our own empire to deal with at this time?* He had not fully resolved the issue with his cousin's desire to forego marrying his son in favor of a Russian! As fate would have it, Eddy succumbed to double pneumonia and died an untimely death. Bertie was also annoyed with the love his mother lavished on this granddaughter and had often thought it was at his expense.

"Edward, listen carefully," she stated.

She is addressing me so formally and always knew when my mind started to wonder, Bertie thought.

"I am not going to live forever, but I have a wish and am commanding both of you to follow through with it."

"Yes, Mum," George replied.

"My granddaughter and her family are going to be in imminent danger. There is growing discontent with the Romanovs by the people."

"But, Mum," Edward exclaimed.

"Edward, do not speak until I am finished. Please, no interruptions. Do you understand?"

"Yes, Mum," Edward stated.

It was becoming a lot clearer to George why he was asked to the meeting. His father and grandmother were not compatible. Furthermore, she could not depend on him. He was aware of his father's indiscretions and Bertie's relationship with his father. George suspected that his grandmother blamed her disobedient son for Albert's untimely death. The animosity between them was evident to everyone close to the court.

"There are only a trusted few who know what I am about to share with you. I have placed a letter with my other private papers with their names on it. These are the only people you are to trust. No one else under any circumstances."

He replied, "Is Sir—"

"Edward, no! He is not on the list, and you are not to share anything with him."

Edward had a special affection for this man, and his mother knew it would be a risk to tell Edward. However, she had no choice, especially if Edward would be wearing the crown when action had to be taken.

"The people of Russia despise my granddaughter. The unrest among the people grows by the day. There is talk in some circles that there may be another assassination of the monarch. That is how those barbarians handle their discontent. I want you to follow my command and see to it that my granddaughter and her children leave the country safely. I am certain that will be very difficult because Alexandra will probably not leave her husband. I am trying to convince the powers to be to at least let the children leave." The queen glanced at her son and grandson. "You must take great caution because there are undercover agents throughout the world. If it is ever discovered that I was behind this plan, it could have major detrimental effects on the British Empire and our alliances around the world."

A scowl appeared on Edward's face. "Edward, I am not asking whether or not you agree with the plan. I am directly commanding you to follow my orders. I want your word as an heir to the throne."

"Yes, Mum," he softly said, looking out the window.

"That is not very convincing," she responded. She was beginning to become annoyed by his insolence.

Edward, realizing her anger and the dire consequences, looked at her and said, "I give you my solemn word as direct heir to the throne and will take an oath to obey my sovereign, the Royal Empress of the British Empire."

George repeated what his father had said.

"Thank you, gentlemen. Our business here has concluded. You are excused." The queen turned away from the princes and faced the window as they walked out the door.

Russia, 1901

Alexandra sat at her desk and wrote in her diary: *I love Nicholas with all my heart. He is so good to me and passionate. Everything I could imagine and more.*

She heard something and looked up. The wind blew gently through the window and rustled the drapes. The full moon filled the chambers with light.

Nicholas appeared in front of her. He was small in stature but muscular. His military training helped keep him fit. Alexandra felt a tinge of excitement travel down her body as she gazed at him. He was aroused. Alexandra delighted in observing his naked body.

Nicholas lay down beside her. At first, he gently caressed her body with his warm hands. Her breasts swelled with anticipation of what was to come. His warm, moist tongue encircled her nipples, and his lips traveled down her body. It was as though he knew each sensual part.

She was now excited, moist, and she wanted him. Her body quivered as he entered her. The motion of his body against hers brought her to ecstasy. As he repeatedly thrust down on her, Alexandra felt his enlarged phallus deep inside of her. She felt progressive waves of building rapture. *More. Good. That is perfect.* Alexandra was breathing heavily.

The strength of his body and the gentleness of his touch created a perfect blend that excited her even more than she could fantasize. Their bodies were intertwined as one, and where one ended and the other began could not be discerned.

"Now. Oh please now," she yelled.

Soon he began to fill her, and she felt rapid, intense contractions as the molten lava flowed within her. Their excitement and pleasure were one, and they remained together, motionless throughout the night.

Nine months later, Anastasia was born. However, it was bittersweet for Alexandra. Her pregnancy prevented her from traveling to England to be at her beloved grandmamma's funeral. With the death of Queen Victoria, Alexandra had no other older authority figure to turn to for advice. How she missed her. *Our children will never know her,* she thought. She cried a torrent of tears and was in despair. What a loss for England and the British Empire.

Alexandra hoped she would be able to give the same love and affection to her own children. She hugged Anastasia and said, "Your great-grandmother would have been so proud to hold you." She began to weep.

Anastasia looked up at Mother and smiled.

Alexandra gazed down at her daughter and said, "Thank you, Grandmother. I know you are here with us."

The long-awaited son and heir to the throne would not be born for several years. However, a dreaded blood disease would curse his birth. Ultimately, his medical affliction would lead to major hardships for the Romanov family.

Anastasia was a special child. She entered the world in a peaceful manner, and the sun always seemed to shine whenever Anastasia was around. She resembled Mother, but her disposition was more like her great-grandmother, Queen Victoria. Anastasia was as much at home with the servants as she was with the people of the court. Anastasia was loved by all, and she was also very much like her grandmother, Alice, the Grand Duchess of Hesse.

Anastasia's great-grandmamma would never know her, but Victoria's influence would be felt due to her carefully orchestrated plan prior to her death. Only the letter written in the queen's hand would identify those who would ultimately know Anastasia's fate.

The unrest in Russia was increasing by the day. The tsar believed he was immune from what he considered a "select few." If it were not for a trusted friend who knew one of the servants, Alexandra would have never known the tenuous situation that was prevailing in Russia.

The people never particularly cared for Alexandra. As distrust for Kaiser Wilhelm of Germany grew, so did the Russian people's mistrust of the tsarina. There was even talk that Alexandra was a spy. No matter what she tried to do, it was never acknowledged. The forces were against her and the family. Her subjects did not know that Alexandra was a strong advocate for most of the people.

Anastasia wanted to speak to Mother and was told that she was still in her chambers. She walked into her bedroom and saw Mother in bed. "Mama, are you in pain?" She slowly approached Mother's bed and sat next to her.

"Yes, Anastasia. My leg is throbbing today. I will have to stay in bed."

Anastasia looked at Mother and placed her warm hand on hers. "Mama, it will get better. Can I get you anything to make you feel better?"

"No thank you, Anastasia, but that was a kind thought. Why don't you go out and play with the others?"

"I would like to spend some time with you. I will go to my room to find a book to read to you."

"That won't be necessary, Anastasia."

"But I really want to, Mother." Anastasia stood up and walked quickly to her room. She was worried because Mother had been in substantial discomfort for some time. Anastasia could not understand why Mother had to suffer and why the doctors could not find a remedy. Anastasia looked through her books and found what she thought be the most perfect one, a book of children's poems. She ran to Mother's room, but one of the servants stopped her.

The servant whispered, "She is sleeping."

Feeling disappointed, but knowing that sleep would be good for Mother, Anastasia walked back to her room. She sat down on her bed, reached under her pillow, and pulled out her diary. She opened it and began to write:

> *My dearest mother is suffering this morning. How I hate to see her in so much pain. Her face was so pale, and she is unable to do anything. Father is away and cannot be here to help her. I tried to read to her, but she fell asleep. I will wait until later and then return. I guess I will go and find the others and play. Until later ...*

Her brother was in his room, playing with his toy soldiers. "Alexei, where are our sisters?"

"They are doing their lessons."

Anastasia was getting bored. "Let's go to the kitchen to see if John is there."

"You know that Papa does not want us to play with the servants. We will get in trouble."

"He is not here, and Mother is sleeping anyway. You are just afraid."

"I am not scared," he yelled, picking up a pillow and throwing it at her. "You are stupid. Get out of my room."

Anastasia picked up the pillow and threw it back at him. "Take that!"

Alexei ducked, and the pillow hit a lamp, causing it to go crashing to the floor.

"Now see what you have done," he said, raising his voice and approaching Anastasia.

Anastasia was angry; however, she knew it would be a grave mistake to have a physical altercation with her brother. She could seriously hurt him, especially with his delicate blood disorder. Anastasia turned and ran out of his room. Before Alexei could follow her, one of the servants entered the room and asked what had happened.

Anastasia ran down the corridor and headed to the kitchen. John was sitting on a stool and helping his mother peel potatoes.

They both looked up, and John's mother exclaimed, "Anastasia, it is nice to see you today, but you know you are not supposed to be down here."

Anastasia replied, "I am bored and want to play with someone."

"John, take off your apron and go with Anastasia. I am warning both of you not to get into trouble."

Anastasia and John laughed as they ran down the steps to the courtyard. Anastasia saw her sisters in the distance. Olga looked at Anastasia, but Anastasia chose to ignore her since her older sister would be displeased by her choice of playmates.

John and Anastasia played for hours. John knew he needed to assist his mother in the kitchen and should return to the palace. Anastasia wanted to return to Mother to check on her condition.

That evening, the full moon lit Anastasia's bedroom, and she had difficulty falling asleep. She was extremely restless, especially after what she heard the guard say that afternoon.

The wind blew the curtains and knocked her hairbrush off of her dresser. Anastasia looked over to her window and saw her curtains moving. She threw her blankets off and slowly approached the window. Yawning, she closed the window and returned to bed.

It was not long before her personal servant heard Anastasia screaming and rushed into her room.

Anastasia was in a fitful sleep and shouting, "No. Don't. Please stop!"

The woman sat beside her and shook Anastasia.

Anastasia opened her eyes and screamed again.

Alexei, hearing the commotion, ran into his sister's room, but there was no consoling her. She yelled out for Mother.

Alexei ran to his mother's room.

"What is wrong, Alexei?" she asked.

"Mama, Anastasia had a bad dream and is crying and calling for you. Please come. I am frightened."

Alexandra usually let the servants deal with such matters, but she was concerned about Alexei's reaction and the effect it could have on his delicate condition. She was in considerable pain, but she managed to stand and walk to Anastasia's room.

Anastasia looked up and shouted, "Mama! Mama! Something terrible has happened."

"It will be all right, Anastasia. I am here now. What happened, my *malenkaya*?" Alexandra walked Anastasia back to her bed and sat down next to her. She excused the servant and motioned for Alexei to return to his room. "I will be in soon, son."

Alexei returned to his room.

Anastasia was trembling. Mother gave her a hug and said, "It will be all right. It will be all right."

"No, Mama," Anastasia said. "It is not going to be all right. These men came."

"And?" Mother said, continuing to hug her.

"They took us to this room, all of us. They had guns. Oh no, Mama. I was so frightened," Anastasia was crying.

"It will be all right. You were dreaming," Mother said.

"I am so terrified. I do not want anything to happen to us."

"Anastasia, I am here. You are in the palace. We are safe, and I will not let anything happen to you. Lie down and let me rub your back."

Anastasia placed her head on her pillow.

Mother leaned over, kissed Anastasia's forehead, and began to rub her back. "You had a rough night, but everything will be all right now." Alexandra started to hum.

Anastasia closed her eyes and fell into a deep and peaceful sleep.

Alexandra sat with her daughter for a while and then quietly went to Alexei's room. He had fallen to sleep. Alexandra lay down next to him.

Alexandra then entered the room and turned to Nicholas.

Nicholas realized that she was upset. "Alexandra," he said, "what is wrong?"

"The children," she said.

"What about the children?" he asked.

"Anastasia just had a very disturbing dream. I believe it was from an incident that happened today. Anastasia overheard one of the guards speaking to one of the maids. He said that our days are numbered—and that soon there will be no imperial family," Alexandra explained.

Nicholas looked up. "That is ridiculous. Who was that guard? I will have him removed."

Alexandra looked at her husband and replied, "You can remove him or even shoot him, but it does not take the threat to you and your family away. Is the monarchy more important to you than we are, Nicky? I am scared and fear what they are going to do to us. When you leave for the front, there is no one here to protect us. You are well aware that my presence in court is just tolerated. If it were up to your family and the people, they would have had me removed long ago."

Nicholas was shocked by his wife's reaction. "Alexandra, my love, no one is going to hurt you or the children. My family cares about you and the children, and my soldiers are loyal to me."

"Nicholas, you can believe whatever you want, but you are not facing the facts and the basic truth. We are losing the war; people are poor, hungry, and frightened. They want change, and the monarchy is not giving them that change. There is major discontent, and you will not recognize it even if it is spoken right here at the palace among the staff."

Nicholas glared at his wife. "You are going to take the word of an angry guard against your husband? I will find out who that man is and exile him to Siberia. We will see what he will be able to do to us from there."

"Nicholas, listen to yourself; that is not the answer. You need to think about us—and our future. We need to leave before something terrible happens. Even Rasputin thinks so."

Nicholas pointed his finger at his wife. "I should have known that 'he' was behind this. All he is interested in is my demise."

"No, Nicholas. This has nothing to do with Rasputin."

"How can you have any confidence in anything that man says? He is the one who is despised. It is he who they want removed—not your Nicholas, not the tsar. The country needs me. They depend on me. I am in the field with my troops. My men know who is willing to sacrifice. That horrible man has filled your head with all these false truths. I will be damned if I will let him control you any longer. He is not welcome in my presence."

Alexandra tearfully exclaimed, "Nicholas, how can you say that? Rasputin saved your son's life. Don't you care about the future tsar of Russia?"

"I certainly do care, but my wish must be obeyed. If he is seen at the palace again while I am here, he will be arrested. Rasputin is a deplorable man, and as soon as you realize it, you will be able to devote yourself to Russia, our homeland, and our future together. We will not speak of this matter again. Understood?"

Nicholas walked out of the room. He was disgusted and did not wish to speak of this issue again.

Alexandra was scared. She was fearful that her husband would be assassinated like his grandfather before him. She knew time was of the essence, and something had to be done. Alexandra realized that it was time to leave the country, but she knew Nicholas would never abandon his post—and she would never leave him.

What about the children? Could she convince him to let the children visit relatives in another country? That would not be unusual. After all, he had just returned from a visit with his cousin, George, heir to the throne of England. If they were not permitted to leave the country, what if the children were smuggled out of the country and other children took their places? It is reasonable that children change as they enter to adolescence. The imperial family will just not make many personal appearances for a while.

Nicholas is so focused on his son and the military that this would seem to be the best time to make my move, Alexandra thought. *Could I deceive him?*

The empress was extremely confused, stressed, and close to panic. She realized that she must speak to Grigori Rasputin. He was the only one she could trust. He had saved her son, and she needed him. She sent for a courier.

Rasputin was one of the most trusted and hated men of the court. Her devotion to him led many to question her allegiance to the country. Although the Russian court mistrusted him, the other courts in Europe knew of his relationship with the empress and knew they could trust him. Once he assisted with her son's illness, she was forever grateful and dependent upon him. He appeared shortly after he received the note from the empress.

Alexandra said, "I really needed to see you."

"Are we alone?" he asked.

"Yes," she replied. "There is no one here but us. I need to tell you that you are no longer welcome at the palace when the tsar is here. He has ordered that you be arrested if he sees you here. You must take caution. I really believe that he means it," the empress said.

"Your Empress, with all due respect, he is probably angry and will feel differently by morning," Rasputin replied.

"But, Rasputin, I have never seen him so angry at me," the empress insisted.

"My dear, I am not worried." Rasputin walked close to the empress and placed his hand on her shoulder. "Is your son, the tsarevich, all right?"

"Yes, it is not that. I am so fearful of what is happening around us. I do not believe we are safe," Alexandra exclaimed. "It is not what is happening but what the future holds. In today's world, you cannot count on anything."

"I know you feel that Europe will save you from the devastation thrust upon the monarchy by the Bolsheviks. You have been told things. However, you cannot rely on what has been said to you. I have reason to believe that the Romanovs' days are numbered. You cannot trust anyone, especially the provisional government."

"Rasputin, what if you are wrong? Cousin George will not let us down," she insisted.

"I know how you feel, but he is thousands of miles away, and your association could threaten his own monarchy. You cannot forget that you have a direct link to Kaiser Wilhelm of Germany."

""What are you trying to tell me?"

"You do not have much time. You must consider options," he said.

"What did you have in mind?" Alexandra said.

Rasputin looked around the room, walked over to the door, opened it, and then shut it. "I have been in contact with those who have the means to get you and the family out of the country. We have discussed this before. You must speak to Nicholas about escaping, but do not mention a word to anyone else. Not even your trusted servants or family. Only speak to Nicholas. If he will not leave, try to convince him to let the children go."

"You are making me very uncomfortable." She began to cry. "Nicholas will never leave his homeland. He still thinks that this whole thing is political nonsense and will go away."

"I know what he thinks, but you are all in danger. It was your grandmother's wish, you know."

"Stop, stop it now. I do not want to hear that."

He ignored Alexandra's outburst and said, "She was a wise woman and knew even back in the late 1890s what was developing. The Bolsheviks are barbarians and persistent, and they will not let anything stop them. They will use you to their advantage and then eradicate you. The country's economic conditions worsen by the day. The people are desperate and will believe anything and anyone who will give them hope. They blame the tsar for what is happening. Please, Alexandra, I do not know when I will be able to speak to you again. There are people everywhere who know our every movement." He looked at her with compassion and concern.

Alexandra asked, "What do you want me to do?"

"Leave Russia at once."

"I cannot ..."

"But—"

"Please do not ask me to do something that I cannot do."

"Then you must consider the children."

"How can I abandon my children?" she replied.

"You must consider their safety and well-being. You are their mother. The family name must persevere. You cannot let it vanish."

"The Bolsheviks would never harm a woman and her children."

"I am not certain that is true. Nor do my sources think that is true, from what I am hearing. If you do not want them all to leave at once, then at least consider the youngest."

"That is out of the question. Nicholas would never let his son leave the country."

"I was not referring to him. He may be too sick and vulnerable. If he were to be accompanied by his doctor, there is no question that he would be caught crossing the border. I meant our beloved Anastasia."

Alexandra appeared shocked and frightened. "How can you even ... my sweet Anastasia?"

"Yes. She would be the first, and then the others can follow."

"Rasputin, people will ask where she is. She could be visiting a relative and be away from court for just so long."

"I have made arrangements to cover for her removal from the court. Please trust me, Alexandra."

Tearful and distraught, Alexandra replied, "If you promise that she will be safe. Even if you do, how can I be sure?"

Walking toward the door and opening it, Rasputin closed the door and said, "Prior to her death, your grandmother put a plan into motion that would be executed in the event it was needed. Even after all these years, it is still in place."

"Does King George know what is going to happen?"

"You know, Alexandra, that is a question I cannot answer other than to tell you that there is reasonable certainty that she will be safe. Her identity will need to be changed in order for the plan to be successful."

"Will that be true of the others when they follow?"

"Yes," he replied. "I cannot give specifics. It is in your best interests not to know. You have put your son's life into my hands. I know you trust me."

Alexandra asked, "What do you want me to do?"

"Under no circumstances, at this time, are you to say anything to anyone, including Nicholas and Anastasia. I will contact you one evening when it is safe. Be prepared to leave the palace with Anastasia at a moment's notice. She is not to take anything with her. I will explain more when I contact you."

Alexandra was having considerable difficulty composing herself. "Please do not leave right now."

Placing his large hand on her shoulder, he replied, "I must go. Time is of the essence."

Grabbing his hand, she urged him, "Please, Rasputin."

He unclenched her hold, and without any further hesitation, he left. However, unknown to the empress he did not leave the palace right away.

He followed a maid down the corridor.

The maid sensed his presence and began to walk faster, but his long legs and stride overtook any attempts she made to reach her destination. She did not know what his intentions might be, but she thought the worst. He was gaining on her, and her body trembled with fear. There was no one around, and even if she screamed, she was too far removed from an area where she would be heard. She felt a large hand on her shoulder. She turned and exclaimed, "What do you want from me?"

"You will enjoy what I have for you," he said.

She was horrified by his audaciousness, especially coming from an individual who presented himself as a holy man. He took his hand and placed it around her waist, drawing her closer. She wanted to resist his advances, but his eyes mesmerized her. He spoke in a soft but suggestive manner.

He lifted her and carried her to a room. He knew his way around the palace and walked with a certain confidence that his desires would be realized. He gently placed her on a bearskin rug and undressed her. Each deliberate action had its purpose, and soon she was nude. Her smooth, pale body was in marked contrast to his rough, dark skin. He took off his shirt, and his brawny chest was exposed. He kneeled down next to her, and still making direct eye contact, he smiled and kissed her. His long, coarse, beard scratched her as it rubbed against her exposed breasts.

He stood and said, "Divine Providence has sent me to please you."

She felt dazed, and with each successive comment, she was becoming more under his control. He unfastened his clothes and removed them. He was massive and aroused. She knew what he wanted. He spread her legs with his hands and then moistened her with his tongue. He felt her reaction as the movements of his tongue excited her. He attempted to enter her with his huge, engorged phallus, but she was too small.

She cried out with pain, but he was almost ready and would not yield to her tenderness and discomfort. He placed his hand over her mouth and forced himself into her. He entered her, and she was torn open. Blood began to pour out of her. He disregarded what he had done and continued the repetitive thrusting action.

He did not realize that his large hand blocked her mouth and her nose, suffocating her. He uttered, "I will now fill you with my divine seed." He felt the intensity of his body and then a multitude of contractions. "Oh yes," he yelled out. He looked down.

Her motionless body was covered in blood.

He checked her pulse and realized his excitement resulted in her demise. He said, "A divine sacrifice."

There were no feelings of remorse or guilt. He cleaned himself off with her clothes, wrapped her in the bloodstained rug, dressed, and left the palace. He would dispose of the body. Her whereabouts would never be known.

He drank that night until he passed out. Many knew about his wanton and reckless behavior. The empress was blinded by her devotion to him and felt that it was just idle gossip by those who were threatened by his "powers."

❧

Alexandra heard footsteps in the hallway. She ran to open the door, expecting to see Rasputin. To her surprise, it was Nicholas.

"Nicholas, I need to speak to you. Please. I feel awful about the way things were left."

"My love, I was just angry. I am sorry if I upset you. I do want to discuss the situation, but perhaps we can better address this issue tomorrow. I have a pending issue with the military tonight, and my presence is warranted. I just wanted to be sure that you were all right."

"Sir, you need to come now," a soldier shouted.

"My dear Alexandra, we will have to speak later." He walked over, kissed her, and left.

She waited several hours for Nicholas. He removed his garments by himself. The servants had already retired for the evening, and he did not wish to disturb them. The inner turmoil of the country was ripping him apart. He looked down at her.

Their eyes met, and they were at once joined as one.

"Nicholas, you look so tired. I am frightened. We ought to consider leaving the country with the children. We are not safe here."

"I have been assured we have nothing to fear."

"How can you be so sure? There are uprisings almost every day."

"I need to leave in the morning for Petrograd."

She stood up and looked into his eyes. "Nicholas, how can you leave the children and me at a time like this?"

"My dear, everything will be all right. I promise. I would never let anything happen to the woman or children I love."

Alexandra thought her husband really believed that he would be safe. He entrusted his life and that of his family to his military. Nicholas would not even consider the possibility that his men might turn on him or deceive him.

The moon's light pierced through the curtains, shining upon Alexandra's body. He was able to see her body through her sheer nightgown. "I need you, my dear." He removed his boots, took off his uniform jacket, and embraced her.

She felt his arms around her, and for a moment, she felt protected and safe. She kissed him and moved her hand over his chest. She unbuttoned the first few buttons of his shirt and pulled it over his head. She continued to kiss him, and her soft, warm lips traveled down his neck to his chest and nipples. She continued down to his waist.

Alexandra looked down and saw him bulging beneath his trousers. She unbuckled his pants, and Nicholas quickly removed them. Her tongue caressed his phallus, and Nicholas groaned with excitement. She continued moving her tongue and mouth as he became more engorged. He backed away for a moment, and then he lifted her and placed her gently on the bed. He aroused her passion and her hardened breasts. Her nipples protruded through the fabric of her silk gown.

His thoughts of the world at that instant left him, and he was consumed by the moment. He caressed her and slowly massaged the inside of her thigh. He wanted her, and she wanted him. He continued to kiss her, and he removed her garments and threw them on the rug. He kissed her breasts, and then he felt her warm, moist response to her sexual pleasure with his tongue. She screamed with excitement.

When Nicholas mounted her, she felt his heart pounding. She was breathing heavily, and her body trembled with inner warm waves of excitement. She was ready and needed him. She guided him within her and felt his power emerging between her legs. They moved together, and his tongue knew every stimulating crevasse. He never lost his vigor to please her. She was becoming lost in her rapture, and she knew that all too soon, they would be one.

When Alexandra arose the next morning, Nicholas was gone. He left her a sealed note that he was off to the field. It was apparent that the note had already been opened. She was not certain when he would return.

⁂

Alexandra realized that she needed to take control of the children's fates. She knew there were informants everywhere—and any change would be considered suspicious.

She began making changes with the personal servants to the children. She carefully orchestrated the situation by sending several servants to another palace to await their arrival. It was not unusual for the servants to make such a departure prior to the imperial family.

One evening, she called for the children. When they arrived, she said, "I will be making some changes with the staff. You do not need to look so unhappy. Sometimes change is good."

"My lady?" a servant said.

"Yes, Maria? I thought I told you I did not want to be disturbed."

"But, my lady, you have a visitor," Maria said.

"Did you not understand that I do not want to be disturbed? I am speaking to the children," Alexandra responded.

Once again, Maria insisted, "I told him your wishes, but he said it was urgent."

"Him?" Alexandra asked.

"Yes, Empress. It is your trusted servant, Grigori Rasputin," Maria responded.

"Please don't leave, Maria," Alexandra requested.

"Rasputin, can it wait? Please Rasputin, I was speaking with the children. I told the staff I did not want to be disturbed," the empress uttered.

"Maria, didn't I distinctly tell you and the staff that I did not want to be disturbed?" Alexandra asked.

"Yes, madam," Maria replied.

"As for you, Rasputin, we will speak at another time," Alexandra said. "Please stop by tomorrow."

"Maria, please assist the children with the nightly routine. I will be upstairs shortly."

Alexandra turned, winked to Rasputin, and said, "I am sorry, but it is better if you leave." Alexandra spoke loud enough to be certain Maria and any other servants in the immediate area could hear her.

Alexandra went to the children's rooms, wished them a good night, and then returned to her chambers.

Several hours later, she sat at her desk. She heard steps near a secret entrance on the other side of the wall. Her heart was pounding. *With Nicholas away, would the underground use the opportunity to take us away? Did I wait too long? Was my cousin correct in not trusting any of them?*

The door slowly opened. "Oh, it is you," Alexandra stated.

"Why? Who were you expecting?" Rasputin asked.

Alexandra replied, "I thought it was you, but I heard footsteps."

"Enough. It is time to go. It is past midnight, and most of the servants are asleep. I have been contacted and made the arrangements. There is a carriage waiting for you. Please go and awaken Anastasia. Do not take anything with you. Wear your cape with the hood—and meet me at the west side of the palace. If anyone should stop you, tell him or her nothing. If they press you, tell them to escort you downstairs. We will take care of them. We must hurry; there is no time to waste."

Alexandra, without hesitating, went to Anastasia's room. She was sound asleep. She appeared so peaceful. Alexandra kissed her on the forehead, and Anastasia opened her eyes.

"Is everything all right?" Anastasia asked.

"Yes, please get up, dress, and do not ask any questions. We are going out," Mother said.

"But where are we going? Are we leaving the palace?"

"We will speak later—not now. We must be quiet."

Anastasia quickly put on her black cape. Before she left her room, she took a brush with an ivory handle from her dresser and slipped it into the pocket. She followed Mother down the darkened corridor and descended several staircases to the basement.

"Where are the others?" Anastasia asked.

"Please, Anastasia. We need to be quiet. I do not want anyone to hear us," Alexandra stated.

Alexandra had difficulty walking down the stairs due to her sciatica. She often had crippling pain that ran down her leg, and it often caused her to be confined to bed. The dampness of the subterranean levels of the palace was further aggravating her condition.

Anastasia, sensitive to Mother's discomfort, said, "Mama, let me help you."

Alexandra leaned against Anastasia as they walked down the winding, narrow stairwells. They heard rodents scurrying around the floors. It was a struggle, but they eventually reached the door that led outside. Alexandra had difficulty opening the large door. Years of wear had warped the door.

Anastasia rushed to her side and pushed with all her strength.

"Wait!" a voice said from the darkened alcove.

Alexandra and Anastasia were startled. Their hearts were rapidly beating. They turned to the voice. It was Rasputin.

"What are you doing here?" Alexandra asked.

"We have no time to talk." He took his muscular hands and pushed. The door opened, and Alexandra was stunned when she saw a man in uniform on the other side. Her heart began to pound, and she backed up.

Anastasia asked, "Mama, what is wrong?"

Rasputin said, "It is all right. Just follow him. I will be remaining here. This is as far as I go. No need to question me; this is how it needs to be."

The empress would not settle for his curt response. "Rasputin, how could you treat us like this after all these years? I trust you and feel safe and secure when you are around. To abandon us at this time is not right. I do not know these men and what they might do to us. You may have faith in what they have told you, but these are troubled times. No one's word is sacred. There is absolutely no one who can be trusted. Anastasia and I are defenseless against these men." She glared at him.

Rasputin walked over, leaned close, and whispered, "These men were sent by King George." He placed his finger over his lips to express silence.

"Please excuse me, Empress. We need to leave. I do not mean to be impertinent, but we do not have the luxury of time on our side."

The empress began to walk, but her cape had become impaled on the large wooden and metal door. Rasputin reached over and freed the material, allowing the empress to walk with assistance from her daughter.

Rasputin said, "I am sorry for what I need to do, but there are some things that are better left unsaid. May the Lord be with you on your journey—and may our Anastasia find peace and tranquility in America." He made the sign of the cross and turned and walked into the night. Rasputin's shadow soon faded into the darkness that surrounded them.

Anastasia and Mother turned at the same time as the fellow approached them and directed them to follow him. He spoke with a distinct British accent. "We will be walking for a short while, Your Majesty, until we arrive at a carriage outside the gate. We felt it best not to leave from an area where others may be able to hear us," the man exclaimed.

The empress, trembling and unsteady, reached out for Anastasia's hand, and together they followed the British Secret Intelligence Service officer to the waiting vehicle.

Anastasia looked into Mother's weary eyes and said, "It will be all right, Mama. I know. Rasputin has made certain of that. I just know we can count on him. We love him, and he loves us." Anastasia patiently awaited Mother's response.

The SIS officer observed the difficulty the empress was experiencing with walking and approached her. "Your Majesty, you appear to be in considerable pain. May I please offer some assistance? The terrain on this side of the palace could be rough to traverse."

She replied, "That would be appreciated."

He carried her while Anastasia walked close behind them. Anastasia took what would be her last look at the palace. As they continued, the edifice faded into the night. It was dark, and the only light was from the crescent moon.

The British did not trust Rasputin, but they knew he would be their entrance into the palace.

The empress did not trust anyone, but she placed her trust in this man who was despised by many. Rasputin would not be accompanying the duchess to the final destination.

An SIS officer would be escorting the empress and her daughter. SIS officers would also be following Rasputin until his fate was sealed. They knew he would not betray the empress, but he could not be trusted beyond that. The Russians in charge were growing more powerful, and Rasputin was in the way. He would need to be discarded as soon as the time was right. The British SIS and the Russians were already conspiring.

Anastasia appeared surprised and began to wonder what was happening, but she kept her composure when a second SIS officer appeared in the carriage.

Looking at the expression on Anastasia's face, the SIS officer who accompanied them spoke Russian and exclaimed, "It is all right, Duchess; these men know what is happening."

Anastasia began to feel uncomfortable with the situation, especially when she gazed at Mother. "What is going on?"

"You need to sit quietly and let your mom explain to you where you will be going," the SIS officer demanded.

Anastasia wanted to know why she was leaving the palace in the middle of the night and no one else from the family was accompanying them.

It was a long trip, and as the story unraveled, Anastasia began to cry. "Where are the others? Why am I alone?" Anastasia felt very much alone. She could not understand why she was being separated from her brother and sisters.

Alexandra realized how distraught her daughter was and placed her arms around Anastasia. "I am sorry, my dear, but it had to be this way. If anyone knew, your safety and that of the family would be at risk. Each of you has to be protected at all costs, and your great-grandmother wanted us to be safe and made arrangements for us."

Upset, crying, and looking at Mother directly, Anastasia asked, "Then why am I the only one leaving?" Alexandra kissed Anastasia on the cheek and continued to give her a tight hug.

Anastasia was trembling, and Alexandra tried to console her. "I know this is difficult for you. It has been something that I have thought about and have worried about for a long time now. Your dad and I love you a great deal. We would never have chosen to be separated from you. There is a part of me that will be lost without you. We are in troubled times now. We are all in danger. It is best that we begin to leave the country. It will be safer if we leave one at a time. We probably should have left long before now, but you father felt it best for the country for us to remain. You know how he feels about the preservation of the monarchy. Perhaps if we knew then what we know now, things would have been different. Out of the graciousness of our relatives overseas, you will have the opportunity to escape this tyranny—and the others will follow."

"But what if things get worse, and you cannot leave?" Anastasia asked.

"My dear, we have to believe that our Divine Maker will allow us to join you. We will continue to pray. Although you are not with us, we will be together spiritually." Alexandra withdrew her arms from around Anastasia and looked directly into her bloodshot eyes. "You will never speak of this or share what I will tell you with anyone. I know our secret will be safe with you."

Alexandra went into detail how the forces in Russia were against the imperial family and how the family discretely made arrangements to remove Anastasia from Russia. Anastasia listened attentively. Her face grew paler and paler, and tears streamed down her face.

"Please try to keep your composure, my dear child. You need to hear every word, and we do not have much time. A special courier has been chosen to take you and one of the families from Russia to England. You will be one of the five children of this family. Their daughter, a great likeness to you, will return to court with me. The family desires to leave Russia because they have been persecuted for years and have had to move from town to town. It will be easier for them to leave the country. The revolutionaries are sympathetic to them. They have few belongings. When you arrive in England, your cousin will have made other arrangements. Your sisters should follow later. Remember: trust no one. Our lives can be in great danger if anyone finds out who you are. Even if you should by chance come into contact with family, do not share with them who you are. You will be known as Sabrina, and your identity is no longer Romanov. We will be stopping at an inn shortly, and the SIS agent will make the change. Let us say our good-byes here. We will not have another opportunity."

Alexandra gave her daughter a hug, knowing that she would probably never see her daughter again. She felt her warmth and tremors. Alexandra knew Anastasia possessed the will and fortitude to stand up to adversity.

A light rain enveloped the land. The rustic inn would be the only stop before Alexandra met her "cousins." The formality would convince the coachmen, and if questioned, they would be able to give a detailed account of the inn.

The stone inn was expecting the guests but the innkeepers were unaware they were the imperial family. Special quarters had been arranged where they could rest while the horses were attended by the inn staff and coachmen. The SIS officer would make all of the arrangements with the family for the exchange. Alexandra was no longer worried because Rasputin had entrusted the SIS officer with the plan.

Alexandra did not know if she could bear the loss of her youngest daughter, but she knew that Anastasia would have a better chance of surviving outside of Russia. She was also aware that if Nicholas ever found out about her deception, their relationship would be wounded— and the scar could last for many years.

"Whoa, ye mares. Whoa—we have arrived," the coachmen yelled.

"But, Mother," Anastasia exclaimed.

"No, my dear." Alexandra took her index finger and pressed it against her lips. "Not another word." Their eyes were red.

"What is this in your pocket, Anastasia?" Alexandra asked.

"Just a brush for my hair," Anastasia proclaimed.

"You will not need this. Give it to me."

Alexandra placed the brush beside her on the seat.

As they descended from the carriage, the staff of the inn greeted them at the door. "We must hurry if we are to return to the palace tonight."

Alexandra left the coach first.

The SIS agent assisted her. He was aware of the difficulty she having with walking and provided her the needed support.

Anastasia looked back at the seat. She saw the ivory brush and wanted it. Despite Mother's demand not to, she slipped the brush into her cape and continued to exit the coach.

As they entered the darkened inn, only a few candles lit their way to a small room upstairs. Alexandra opened the door, and she saw the SIS officer standing beside a young girl. At first, Alexandra was astonished; there was a strong resemblance.

"Anastasia, change into her clothes—and then we will be gone. I will be traveling to our cousins and then returning to the palace with this young woman, and you and the SIS agent will continue on your journey," Alexandra explained.

As Anastasia removed her clothes, she almost forgot the brush in her cape. She took the cape and reached inside the pocket. Anastasia took the ivory brush and placed it into the pocket of her dress. She then placed the cape on the chair beside her.

Alexandra entered the room. Mother took her clothes and cape. Anastasia looked at Mother. She knew there was little time, and as a candle burned down to darkness, her heart would burn with the absence of the light from Mother's love.

I am Sabrina now, and so should it be. Anastasia will never be spoken of again.

The SIS officer and Sabrina were on their way, and the empress and her fictitious daughter headed to the family in the country. Alexandra placed her hand on the seat. Where is the brush? She looked and searched, but it was nowhere to be found. Did Anastasia take the brush back? Did it fall out of the carriage? What had become of the brush?

She rode back to the palace with the young woman who would

never see her parents again. Alexandra felt responsible for her. She would be taking the place of her beloved Anastasia.

"Your Majesty," the young woman said. "This is extremely difficult for me. I miss my family already, and I just left them."

Alexandra replied, "My dear, I am no longer your empress. I am your mother. Please refer to me as your mama. Consider this a new adventure. I will try to make the journey as pleasant as possible. You are aware that we are all under a tremendous amount of pressure. There are many unknowns." The empress stared at the young woman.

The child asked, "Excuse me, Your Majesty?"

"No, please. I know it is difficult, but for our safety please refer to me as Mama."

"Yes, Mama. Why do you stare?" the young woman asked.

"Your resemblance to Anastasia is remarkable. That is the only reason. When we return to the palace, you will spend several days with me. I will personally review some things I feel you must know. Under no circumstances are you to say anything about your prior existence to anyone—whether they are family, friends, or servants. It could place you and the family in great danger."

"Yes, Mama."

"That's my Anastasia. Now let us get acquainted." Alexandra reached for Anastasia's hand.

Alexandra spent most of her mornings tutoring her surrogate daughter. There was so much to learn, especially if her identity was going to be kept from the staff. Her sisters adjusted well to their new sister. Her temperament was a better match, although she knew they missed Anastasia.

Alexei was most affected. He and Anastasia had been inseparable. His best friend was now gone. He often walked by her room and looked in. He tried to connect with his sister, but it just was not the same for him. Alexei became increasingly more solemn. Not only was Anastasia gone—but so was Rasputin.

"My dear, do you miss your family as much as we miss our daughter?" Alexandra asked.

"Oh yes. There is not a day that goes by that I do not think about them. I do believe that someday we will be reunited."

"I hope you are right," the empress replied. "I am certain that as time goes on, there will be a plan for all of us to leave Russia. My family will not desert us. When I met with my Cousin George several years ago, he led me to believe that I would be able to count on him."

"Your Highness, excuse me, Mama, I pray everyday. I am certain my prayers will be heard."

"Thank you, my dear." The empress reached over and gave her daughter a hug. "You are a special person, and I am thankful that our paths have crossed. I am waiting word each day, and when I hear something, I will let you know. You can never tell when it may come. Remember: although we speak, you are never to say anything to anyone."

"You never have to worry about me. I appreciate all that you have done for my family, and our secret will be kept in confidence."

"Now let us talk about how we are going to deal with my husband's mother," Alexandra stated, looking her daughter and smiling.

CHAPTER FOUR

Crossing the Channel

Europe 1916

Men attempt to have power over their destiny by imposing their will on others. Wars are a means of this control that cause havoc on the welfare of others. The premise that is stated is often a screen for the leaders' need to gain even more dominance. Their compulsive need not only leads to death and destruction but often to their own demise. We could view history as a blueprint of what is yet to come. However, leaders rarely learn from mistakes from the past. The need for supremacy compromises the peace at an effort aimed at challenging fate.

Anastasia and the SIS agent hastily made their way to a small village. This would be the last time she would see her beloved homeland. The goal was first to unite Anastasia with her new family. Rasputin and the SIS had made provisions available at the border. Once they crossed the border, it would be a long journey. There would be little time for the transition due to the weather conditions that would be changing.

Winter was a difficult time for traveling and would make the journey virtually impossible. In addition, war was raging throughout

Europe. This war would ultimately create the conditions that would lead to the downfall and removal of Anastasia's father from power. There would be checkpoints along the way and agents to assist with the crossing.

Victoria, through diplomatic channels, had developed the plan years before her death. All that was needed was to activate it. The war had made some things more difficult, but the family, which was now extensive throughout Europe, facilitated the process. It had been the queen's belief that land travel across Europe would be a better way for Anastasia's escape than through the waterways of Russia.

Anastasia as her new namesake, Sabrina, met her adopted family. Although she had little physical resemblance to them, she was a mirror image of their daughter who was on her way back to the palace. Sabrina, in spite of Father's disapproval of associating with commoners, had often interacted with the palace staff children. She quickly adapted to the situation and to her brothers and sister.

Sabrina was the youngest. Father was a stern-looking man, and Mother appeared quite meek. The family had a strong spiritual belief system that helped to bear life's heavy burden. All they had known were poverty and despair.

The Russian military was a formidable threat and would often abuse these unfortunate people and burn their villages. They would have no choice but to constantly be on the move. Their only hope was to travel to America for religious freedom and to be free from prosecution. That was costly, and the chances were slim to none until now.

They would have the means thanks to the British Crown and their newly found daughter, Sabrina. However, life would not be plentiful; any attention drawn to them could be perilous to them or—more importantly—to the imperial family.

The days were long, and the nights were short. They were constantly on the move. The terrain was rugged, and the weather was forever changing. The stench of the animals and the men was offensive. The fragrance of the palace boudoir was long gone. Sabrina's smooth, pale skin was now tanned, and calluses were formed on her hands and feet. Her hair was snarled, and there was no time for personal grooming. Their commode was the good earth, and the hygienic wipes were leaves. They were making progress and would soon reach another border.

Sabrina felt that it would be a possible hazard, and the uncertainty unsettled her. She did not know what to expect. What would happen if Sabrina were recognized? She guessed that would be doubtful. Her body certainly did not resemble royalty. The look on her face must have been telling.

Sabrina's older sister, Anna, stated, "Don't worry, everything will be all right—just stay close to me." Sabrina felt a great sense of loss. All she kept on thinking about was Mother's last words: that she would be the first, and the others would follow. Her heart felt empty, but she had to persevere. *I will prevail. My family is depending on me. I cannot let them down.*

They reached the next border at dusk. The light was barely visible from the austere building that was seen through the country mist.

There were two guards at a wooden gate. A primitive structure housed the men. "Where are you folks going?" They gazed at them and sneered.

One of the guards seemed friendlier but reserved.

The other was sarcastic to the point of abuse. He waved his gun in front of their mother in order to provoke their father.

The other guard shouted, "Leave them alone. We can have our folly with the next ones that cross." The guard coughed up a wad of phlegm and spit upon the ground, missing the mother by several inches. "I am tired and hungry and want something to eat," the guard said as he harpooned a loaf of bread with his bayonet. "Here, my dear fellow, is your dinner. Let these kikes starve."

The other guard walked over to his comrade, and in a stern voice and with an outstretched arm, he firmly stated, "Get over here. Let me handle this." He approached the wagon, gave a brief glance, handed them back the bread, and sent them on their way.

"You are too kind to these nomads. They deserve to die and be thrown to the pigs."

Sabrina's legs trembled, but her older sister placed her hand on her thigh and whispered, "It will be all right."

They soon crossed the border and were on their way.

As they headed west, another caravan met them. There was what appeared to be another family. They had three grown sons. The men were introduced as their sons, but it seemed to Sabrina that there was something about them that led Sabrina to believe they were traveling incognito. The men were in their twenties, well built and well spoken.

Sabrina never shared her belief with anyone, but she felt a sense of security knowing they were near her side. Traveling as a small caravan would further disguise them. The nights were chilly now, and their new friends had extra clothes and blankets that they readily shared.

One night, Sabrina heard the men speaking when she was supposed to be sleeping. They spoke about their plans. She began to feel hopeful, and from that point on, she was less concerned about reaching her ultimate destination.

They were approaching Austria-Hungary, and Sabrina knew there would be little difficulty there. Her great-uncle had major influence, and she assumed he would assist them on their way to France. Sabrina realized that he was not her great-uncle anymore. She was a Jewish immigrant—not a grand duchess.

To make matters worse, Russia was at war with Germany. How were they going to cross the border? Sabrina panicked for a moment and thought they were going to become prisoners or be killed. Her great-grandmother could have never predicted that they would be in the midst of World War I.

The men approached the gate and handed the guard several documents.

Sabrina looked from a distance with bated breath. She felt her heart pounding, and the palms of her hand began to sweat. She began to quiver but kept a stoic exterior.

The guard stepped out and proceeded to walk in their direction. He walked over to Father and handed his papers back. The guard said in a deep voice, "Is this your family?"

Father said, "Yes."

The guard placed his hand on his revolver that was on his belt and exclaimed, "Be off with you now. Those people over there have been waiting for you. It is almost sunrise. Be off before the sun rises or you will not be able to cross."

When they reached where their father was standing, the guard blocked them. "Sir, is there something you forgot?" Father walked over to him. Once again, the guard placed his hand on his revolver. "I believe you mean this." Father handed an envelope to him. The guard took the white envelope, broke the seal, looked inside, and said, "You may now all pass."

Sabrina took a sigh of relief as she slowly followed her sister across the border. The guard gazed at her, and when their eyes met, Sabrina looked down. She tripped on her long skirt and fell to the ground. One of the three young men rushed to her side, placed his arms around her waist, and lifted her up.

"Are you all right?" he asked.

"Yes, just a slight scrape to my knee, but I am sure it will be fine. Thank you for your help."

As he began to speak to Sabrina, the guard looked over and directed them to move on. The guard motioned to the guard at the gate to permit the other families that were traveling with them to pass. As they crossed the border, another caravan that would hasten their travels through France to the seaport joined them. They would all cross the channel separating the two countries by boat and arrive in England.

A cargo ship waited at the port. There would be no frills bestowed on them. It was yet another way not to draw attention to them, especially when they would arrive in England.

Several of the men who accompanied the caravan were to become seamen. They boarded the ship, and by dawn, they set off to England. The sky was bright pink that morning, a sign that Sabrina would later learn as the seamen did: *Be warned.*

The ship's quarters were tight and something that Sabrina would have to become accustomed to on her journey east. She slept with her older sister in a berth that jutted out from the wall. The others shared similar space in the same cabin. Although they were on a cargo ship, the supplies were scarce.

Her mom was most concerned about the movement of the ship.

She had heard from others that seasickness was an extremely bad condition. Sabrina was used to the imperial yacht, but this ship was a far cry from that vessel. They were told not to go up onto the open deck unless accompanied by one of the parents.

At first, the sea breeze from their small porthole felt refreshing. The water was rather calm, but shortly after they were out to sea, the wind gusts amplified. The water became extremely rough. The waves crashed against the bow as though they were going to break the ship in half.

The ship was rocking, and everyone was being tossed from side to side. Mother was becoming increasingly ill. Her complexion deepened to a shade of green. Her brothers were not doing that well either. The water from the massive waves poured over the railings of the ship and splashed upon the decks.

Someone yelled, "Man overboard."

Through the porthole, Sabrina was able to observe a gallant effort to save the poor soul, but it was to no avail. No lifeboat would be able to stay afloat in the engulfing sea. Sabrina had been alarmed at the border, but now she wondered if the jaws of the sea would swallow her up. To come so far and not reach port would be dreadful. There was no one who could save them out there. She prayed and repeatedly thought of her arrival in England.

As the morning sun rose above the horizon, so did the sight of land. Sabrina was grateful for the brave men who saw the storm through and made it to port. Sabrina did not know what to expect, but she was disappointed when they arrived. There was no one to greet them, and it appeared as though they were on their own.

Sabrina saw Father speak to a man in the market, but as quickly as she observed him, he was gone.

Sabrina heard her sister tell her brothers that they would leave on the next ship to America. *What happened to my great-uncle? Didn't he want to meet me? Once I travel to America, no family member will ever see me again. Mother was right. I am no longer Anastasia. I am a commoner.*

As she walked slowly down the street toward the ship, Anna grabbed her hand and squeezed it. "Don't be disappointed, Sabrina,"

Anna whispered. "There are reasons for everything. We will speak later."

Sabrina was later to learn that Great-Uncle Edward had spoken to his friend against his mother's wishes. This had breached the queen's confidence, and there were several people who found out about the queen's plan. However, with Edward's death and now his son on the throne, it was understandable why the king would not make arrangements to meet Sabrina. Such an encounter would probably endanger her and her family.

Sabrina believed the man who met with Father at the dock was an agent of the king's SIS who briefed Father on the plan. However, by that time, it was too late to correct the wrong that had been done. There was a double agent who was supposed to meet the family at the dock. Thankfully, King George realized what his father had done and had the SIS uncover the name of the double agent and his associates. They were systematically removed at the same time that Edward's confidant was incarcerated.

CHAPTER FIVE

Aboard Ship

S abrina's mother was still recovering from her ocean voyage from
France as they ascended the gangway to yet another ship. The
United States would be their final destination. New York City awaited
them, a paradise where they would be free from the confinement and
burden of the Old World. The transatlantic experience was to be one
of many intriguing adventures, some of which would end in tragedy.

Sabrina's first experience aboard ship would involve a banana.
Who would ever think that this fruit would have such an impact on a
young girl? She had never seen a banana. In spite of the riches of the
court, they were never served this fruit. Why? Sabrina did not know.
She was handed this yellow bounty, and she proceeded to peel it, throw
away the edible fruit inside, and consume the skin to the delight of the
crewmen. They found her behavior comical to say the least, and with
their belly laughter, they exclaimed that she had just thrown out the
fruit and eaten the part that was to be discarded.

Sabrina asked, "Doesn't one usually throw out the pit and eat the
outside?"

The last accommodations on the cargo ship were luxurious
compared to what they had to endure aboard the transatlantic vessel.

There was such a great need to accommodate so many people that they were squeezed in like sardines. The berths were closer and smaller. They shared the same room with several other families.

As with their land journey east, there was no real bathing, and the varied smells in such close quarters made the situation unbearable. To make things even worse, there were several infants with dysentery in their quarters.

The days were better than the nights since they were able to go aboard the decks on most days. The sea air was a delightful departure from the foul smells below deck. They liked to interact and play with the other children. Almost anything served as a toy. A bottle cap, cork, or empty container created a novel game or two. The nights upon the sea were worrisome. One was able to hear the sound of the rats inside the ship's walls, rustling about in a quest for food. Although there were several cats aboard, the rats multiplied far faster than they could be caught.

It was a long time to be out to sea, and people could not always refrain from cardinal pleasures. Next to Sabrina's family, there was a young couple. Sabrina really did not understand at the time what was happening, but all she heard was heavy breathing and several sighs. At first, Sabrina thought they were not well. Later, she realized that they were affectionately enjoying one another. How was she to know any differently?

There was someone aboard who looked very familiar to Sabrina. He was an older man, and she believed that she had seen him around the palace. He did not recognize her. Sabrina was certainly not going to say anything, but she wondered who he was and why he was on the same ship.

Sabrina met an older, kind lady who had emigrated from Russia to England. She had experienced difficulty procuring a visa to America but had recently managed to secure the necessary papers. She introduced herself as Mrs. Krohl. She was fluent in three languages: Russian, English, and Yiddish. Sabrina was to learn that Yiddish was a universal language that Jewish people spoke. Mrs. Krohl and Sabrina used to sit for hours and discuss Russia and England.

Sabrina had a strong desire to learn about England, especially when Mrs. Krohl indicated that there were members of her family who had knowledge of the royal family. She listened attentively about the tales that were told.

Mrs. Kohl's stories about England seemed very similar to what her mom had told Sabrina about her grandmother. Sabrina was puzzled by how this woman would be acquainted with such details. Sabrina was unable to discuss this with her because it would have disclosed information that could violate who she really was. Sabrina just listened with curiosity.

Mrs. Krohl was not very flattering about the imperial family of Russia. She related stories how they prosecuted the Jews and forced many into lives of poverty, despair, and ruin.

Sabrina was astonished by these revelations, but she was not able to say anything that would have given away her identity.

Mrs. Krohl was certainly bitter, and it was understandable why she left Russia shortly after her husband died. Her family had sent her money in order to bribe the Russian officials and secure a visa. She remained in England for a number of years until she met an American gentleman and chose to relocate to America.

Mom's health was beginning to deteriorate. She spent her days confined to bed. Sabrina's older sister sat by Mother's side to assist her if needed. Sabrina's father and her brothers did chores on deck. Every hand was needed. There was an overabundance of required duties to perform each day to keep the ship on course to America.

While the men tended to their tasks, Sabrina liked to explore the ship or play with the other children. There were some areas that were restricted, but Sabrina's sense of adventure won out over compliance with the ship's rules. The door that led below their deck was closed. Sabrina often wondered what her exploration would discover. Sabrina slowly opened the weather-worn door. There was a dark, damp, and musty odor emerging from the deck below. It was very quiet.

As she proceeded, some light was filtering through from the outside. There were crates piled high on one side. On the other, there were bushels of food. Sabrina heard the water along the sides of the ship as the bow plowed through the massive ocean. The floor and wallboards creaked. Little critters ran between the crates and bushels.

It was very eerie, but she was curious about what she would find. It was an adventure, and Sabrina wanted to continue.

The boat moved to the port, and the light beamed down on a figure in the distance. At first, she froze and then carefully jumped behind a crate. There stood a crewmember. He was a handsome fellow, and she recognized him by his red beard. He was shirtless and his muscular, sculptured body was tapered down to his waist.

Sabrina could not see beyond that point and moved closer. His tanned torso was in marked contrast to the rest of his rugged body. Sabrina was embarrassed by the appearance of his smooth white, firm buttocks. *What would she do if he turns around? I need to leave. But what if he sees me? I am best to stay where I am at least until he leaves.* Sabrina heard a voice. She ducked further down. He was talking to another person.

"I have been waiting for you," the red-bearded man said.

"Are you sure it is safe?" the other crewmember asked.

"No one is going to come in here at this time of day. Anyway, we can hear them once they open the hatch."

Evidently Sabrina entered this deck by a doorway they were not aware existed.

The red-bearded man spoke said, "Come to me."

Sabrina lifted her head and saw a crewmember she did not recognize approach the red-bearded fellow. He removed his shirt and began to kiss him. His lips caressed his body. He moved down his body to his waist, and when the man turned, Sabrina gazed at his erect phallus. He was noticeably aroused and large. Sabrina was somewhat puzzled by his appearance. She had never seen a nude grown man. There was her brother, but he appeared much different. He used to run around the private rooms of the palace after he took a bath. The servants used to chase him around and try to catch him.

"You are very excited," the man replied. His massive phallus emerged from his bright red hair. Sabrina was startled. Inside of herself, she felt a tinge of excitement. Sabrina had never felt this way. What was happening inside of her? His lips encircled him.

The man cried out, "More, please more. Your warm tongue feels so good." Although he sounded like it was pleasurable, he made groaning sounds. The man continued his movements to what seemed to be the other's delight. The red-bearded man put his head back and moaned with delight. He took his hand and moved the other man's head back and forth as the man held his phallus within his mouth.

I must go, she thought. *If I am found, they will hurt me.* But she did not move. Sabrina was mesmerized by the moment. The bearded one stopped, and the other man turned and bent down. The rays of light made their sweat-covered bodies glisten.

She did not know what to expect, but the bearded one took his hand and entered the other man's anus with his finger.

"Ah good," the man cried out.

He then took his erect phallus and entered him, moving in back and forth.

The other man sighed with each forceful thrust. "You want it, don't you?" the red-bearded one shouted.

The other crewman was making jerking movements with his hand on his phallus. His hand moved faster and faster as he massaged his aroused shank. Then the bearded one made several repetitive, jerking movements that ended with a gratifying utterance. His sweat-laden torso fell upon other man's body and blanketed him. The other man cried out with excitement as a white fluid emerged from his stiff phallus. He turned, and they embraced for a while, locked together by their lust.

After several moments, they dressed and left.

Sabrina did not realize at the time what had befallen her eyes. She was aware of men's attraction to women, but never did she realize that men could be attracted to each other. Was it the isolating aspects of the sea that brought men away from port and women—or was it more than that? What do men do in the battlefield when they are away for long stretches at a time? *I must be going before I am missed. I hope no one asks me what I did this afternoon. What is going to happen when I see these men on deck?*

Sabrina emerged from the deck door with an adventure that was certainly different from what she would have ever predicted. She usually kept her distance from the crewmen so the likelihood of their crossing paths would be minimal. However, the situation Sabina experienced would be one she would remember for a long time.

CHAPTER SIX

The Morning After

W hen Sabrina returned to the main deck, people were moving about as they would on any other day. Shortly after, she looked out to the horizon and saw dark clouds and a mist that appeared to be a storm in the distance. It was interesting for Sabrina to experience the warm rays of the sun aboard ship and view a dark shadow and rain showers in the distance. The open expanse of the sea with no obstructive manmade or natural structures provided this breathtaking vista. *Nature is a marvelous wonder*, she thought. Although she was reflecting on the beautiful moment, the crew was becoming increasingly more distressed.

"All passengers return to your decks below," the captain ordered. "Man your stations. Secure all hatchways—and be prepared. The worst is yet to come."

As people were hurrying around, the wind started to gain momentum.

Sabrina felt a gentle but determined hand whisk her in the air. "Sabrina, we need to return to our deck. There is a major storm brewing out there." Dad took her down to the deck and placed her by Mother's side. When the family was accounted for, he went back on deck to help the crew. Father was a capable man whose assistance would be needed.

Sabrina was able to hear the waves bursting against the ship. The wind was howling, and the ship felt as though it were diving into the sea. Water rushed onto the deck from outside the ship. She began to worry about the men on deck. Sabrina heard loud talk and people yelling, "Men overboard. Tie yourself to the rope—or you shall be engulfed by the sea."

The strength of the wind was formidable. The crew was drenched, and the wet deck was beginning to fill with sleet. This further compounded the problem by making the deck slick.

A crewmember on an upper platform lost his balance. He tried to hold on, but a gust of wind toppled him into the sea. The only reminder of him was a piece of his shirt that was caught by a piece of protruded metal on his way down into the sea. The crew tried to save him, but the height of the waves and the undercurrent consumed him within minutes. Father tried to save him and two others, but it was to no avail. His muscles ached after from the strain of reaching beyond his capacity. The crew and the captain appreciated his efforts, but they were not enough.

Sabrina heard the loud sound of ice pellets hitting the deck. They pounded for a half hour, and then the rains came. Soon the intense movement of the ship decreased, the pounding of the sea diminished, and the rain ended. The hatch opened, and the sun was shining brightly.

The storm was over, but not before it had taken three lives. Two crewmen and one passenger were now beneath the sea. The woman who lost her beloved husband would now be in mourning. She and her children would be starting off in America alone. It was a sad day for them, but his efforts helped avoid major disaster for everyone. For that, they were grateful.

There was an undercurrent of melancholy on the ship for the next few days. Sabrina stood at the railing gazing out to the beautiful sea.

The imperial yacht was Papa's salvation. He loved the sea, and our holidays with him were special. We would all dress in our white-and-blue outfits and play on the decks while the staff gazed at us. I never gave it much thought what they were thinking. Occasionally,

I would ask some of the staff children to join us. Papa would not like this practice, but Mom did not mind. Mama used to amuse herself in the palace when she was younger with the servant's children and felt the interaction was healthy. Our meals were formal. I remember the white linen and the crystal glasses and the dishes with our royal seal. Brother used to sit next to me, and our behavior always seemed to receive critical looks from Papa. Mama would shake her head from side to side.

Tears formed in Sabrina's eyes and started to roll down her cheeks. She felt so alone and empty.

What are they all doing now? Will they eventually join me, or will they succumb to the radical plight of the Bolsheviks? She placed her head down on the rail.

"Sabrina, are you all right?" her older sister asked.

"Yes," Sabrina replied. "I was just thinking about some things."

"It is time for lunch. Let's go together," Anna suggested.

Anna tried her best to console Sabrina during the times of melancholy and reflection. She knew how much she missed her family, and she too missed her younger sister. Although they resembled one another, they were very different. Anna never made reference to their differences, but Sabrina was able to tell by the way she gazed into her eyes. They were from worlds apart, and as much as Sabrina tried to assimilate, it was very difficult to understand this family. They were from an impoverished class, and they were of a different religious persuasion. Anna was a good teacher, and Sabrina was certain that she would be better able to relate in time. The servants were poor too, but living in the palace was very different from living in the rural areas of Russia.

Sabrina's heart felt like it was going to break. She could not understand why she had to be the chosen one. *What was Rasputin thinking? Why didn't the oldest go first?*

Sabrina was so concerned about her poor brother without her. *What if he gets injured and starts to bleed. There is not anyone around who will protect him like I would.*

A chill traveled down her body. Sabrina's hands began to tremble. She had not felt this way for a long time. She remembered when the servant boy locked her in a trunk and then left the room. Sabrina had thought she was going to suffocate. It was not until an hour later that one of her brothers wandered into the room and heard her frantic voice. She had pounded her fists against the sides of the trunk. Sabrina never did say anything. If she had told someone who had done this foolish thing to her, the guards would have whipped the servant boy— and his parents would have been banished from the palace. As far as anyone knew, Sabrina was playing and got trapped in the trunk.

"Sabrina, do not forget our English lessons after lunch," Anna called out.

Mom and Dad felt it was essential for all of the children to learn English because it would be easier for them to adapt in America. Sabrina was learning the language quickly since most of the crew and passengers were from England and spoke English.

Lunch was nothing special. Bread and soup were the mainstays for most lunch meals. It was easy to prepare, inexpensive, and a little went a long way. They often said, "Oh, there is going to be another for lunch today; one would just add another cup of water."

The sparse, meager, and humble galley of the ship had replaced the splendor of the palace.

"Sabrina, you are pale and quivering. What is wrong?" Anna asked.

"Nothing is wrong, Anna."

"There is something. Are you sure you do not want to discuss it with me? We can go to a secluded place."

"No, Anna, talking about it is not going to change the situation," Sabrina insisted.

"But, Sabrina, you need to share what is on your mind if you are going to feel better."

"Please, Anna, I just need some time."

Anna realized at that moment what was disturbing her adopted sister, and it would probably be best not to continue to probe her. *When Sabrina is ready, she will talk to me. Until then, I will just need to let her know that I am there for support if she needs me.*

Sabrina was very appreciative of her sister's attempts to be there for her, but she could not take the chance that someone would overhear what she was saying if she did share her feelings with her sister. Rasputin made a good choice in choosing a family. Not only were they kind and willing participants in the process, they were understanding and sensitive. If there had to be another family, this was a good one.

Her dad appeared at the table. He did not always join them for lunch because he would usually break bread with the crew. He spent a great deal of time on the main deck, assisting in any way he could. He was a strong, able man and his carpentry skills were a great aid to the crew. He was also a sociable man but highly reflective. He preferred to work by himself. Although he did not speak English very well, he was learning. He knew if he were going to seek employment in America, the more fluent he was, the easier it would be to secure a job and support the family.

Her dad probably wanted to share something with them. Mother was still in bed and spent most of the day in a reclined position. They brought her food, but she ate very little. They were worried about her because she was becoming frailer as each day passed.

"Children, your mother is not doing very well. I ask that one of you sit with her on a regular basis and try to assist in feeding her. She needs nourishment. A little tea at a time would be most helpful, especially when the seas are calm," Father urged.

"Is she going to die?" her younger brother asked.

"I am not a doctor, but without fluid, no one is able to survive," Father replied. All the children looked shocked. "I am concerned at this point. I am not saying this is going to happen; I am trying to prevent something from taking place. The captain tells me this is not unusual. On every journey, there are a number of people who become sick. It all depends on the weather conditions. In looking ahead, the captain thinks it is going to be smooth for the next few days. He has also provided me something that is given to a new sailor that was presented to him by an old friend of his who sailed the seas for many years. That should help Mom as well." He did not want to alarm the children, but he wanted them to know the truth and assist with the necessary precautions.

When it was Sabrina's turn to sit at mother's side, she remembered what Mother had told her when she had a serious illness: *Anastasia, with each passing day, you will get a little stronger. Think positive thoughts; they will help guide you through this illness. Remember, Anastasia, keep repeating to yourself with each day, "I will get better and better."*

Prior to assisting her mom, Sabrina went to the open deck to glance at the sea. She knew if the seas were rough, it would be pointless to try to have Mom eat or drink. She also went to the galley to see if there was any rice. The royal chefs often told her that rice was a good solid food to ingest during times of stomach upset. Sabrina felt fortunate that they were preparing rice for the next meal. She also asked for tea and a little clear soup. She carefully carried those items down to the deck where Mom was on a cot.

When her mom heard Sabrina's steps, she opened her eyes and glanced at her. For a moment, Sabrina was not sure if she knew who she was.

"Sabrina, how kind of you to come down here. I heard it is a beautiful day outside. Wouldn't you rather be playing?"

"I brought you a few things." Sabrina placed the items on the floor and sat on the side of the bed.

Her mom reached out for her hand. It was a slow but determined movement, but their hands eventually met, and her mom placed her hand on top of Sabrina's.

"You feel warm, dear. It feels good," Mother stated. Her thin hand was light, and the wrinkles and blood vessels protruded. The loss of body fat had a major effect on this once strong and robust woman. Tears formed in Sabrina's eyes, and one rolled down her cheek. She turned away, composed herself quickly, and then turned back. "I have just the right thing for you to warm you up," Sabrina said in an optimistic voice.

Mother looked up at her. Her eyes were sunken into their sockets, and black rings encircled them.

Sabrina continued, "I brought some hot tea from the kitchen."

"Thank you, Sabrina, but I can't," Mother replied in a quivering voice.

Sabrina quickly responded, "I know, but let's try just a little." She poured a little of the tea in a small cup and lifted it to Mother's parched lips. "Just a little."

Mother tried to raise her head, but she was not able to gather the strength to do so.

"Mom, don't strain," Sabrina took her arm and placed it behind Mother's neck to assist with the effort.

Her mom complied and took a small sip of tea.

Sabrina carefully placed Mother's limp head back on the pillow and placed the teacup on the floor.

Mother looked at Sabrina, smiled, and fell asleep.

Sabrina realized it was pointless to try to feed Mother in this manner. It probably took more effort for Mother to raise her head than the energy she would receive from the food she ingested. She looked around the room and saw a small blanket on the foot of the bed. Sabrina folded it and placed it under Mother's pillow. Several minutes later, her older brother arrived to relieve her. She looked at him and said, "Saul, thanks for coming, but I would like to spend more time with Mom. Would it be all right if I took your shift?"

"Certainly, Sabrina. I really appreciate it. What should I tell Father?"

"Tell him I wanted to spend more time with Mom, and you will take a shift from me sometime in the future."

She sat with her mom for hours and relieved several of her brothers' shifts. It was important to Sabrina that her mom improved, and she wanted to be there with her. Elevating Mother's head was a great help. She drank some tea and ate some rice. She spent more time awake, and she and Sabrina spoke and began to learn about each other.

As days passed, their relationship continued to grow.

Sabrina enjoyed the private moments with Mother. The sea cooperated, and her mom began to eat, drink, and become stronger. There were even intervals when she arose from the bed and went upstairs to the main deck. The other passengers were glad to see her and greeted her openly.

The captain made a special effort to speak to her. He understood some Yiddish from years at sea, and Mom knew some English. Sometimes Anna and Sabrina assisted their mom with the communication.

Being out at sea, the passengers began to know one another quite well. Relationships were formed, and friendships were developed.

These would be important once they arrived in America. Those who immigrated to a certain area would remain close and be a support system for one another. Sabrina was uncertain where her family would ultimately live, but she was certain it would be in a populated place so that they would blend in with the general populace.

Sabrina had overheard Father mention that they would probably remain with another family in New York for a while. Her sense of adventure could not wait. She had heard so many things about the big city, and soon she would find out what was true and what was in the imagination of others.

Sabrina's English had improved, and she was able to understand what was being spoken. She had some difficulty with speaking, especially if the conversation continued for any length of time or was expressed very quickly. However, she was learning three languages simultaneously: Yiddish, a form of German, and English.

Sabrina's hands remained callused, and her peach-colored skin was darkened. Her hair had been cut, and her feet and legs had several sores and scars from a variety of minor injuries. It would probably be a miracle if anyone would recognize her, but there was always that chance. Mother, father, brothers, and sister protected her and rarely left her alone. If Sabrina were out of sight, she would be strongly disciplined upon her return. This family was very committed to her safety and welfare.

The sun began to set on the horizon. It cast its multitude of colors upon the sea. The pink, blue, yellow, and orange hues were breathtaking. It was one of Sabrina's favorite times of day, especially when the sea was calm. It appeared like a placid lake. It was vast and expansive—but tranquil and inviting. It was like a mirror casting its reflection. Soon the color would vanish, and the darkness of the night would blanket the sea and cover its mysteries. Sometimes the light of the moon would invade its mystique and scatter its rays of light upon the surface. The passengers could easily forget its other natural state and how it could change in an instant and wreak havoc and devastation. They all knew that harrowing experience too well.

Dinner was completed, and the families exchanged stories about the past. It was amazing to Sabrina how quickly people began to establish relationships with one another—some even before the ship set sail. Some people who never knew one another had family members who knew one another. It was certainly a small world—and it was getting smaller with each discussion.

In the distance she heard the crew making a noise. They were saying, "A bird has landed on the mast."

Sabrina knew all too well what that meant. Land was close, and they would soon reach their destination.

CHAPTER SEVEN

Land Ahoy

B y morning, passengers and crew alike were bursting with excitement. The final destination to America was going to be realized within a day. Mother was feeling much better now. The sea closer to land was much calmer. Sabrina's sense of adventure was verging on excitement. As she looked over the railing across the open sea, on the horizon she saw what appeared to be a faint land mass. *Was it another mirage, or were they that close to land?*

"Sabrina," Mother shouted, "you need to gather your belongings. Tomorrow we will be docking in New York. When you are finished, please ask Anna to assist you with your brothers' clothes. I want everyone ready to disembark. I heard there was an extensive check-in procedure. I will speak to your father about the papers for each of you."

That evening, people rejoiced. It was a time to reflect, a time to wonder about the unknown, and a time to say good-bye. Many people would be leaving the ship for other destinations. So many of the people left their homeland for a brighter future. The toil and heavy burden of poverty and despair were beyond reproach. Now they may have an opportunity to have a better life.

As night set upon the sea, the movement of the ship once again fell prey to unsettled weather. Another storm was approaching. The wind gusts increased in intensity. The squalls rose, and the waves were twenty feet high.

The captain called out, "All passengers below, and all hands on deck. Fasten and secure everything." His intense voice echoed through the deck.

The rain began as Sabrina entered the hatchway. The door behind her blew shut. The sound of water thrashing against the ship intensified the fear of all below.

As conditions continued to worsen, Mother returned to bed.

Father ascended to the deck and Sabrina's eldest brother accompanied him. As they opened the hatchway, water poured into the deck. Somehow they managed to close the hatch. Sabrina heard Jake call out, and then his voice was muted by the sound of the rain beating against the deck and the wind howling through the ship.

There was something within Sabrina that resonated—a negative and anxious foreboding feeling. *What is going to happen? We are so close but so far away.*

The captain knew of the impending danger. A glance at his face and the sound of his voice were all that Sabrina needed to know that the future once again was in question. She felt an unsettled feeling in the pit of her stomach.

Lightning and thunder accompanied the torrential rain and whirling wind. The rain abated, and hail began to fall. It pounded the deck with ice pellets the size of walnuts. The decks quickly became slick, which further endangered the crew. *How many more men are going to be swallowed by the sea?*

The hatchway blew open. Several of the crew hastened to secure it. As they closed it, she gazed out and saw a giant mass of water covering the deck as it struck the bow. As she walked over to Mother, she appeared pale and had a horrid look.

"Mother, what is wrong?"

She did not speak, and she stared aimlessly into space.

What did Dad tell her before he ascended to the upper deck? Why did he allow Jake to follow him? There I go again thinking, thinking, thinking—analyzing, analyzing, analyzing—my mind is ready to explode. Why me? Why me? I long for the tranquility of the palace. I need to be strong. Mama and Papa would want it that way. There is no other option.

Sabrina walked over to her mom, placed her hand upon hers, gently squeezed it, and said, "Everything is going to be all right. Don't worry. I will be here for anything you may need. We must have faith. It has brought us this far already, and by morning, it will all come together." Sabrina thought the morning might never come for some if not all of them.

The ship was rocking from bow to stern. The bow dipped as it tried to pierce through the engulfing sea. Water was gushing in through the hatchway. There were already several inches, and it was accumulating at a steady rate. Sabrina called out to her brothers, "Lift everything up and place it on the cots. We need to protect what little we have."

Mother turned her head toward Sabrina, acknowledged her comment, and then closed her eyes.

Up on deck, the crew was finding it increasingly difficult to control the situation before them. Several men had already fallen overboard, and others would soon join them. It was difficult to steer the massive vessel due to the wind and turbulent conditions of the sea.

"Jake, you must go to the lower deck immediately," Sabrina's father demanded.

"Father, I want to stay with you," Jake replied.

"It is too dangerous."

"But—"

"There are no buts. You must yield to what I have told you. These conditions call for a seasoned sailor," Father cried out.

"Then why are you here?" Jake sarcastically replied.

Becoming extremely frustrated at his son's demeanor, Sabrina's father yelled, "Jake, now!"

"But—"

"No. Now! And that is final."

As Jake hurried toward the hatch, the sound of metal cracking was heard. His dad gazed up and saw a steel beam separating from an upper deck, and within seconds, it came crashing down upon Jake. It crushed Jake.

His dad ran toward him, but it was too late. He was instantly killed. His limp body was under the beam. His dad cried out, "Oh, Jake. No. No. No!"

A strong gust of wind scooped Father up and threw him against the rail. He miraculously grabbed the rail and held on. His hands clutched the rail with such force that it took two crewmen to help free him. The crewmembers assisted in lifting the beam so Father could pick up Jake and carry him below before the storm thrust them both into the sea.

Sabrina was looking in a forward direction when the hatchway opened. A gush of water preceded the image of Father.

As he entered the hatchway, he was carrying what appeared to be a bloodstained body. *Who has the storm taken this time?* A chill traveled down her body. Sabrina realized he was holding Jake.

Tears of grief flowed from her dad's eyes. He slowly approached Mother.

Sabrina's brothers and sister converged to their mom's bedside. The sight of their father carrying Jake stunned them. They looked away, but the vision of their slain brother broke their hearts. They began to cry uncontrollably. There was no consoling them.

Sabrina's mom opened her eyes. Sabrina would never forget that look. Sabrina's eyes met her dad's, and they both stared at each other for a moment.

Her mom put her hands over her face and passed out. Her dad and her brothers prepared the body according to Jewish tradition and wrapped him in a white shroud. For the remainder of the night, they sat vigil around the body. Others joined them in prayer while the storm raged above the deck.

That evening, Sabrina found it difficult to sleep. She was extremely anxious, and her sleep was restless. She finally fell into a deep sleep after several hours.

Sabrina had a dream about her birth family. Father was comforting her in her dream when she felt her body shake.

"Sabrina?" Anna said. "Are you awake?"

Sabrina opened her eyes and looked at her. She was somewhat in a daze and wanted to go back to sleep to be with her papa. She was stunned and dismayed when she realized it was only a dream. "I am up now!"

"I am sorry, Sabrina, but I just needed to speak to someone," Anna responded.

"That is all right, Anna. I was just dreaming. Let us walk upstairs to the deck. There we will be able to find a place where it might be more private." They went to the upper deck and sat down in an isolated area to talk about the death of their brother.

The morning brought a beautiful sunrise. They lost eight men—six to the sea and two to fatalities aboard the ship.

In the distance, Sabrina saw a green figure rising from the sea. Sabrina heard someone say, "It is the Statue of Liberty guarding the gateway to freedom."

They would be the last to disembark because of Jake.

Dad approached Sabrina and said, "I know it was a difficult night for all of us, but Mom needs you more than ever. I know I can count on you and Anna. Please follow Anna's lead. I have explained to Anna the procedure of disembarking and immigration. We will just have to wait. It might take several hours. Sabrina, do not answer any questions. Let Anna or myself answer for you. There should be someone at the pier when we dock to facilitate the process. Sabrina, do not speak to anyone outside of the family. We can all be placed at risk and possibly deported back to Russia."

As the ship continued to approach land, the city became more visible. Sabrina could not wait until they were on solid ground.

Her dad knew Sabrina well and advised her accordingly. She really did not know what to expect, but she was certain he had been briefed prior to taking sail.

The captain appeared and placed his hand on Father's shoulder. "I am sorry for your loss. He was a valiant young man who wanted to assist us with the plight of the storm. So many lives have been taken by the sea during these voyages."

Father looked at him, and although he did not completely understand everything he was saying, he knew the captain was conveying his deepest and sincere sorrow. He looked at the captain with tears in his eyes and replied, "Thank you, Captain."

The captain nodded, handed him a large white envelope, and left to attend to other matters.

Father was also approached by many of the seamen who paid their respects.

A gentleman who spoke Yiddish said, "The Lord works in mysterious ways. We cannot always know what his purpose may be, but in the end, I do believe it all comes together."

Father was never the same after the death of Jake. It was just too much for him bear. Father would sit in silence. When parents lose a child, a major part of them dies with that child. The sparkle in his eyes was gone forever.

When the cargo ship docked, several men from immigration walked up the gangplank. They were wearing black suits and proceeded quickly. They handed some papers to the captain, exchanged some words, and then motioned to the family.

"Do any of you speak English?"

"Very little," Father replied.

"I will secure a translator. I know that one of the officers speaks Yiddish."

Dad acknowledged by nodding. The men walked back to the gangplank to await the officer's arrival. The family would be last to disembark. They would need to be debriefed by the medical personnel.

It was not the best of times. Influenza had taken many lives, and they needed to be certain that their son did not succumb to the virus. The captain was familiar with the procedures and many of the officers. He had sailed many times into the port of New York.

Sabrina's heart still was racing and beating hard from the anticipation of the day. She felt somewhat compromised by being silent, but she knew she had to listen to father's demands if the process was to move forward.

Soon the passengers started to disembark. The other families said their good-byes not knowing if they would ever cast their eyes on each other again. It was like saying good-bye to a family member. The days at sea brought people who had never met close to one another. They shared their dreams, sadness, and happiness. The adventures of the sea would bond them forever.

Sabrina thought, *Another farewell, another loss, and another painful association from the past. I wonder how my family is doing back in Russia. Will another sister join me in the near future? I perhaps will never know. It is likely I will never see them again.* A tear rolled down her cheek.

Anna walked over and put her arm around her. "Sabrina, I know it is hard saying good-bye, but we will meet new people and make new friends."

"Yes, Anna," Sabrina replied. However, in her heart there was a major void and emptiness for her birth family. She would never experience their love, the feel of their soft, warm, gentle hands touching hers, their hugs, her mom's soft kisses upon her face, her brother's wanton looks, and her sister's advice. That was all a distant memory that clung to Sabrina and produced a sense of loneliness and despair. Why didn't King George intervene? Why all this secrecy and planning? Rasputin did say others would probably follow her. Was she just having a dream? Would she awake and be in the summer palace— away from all this and with her family.

People were being herded into the Immigration Holding Building. They were not the only ship to arrive. There must have been hundreds of people swarming on the pier. Several people kneeled down and were kissing the ground.

After all the passengers left the ship, three men in dark suits boarded the ship. They walked over to the captain, exchanged various papers, and appeared to be discussing what was contained within them. Several times, they glanced in their direction. As they started to walk over to them, Sabrina's body trembled.

The captain and Father spoke to one of the men who spoke Yiddish. Anna whispered to Sabrina that they were discussing Jake. They asked if the body could be unwrapped so the medical personnel could examine it. However, the captain spoke up, and they did not pursue that request. A plain pine coffin was brought aboard, and Sabrina's brothers and father placed the body gently inside.

Her mom needed to be consoled, and Anna and Sabrina were at her side for support. They all followed the suited men off the ship into the building.

They entered through a side door and did not need to make their way through the masses of people. Once inside, another man and woman entered and escorted them to a private room.

"You will need to split up for a while," the men said. The woman indicated that she would be accompanying Mom and the girls. The immigration agent would be taking Father and the boys to another area. The woman was a nurse and asked her mom a number of questions. When she saw Mother's Star of David, she continued the interview in Yiddish.

When she approached Sabrina, she said, "Haven't I seen you before?"

Sabrina was stunned by her comments.

Anna quickly responded, "No, Madam. This is our first time in New York."

"Oh, you speak English?" the nurse replied.

"Yes, I learned a few words on the voyage from England. My sister only speaks Russian," Anna quickly stated.

Sabrina looked down.

The nurse continued, "I guess you just resemble someone else."

After the examination, they were led to another room to wait for the men.

Father and the boys followed the same routine. They had to remove all their clothes and were examined thoroughly.

The medical examiner said, "You are cut," and he continued the questioning in Yiddish.

The boys felt very uncomfortable by the thorough examination. After what seemed an eternity, they were led to the room where the girls were waiting. As her dad and the boys entered the room, Mom observed the expression on their faces and realized that their examinations were an ordeal. She felt it best not to say anything.

After they were reunited, a distinguished-looking man entered the room and closed the door. He directed them to follow him with their papers. He led them to another room where their papers were certified and then directed them to exit the building. Prior to their departure, he told them that someone would be waiting for them outside and that they should leave immediately. They were also told that arrangements for Jake had already been made, and he would be transferred accordingly. He told them not to ask any questions and to leave. "Welcome to America." He handed Sabrina's dad a piece of paper and said, "If you need anything, use this number." He left the room, and the exit door opened.

To Dad's surprise, his cousin was standing in front of him. They embraced. "There is no time to waste. We must be going now."

Sabrina looked back. There were several armed police officers heading in their direction. Prior to the door closing, she noticed that the distinguished gentleman stopped the police, spoke to them, and did not continue in the direction of the family.

As they passed the newsstand on the way to their cousin's home, a voice said, "Extra, extra, read all about it. February 1917, the tsar of Russia abdicates."

Sabrina glanced at Anna and began to cry uncontrollably.

Anna rushed to her side—and Mom to the other. People were gazing in their direction. Mom shielded Sabrina from public view. The monarchy had ended. What would the future hold for the imperial family?

CHAPTER EIGHT

The End of an Era

Russia 1916

The Russian soldiers tried their best, but the forces against them won out. The people were thrust into a world of hunger, poverty, and disease. There was no reason to believe that any change for the better was in the people's future. It paved the way for a more deadly outcome. Expectation for something better would ultimately be replaced with misery more lethal than what was present prior to the revolution. The spoils of war were upon the people. Tyranny would prevail. It would seem that the death of the imperial family would be in vain.

The spoils of World War I left their mark on Russia. The poverty, sickness, and disease were widespread and were devastating to the general population. The people did not respect Empress Alexandra. Being born in Germany and having close family ties to Kaiser Wilhelm, the Russian people did not trust her. There was talk that she was a spy and aiding the Germans during the war. To make matters worse, she could not always be seen, and she kept the children cloistered on the advice of Rasputin. This man with his spiritual mystique was referred to as a demon.

Rumor had it that the empress had taken Rasputin as her lover. This gave Rasputin a voice in court and control that the populists would not tolerate. Although Alexandra's love for Nicholas was sound, there were those who had an agenda to undermine the imperial family. The unrest among the people was building. Even the tsar's most trusted men were distancing themselves from him.

When Nicholas went off to command the troops, he left the empress in control. Her decision-making skills were poor, and Rasputin's advice undermined her. One evening while the tsar was away from the palace commanding the soldiers, Rasputin entered the private chambers of the empress.

Startled and caught by surprise, the empress exclaimed, "You startled me."

"I apologize, Alexandra, but I needed to speak to you. There is not much time left," Rasputin replied.

"What do you mean?"

"You must leave at once," he declared. "There is going to be a major uprising."

"But the tsar will never leave," she insisted.

"Nicholas must think of the children. We have saved Anastasia, but there are the rest of you. Flee or you will be faced with peril," he declared.

"Thank you for the warning, but I cannot betray Nicholas or his direct orders," she replied.

"I must take leave now, and I will probably not see you again," he declared. With that, he quickly left her chamber.

"Rasputin," she called out, but it was too late; he had already left. Alexandra sat down at her desk, placed her hands to her face, and began to cry uncontrollably. She felt frightened and alone. *What is going to happen to us? One of my most trusted and adored friends will never be in my presence again.*

Rasputin's fate was sealed after he attended a meeting. He was invited to have a few drinks and some cakes. The poison he was given did not have the desired effect. He left the meeting and headed home down the deserted, darkened streets. He knew that something was not right, but he would not be taken easily. Several armed men followed him. Nothing seemed to deter his resolve. Poison and bullets would not kill Rasputin. His assassins finally had to bludgeon him and toss his body into the river. It was a horrible fate to befall him—but a key piece of what was yet to come.

The tsar was becoming increasingly aware that he would need to step down. He was convinced by his trusted advisors that he had no choice but to resign, and in 1917, he abdicated in favor of the Bolsheviks.

Alexandra was aghast at his decision and knew the end was near. The tsar and his family were initially imprisoned in the Alexander Palace at Tsarskoe Selo.

Alexandra waited for her family to intervene, but the powers of Europe did nothing to assist her or her family. Nicholas still believed that this episode would pass and he would return to power. However the provisional government had other plans. They were moved to the governor's mansion in Tobolsk and finally Ipatiev House in Yekaterinburg. There would be no chance of escape, and Nicholas knew what was to follow.

While in captivity, the family spent most of their time together. Several attempts to make arrangements to flee were foiled by the spies that surrounded them. The other courts of Europe were well aware of what was happening, but they did not intervene because of the delicate political issues that existed.

The Ipatiev House would be the last domicile for the imperial family. There they would be on house arrest and for all purposes prisoners of the Bolshevik regime. The house was small and protected the prisoners. A high fence surrounded Ipatiev House. The windows of the house would be kept shut, and to prevent any views to the outside, they would be painted white.

The captives feared that the imperial family would try to escape or signal someone from the outside. They would be highly guarded. The imperial family occupied the top floor of the house. Their quarters were small and sparse.

The stress and impending doom preyed on Alexandra and Nicholas. Nicholas was used to being active with his military and was closed off from the world. He began to realize that he was not going to be granted exile and that his wife was probably right. The barbarians would use the family for their advantage, and once they were not needed, they would be discarded. Nicholas felt terribly responsible for not leaving the country when he had the opportunity.

Alexandra spent most of her time in bed. The heightened stress compounded her sciatica, and the pain was excruciating. The weather in Siberia was not very conducive for her. She could just about manage the stairwell to go downstairs to the bathroom.

Alexandra prayed and reflected about the past.

Alexei was also suffering. He rarely had a pain free day. He missed Rasputin and his influence, which often made him feel better. The duchesses read, wrote, spoke, and attended to their mother and brother. The family adjusted to their new sister. They were aware of the change, but no one spoke of it.

Anastasia spent her time reading and taking walks on the grounds. They wondered when it would be their turn to leave. It was that hope that kept them going in the midst of the terror and degradation.

Nicholas had aged beyond anyone's recognition. He lost weight and muscle tone. His beard was graying. On May 19, he turned fifty. *A half of century,* he thought, *and this chapter in my life has been placed on hold.*

"Nicholas, my love, have you gone for your walk today?"

He looked at his wife. She too had aged. Her face was not of a forty-six-year-old woman. Her suffering over the years had taken its toll. He wanted a perfect life for his bride when he brought her to Russia. He knew she missed her grandmother and her homeland. He was going to make it up to her. Nicholas wanted to provide Alexandra with a life of plenty. From the start, it appeared as though they were doomed. The Russian people rejected his foreign bride and wondered why he did not choose one of their own. Weren't there enough Russian women that he could have had for the asking? His mother was also a major force to contend with during that time. Then there was Alexei and his blood disease.

Alexandra knew she was responsible for this dreaded curse. It was passed on from her grandmother to Mother and now her. How this plagued her over the years. She tried to save the family, but Nicholas would not listen.

I assumed that the military would never yield to the temptation of the Bolsheviks. What a fool I was. And she is still concerned about us all. She wears the crucifix and a locket given to her by Rasputin. She believes his spirit bounds her to the Lord. She holds onto it and prays for redemption. "My dear, you look as though you are in considerable pain."

"There is something I need to discuss with you," she replied.

"What is it?"

"Do you remember several years ago when we discussed leaving the country—and you became enraged?"

"My dear, we should not speak of such things. The walls have ears. There are so many people constantly around us, and this place is rather small."

Alexandra motioned to Nicholas to come sit next to her on the bed. He walked over to the door, stepped outside, saw one of the guards, and asked, "Would it be all right if we closed the door for a little while we—?"

Before he could finish the sentence, the guard said, "Yes. I was just going to have a smoke anyway, and I know the fumes bother the empress. We usually close the door when we smoke."

Nicholas walked over to his wife and sat down next to her.

She reached over and gave him a kiss. "Nicholas, it is important that you not blame yourself. We have been through a lot together, and we will see this through for better or worse."

Nicholas looked at his wife. Her eyes were filling with tears. He took her hand and said, "I am so sorry that I did not listen to you. How stubborn I was to put my faith in the military more than in you. When you mentioned Rasputin, I became enraged. You know I never did trust him."

Alexandra gazed at her husband and softly replied, "But you know that letter that he wrote and the prophecy?"

If it was your relations who wrought my death, then no one of your family that is to say none of your children or relations will remain alive.

"Please, Alexandra, don't remind me. You know I did not have anything to do with his demise. I know it was my relative, but no one briefed me about it. There were a number of people who felt he was getting too powerful."

"Nicholas, stop. You do not have to give me an explanation. I have lived here all these years with your mother. She does exactly what she wants to do in spite of our wishes. I need to tell you something. Please lean closer to me."

Nicholas placed his ear close to Alexandra's mouth. She whispered, "It is about Anastasia."

Nicholas moved his head and glared at Alexandra. "I know. There is nothing about that topic that we have to discuss."

"Nicholas, please do not be angry with me. I had to do what I thought had to be done in spite of your wishes. I cannot express how much inner turmoil I had to go through. I really felt that I was deceiving you."

"As I said, Alexandra, it is best we not discuss it. At the time, if I had found out, I would have been irate. Today is a different set of circumstances, and perhaps we should have all followed that lead, but we didn't. I need to live with my decision as you do yours. I am hopeful that she is still alive and that she and her descendants will carry our legacy with them. I love you, Alexandra, and I do not want you and the children to suffer any more than you already have. Rasputin did a fine job. No one would ever know by looking at Anastasia."

"So you really did know that Rasputin—"

"And do not forget the European contingency." He winked at her.

"So you did know all along. You are terrible."

"No, my dear, just aware of your intentions and needs." Nicholas reached down and gave her a kiss. They embraced, and for a moment, they were together and away from captivity.

"Sir," the guard shouted, "I am back and have been ordered to open the door."

"As you please," Nicholas replied. "Those pigs cannot even leave us alone for a few moments."

The door was thrust open, and the guard walked into the room.

"So much for privacy," Alexandra exclaimed.

"Excuse me?" the guard said.

"Oh nothing. I was just complaining about my leg to my husband," Alexandra muttered.

Nicholas looked at his beloved wife. "It is what it is."

Alexandra replied, "I guess it is."

"Nicholas, there is something else I need to share with you," Alexandra said in a soft voice.

"The door is opening," Nicholas cautioned.

"It does not really matter at this point," Alexandra stated back.

"What do you mean?" Nicholas looked at her with a puzzled expression.

"This morning, I went downstairs. My leg was bothering me so I needed to proceed very slowly. The guards evidently did not hear me walking down the stairwell. I know that because they usually pass a derogatory comment or two when they do hear me. They are for the most part—better I should not say."

"Alexandra, can you get to the point," Nicholas stated.

"They were saying there is word from headquarters that this country and the foreign enemies are approaching and are starting to present a risk to the Bolsheviks and that our presence may be more of a threat."

Nicholas realized what his wife was saying but did not know if she understood the significance. He looked at the calendar on the wall. It was July 16. Nicholas took his wife's hand and said, "I believe the end is near."

Alexandra looked at her husband, placed her hand on his hair, and kissed him. "I know."

Nicholas hugged her. She whispered, "May the Lord give us the strength when the time comes. May our souls and those of our children be saved."

They fell asleep for a while until the children wandered into their room.

Tatiana said, "We should let them be alone. They are resting."

"No, Tatiana. Come in," Alexandra uttered.

Nicholas awakened. "What have you been doing?"

Olga, Tatiana, and Marie sat on the couch.

A few moments later, Alexei came hobbling into the room and sat on Olga's lap.

"Where is Anastasia?" Alexandra asked.

"I think she is reading," Marie said.

Nicholas said, "Do you remember when we went to visit England several years ago?"

"Yes, Papa," Olga replied. "Wasn't I the only one to have seen Great-Grandmamma Victoria?"

"That's right," Nicholas said.

"I loved the *Standart*. We used to have so much fun. I can remember the time at dinner when the server tripped and the tray of food fell to the ground," Tatiana stated.

Laughing, Marie added, "And Alexei took off his bathing suit and ran down the deck waving it in the air."

Alexei said, "And the doctor ran after him and slipped on the deck and slid into Papa."

Nicholas and Alexandra were laughing.

Olga exclaimed, "The expression on the doctor's face when Alexei stuck his tongue out."

Alexandra continued, "Papa looked at the doctor and said, 'You should try it sometime.'"

Everyone was laughing, and the guards ran into the room. "What are you all laughing about?"

The family looked at the guards and continued their amusement.

The guards, perplexed at the family's behavior, walked out of the room.

Alexei said, "Perhaps they should run around the courtyard. It would probably do them some good."

Anastasia walked into the room. "What is going on? I heard you from my bedroom."

Olga replied, "We are just having some fun. Come join us."

Anastasia sat in front of the couch.

Marie said, "Then there was the time when we all dressed for the ball, and Olga descended the grand stairwell and tripped on the last step. The palace ballroom was crowded, and when she fell onto someone, they hit someone who was holding a drink. They, in turn, jerked their arm that toppled a waiter's tray. The glasses of champagne went airborne and gave several people standing in the area a shower. Olga, you are turning all red. Don't be embarrassed; Papa always did say it was a grand entrance by his eldest daughter."

"Thanks, Marie," Olga said, glaring at Marie and raising one of her eyebrows.

Olga said, "And, Marie, do you remember when Alexei took a photograph of you getting dressed?"

"Girls, girls. Before our good time becomes something more than humorous, let us think of something that we would like to be doing if we were back at the palace," Nicholas said.

Once again, the guard walked into the room.

Alexei looked up at the guard and said, "There is really no place for us to go without your seeing us leave the room."

The guard turned around and left the room.

Olga said, "I would like to be taking a bath."

"Not me," Tatiana said. "I would have the pastry chef bring me the largest chocolate cake."

"I would be playing with my train set," Alexei said.

"I would be planning a party," said Marie.

Anastasia looked up at Alexandra. "Paint, yes paint. I would want to paint the beautiful view from my window."

"Mama, what would you do?" the children said together.

"Well, I would like to have all of you in my room together and read a book of poems that was given to me by my grandmother," Alexandra said.

Nicholas looked at his wife, took a handkerchief out of his pocket, and dried a tear. "I would like to take a long ride on my favorite horse."

Alexei said, "Let's go. What are we waiting for?"

"I wish it were that easy," Anastasia said.

The Bolsheviks knew there was an abundance of Russian jewels but were unable to find them. They tried to infiltrate the family through the servants and had already searched the other locations where the family had lived. All correspondence and previous papers had been confiscated. However, to their dismay, Alexandra had burned most of the papers, including diaries and letters.

One of the guards was ordered to try to speak to one of the grand duchesses and gain her confidence. On her walks, Anastasia came into frequent contact with one of these guards. They initially passed glances and smiles at one another and then spoke. The family was not very happy, but they knew if they discouraged her, there could be reprisals.

Anastasia liked the guard. She was naïve as to his purpose.

He asked if it would be all right if he could see her one evening.

She wondered how he would arrange that.

He told her to meet him after midnight at the far fence.

If she left the house, she feared that she would be shot.

The guard told her he would meet her at the door and walk her to the perimeter of the property, outside the fence.

Anastasia wondered if she was going to be the next one chosen to escape.

He told her not to say a word to anyone. The guard spoke distinctly and sternly.

She agreed and quietly sneaked out of her chambers that evening.

One of her sisters awakened. "Where are you going?" she asked.

Anastasia replied, "I am going to the bathroom. Go back to sleep."

Fortunately, although completely dressed, Anastasia had her robe over her clothes.

Her sister turned over and went back to sleep.

The guard met her at the door and escorted her to the perimeter.

"Stop," a soldier said. "What are you doing?"

"Just going to have fun with one of the grand duchesses," he replied.

"Ah I see. Can we have her after you?" the soldier asked.

"She will be too tired tonight after I am through with her. Perhaps tomorrow," the soldier responded. He told the grand duchess to nod.

Anastasia nodded.

The soldier stated, "I am going to have a smoke with some of the other guards. Have fun."

The guard took Anastasia to a desolated, deserted house. When he opened the door, a young woman was inside.

"Who is that?" Anastasia asked.

"That is a friend. She is here for a visit," the soldier replied. He ordered Anastasia to undress.

"Why do you want me to disrobe?" Anastasia asked.

"There is going to be a head count soon at the house. My cousin will take your place," he replied.

"Am I going back?" Anastasia asked.

"That depends on you," the guard said, winking.

"Can you excuse us?" Anastasia asked the soldier.

"Shy, aren't we?" the solder said.

He left the room, and the two women exchanged clothes. The woman went to the door and opened it. "We are ready."

The soldier ordered the woman to return to the house. As she crossed the gate, the other soldiers called out, "Remember that tomorrow is my turn." The guard looked at the woman without realizing it was not Anastasia. The woman continued to the house and went inside. She walked slowly, looking in the bedrooms. When she reached the one that had the empty bed, she undressed and went to sleep.

At the deserted house, the guard walked into the room and found Anastasia in a chair. He walked up to her and said, "Why did you bother to get dressed?" He was slurring his words and held a bottle of vodka. He held the bottle in front of Anastasia's face and said, "Here, do you want some?"

"No, thank you. Aren't we going?" she asked.

"Going where?" He approached and threw her to the ground. "All you royal bitches are the same. You want it, but you tease." She looked at him with terror. He had no intention of taking her anywhere. He lay down on top of her and placed his hand over her mouth. With his other hand, he lifted her dress, ripped off her underwear, and unfastened his trousers. He exposed his engorged phallus.

She struggled, and he brutally punched her in the head. From that point on, she would fade in and out of consciousness. He unbuttoned her blouse and lifted her undergarments, feeling her soft, white breasts. He then entered her.

She awoke and felt pain each time he went down on her. She moaned.

"What's the matter? My cock is too big for your tight cunt?" he yelled.

She spit in his face.

"You fucking bitch," he snapped. He pounded his fist against her face. Her eye was badly bruised. She lifted her head and spotted a bottle close to him. She was getting weaker, and the pain was intense.

She reached out for the bottle and hit him over the head. "You are disgusting."

He was motionless on top of her.

She pushed him off and passed out. When she awakened, he was still there. He was not moving, and a pool of blood surrounded his head. His eyes were open. He was dead.

She realized that she had to leave as soon as possible. She would escape now that she had the opportunity. She quickly dressed and left.

She would reappear in 1920 and jump from a bridge into the Landwehr Canal in Berlin. She would be sent to Dalldorf Mental Asylum for two years. She would claim to be Anastasia. She would be known as Anna Anderson.

Shortly after the woman fell asleep, the imperial family awakened on July 17, 1918. The dampness of the night still grasped the countryside. They were told to dress for the purpose of transporting them to another location. They were instructed to dress in their formal attire, and the servants would follow after they packed the belongings.

Nicholas thought that one of his trusted aides must have delivered one of his notes. However, like all the previous correspondence, it was intercepted.

The provisional government was becoming concerned that the forces outside the country would rise up and intercede.

Anastasia was nowhere to be found. Who was this other person? They insisted on an explanation.

However, the guard told no one to talk.

They had no choice but to move quickly and not to speak. The family was escorted outside, but there was no carriage. There would be no transport.

Alexandra looked at Nicholas. They knew that this would be the end.

She appeared frightened, and her greatest fears were going to be realized. *How could they kill innocent children? Is there no sense of humanity left in this world?*

The guard's friend said, "No speaking—they ordered!"

She continued.

"Gag that one," he commanded.

The remainder of the prisoners, including the rest of the imperial family, were told not to speak to each other.

Nicholas asked for chairs for his wife and son. His request would be honored. As Alexandra sat down, she turned and looked into her beloved husband's eyes. He looked back and blew her a kiss. She smiled and mouthed, "May the Lord protect us."

An order was given, and they were all blindfolded with their hands tied behind their backs.

Alexandra turned, but her daughters were already blindfolded. They stood with their heads to their chests. Their bodies were trembling.

Alexei struggled to become free, and for a moment, he did free himself.

The Bolshevik guards quickly restrained him—but not before he kicked one of the guards in the scrotum. The guard struck him with the handle of his gun, and Alexei fell down.

The guard fell to his knees in severe pain.

Alexandra then felt a soldier's hands on her head as he tied the darkened piece of material around her head to cover her eyes. She continued to pray, and within minutes, the order was given.

Numerous gunshots were fired into the bodies of the imperial family and their servants. Blood spattered on the walls and the floor of the lower-level room. A flock of birds ascended to the air. Several bullets ricocheted off of several of the limp bodies, creating pulsating movements as though the imperial remains were still alive and reacting to their captures in response to the savage attack. The guards were frightened at what they were experiencing and were astonished by the trajectory of the bullets.

Once the thunderous sounds of the guns were silenced, the guards continued their brutal attacks of the bodies with their bayonets. Their mercilessness was accompanied by gaiety and laughter. They took pride in their butchery.

The bodies were transported to a deserted area, further mutilated, torched, and then tossed into a shallow mineshaft that served as an unmarked grave. There would be no formal ceremony. Their pitiful fate was sealed. The Bolsheviks would prevail.

This marked the end of an era.

CHAPTER NINE

Arriving in America

As soon as the family was safe outside, Father gave his cousin a big hug and began to cry. The ordeal of the voyage and going through immigration was too much for him. It was hard to see this strong man become overwhelmed by emotion. His fortitude had paved the way for his family to start a new life in America. Somehow he managed to secure passage.

Sabrina would never know how Father had initially made contact with Rasputin and the British. He would be responsible for his family and for her safety. Sabrina would later learn that she was to the last Romanov to survive the plight of the Bolsheviks. The journey would be bittersweet. He lost a daughter to the imperial family and a son to the sea.

"You are coming to stay at our house," Father's cousin stated.

Father replied, "I have some money. We can rent a flat nearby."

"No, I will not have that. You are family. I insist," he said.

"We are too many," father responded.

"Not too many for your cousin. You will also sit Shiva at our house. I already made all the arrangements."

Father grabbed his cousin and embraced him. He gave him a kiss. "You are more than family to me; you are like a brother."

How father's cousin was able to complete all the necessary tasks within a few hours, they would never know. Sabrina thought. *Is he part of the global plan that was set up by my great-grandmother?*

"Now introduce me to your family."

Father went through all the introductions and stopped at Sabrina. Father was speechless, and tears started to form in his eyes. Mother quickly interjected, "This is our beloved Sabrina, our youngest. My dear husband, it has been a very emotional day for you. We have our whole future in front of us."

Sabrina was aghast at Mom's quick response. If anyone were in hearing distance, they certainly would not have expected anything.

"Please grab your belongings because I live close to the pier. Jake has already been moved to the funeral home," he explained.

Father felt a strong pain to his heart when his cousin mentioned Jake.

"He will be buried tomorrow morning. We will have a graveside service. I made the arrangements because I felt it would lighten your burden. I will secure some dark suits for the boys and yourself. My wife will have a selection of dresses for your wife and daughters. If there is anything you would like to have there or change, please let me know."

"I know this has come from your heart. We truly appreciate what you did."

"Not another word. Our love for you transcends any formalities."

As they walked down the streets, there were people everywhere. Buildings towered over them. There were merchants selling wares on the streets.

They passed an open food market. There were all kinds of sounds and noises. There was a sea of people talking, yelling, babies crying, carriages passing, construction, and a host of other clatter. Sabrina was overwhelmed by the excitement. The hustle and the bustle of the city were in major contrast to the solitude of the palace.

"Children, if anyone hands you anything, do not take it. Stay close to one another—and do not wander. We do not want to lose anyone the first day in New York," their mother said.

After a mile or so, they arrived at a wooden structure that was three stories high. The buildings that surrounded the house dwarfed it.

"This is it. My humble abode awaits you. I helped build it myself. Come in and meet the family." As the cousin entered his house, he touched and kissed something on the doorpost. The rest of the family did the same thing. Sabrina followed their lead but did not know what it was or why she was doing it.

Anna whispered, "That was good, Sabrina. I will explain the tradition to you later."

Their cousin had immigrated to the United States eight years earlier. He was a newlywed who decided to start a new life in the Americas.

There was major construction in the city, and the cousin was quite handy. He decided to become employed as a laborer. He initially worked alone, and then he added several other men. As family and friends immigrated to New York, and were in need of a job, he helped them become established.

The cousin had four crews, and they were all busy. The business was very profitable. His wife helped the women and children adjust to the New World. Rachel assisted with school registration, paperwork, housing, medical services, and food. She served as a translator for those who did not speak English and taught those who wanted to learn English.

Rachel had three boys and three girls. She felt blessed by her children and the success of her husband. The house was full of activity. Any family member or friend was always welcome. The cousin had two other families living with him. Everyone chipped in with the chores inside and out. The cousin showed them their sleeping quarters. It was luxurious compared to the ship.

Anna and Sabrina shared a room with other girls, and the boys shared another room. Throughout the evening, people stopped by to meet them and pay their respects.

The next day, they awakened early to prepare for the funeral. Mother and Father helped each of them get ready for the day. It was a bright and sunny day, and although they were deeply saddened by the death of Jake, the people who surrounded them helped ease the burden.

After the graveside service and burial, Mother and Father would be sitting Shiva for Jake. Sabrina was to learn that Shiva was a religious custom where people come to the house and pay their respects after the passing and burial of a loved one. The ritual lasted seven days, but it did not include the Sabbath, which is Friday at sundown through Saturday at sundown.

They met so many people that week. Each of the family members was exhausted. Their throats were dry from talking. It was as if half of New York stopped by the cousin's house. He was well known in the community, and people came to visit and pay their respects.

After the Shiva period, it was time for Father to find employment. He knew he could always work for his cousin, but he was a very talented and skilled man. If something mechanical needed to be fixed, Father was able to repair it. His cousin wanted Father to head up a crew in Brooklyn where several building projects were underway. At first, Father felt his cousin was doing him favor, but it wasn't until their cousin told Father that he was the one with the knowledge and know-how and his general demeanor would make him perfect for the position. Father ultimately agreed, and within a month, Sabrina's family secured their own living quarters.

There was so much activity in Brooklyn. Land was being sold, and houses and apartments were being built. Father did well for himself, but Sabrina didn't believe he ever felt satisfied. They had a backyard where the boys used to play. Mother purchased chickens, and Father built a structure to house them. Mother also wanted a goat, but Father was against any additional animals.

"Mother," he said, "we are in a developing city, and the neighbors would not look too fondly upon us purchasing a goat."

Sabrina was certain that Mother strongly disagreed with Father's assessment but had to yield to his wishes. They planted vegetables. Sabrina had never seen vegetables grown from seeds. She was amazed at their transformation as they grew.

Mother bottled the excess vegetables so they were able to consume them throughout the year. Their apartment had been converted, and they had gas lighting, a stove, and an icebox. The iceman came once a week to replace the block of ice. Sabrina was learning to cook, and Mother was very patient with her. They had indoor plumbing, and

Anna and Sabrina had their own bedroom. The boys were together in their own room. Mother and Father shared the third bedroom.

Anna and Sabrina spent many an evening speaking to one another long into the night. The only topic they were prohibited from discussing with anyone—including themselves—was the Romanovs. Sabrina never did recover from the devastating news about her family. She knew in her heart that after the tsar abdicated, her biological family would never be in her life—and none of them would come to America. As they sat Shiva for Jake, they also sat in silence for Sabrina's family. Her new family probably realized that she was mourning them, but they never spoke a word.

The months went by, the seasons changed, and the family assimilated into Brooklyn. It was a rather large city in comparison to the smaller towns in Russia, and Sabrina was amazed by how close the Jewish people were to one another. Everyone seemed to know everyone else.

Sabrina was the "pretty" Jew from Russia who now lived in Brooklyn. However, as the time passed, she became just a young woman from Brooklyn. Anna was the first to marry. The marriage was arranged informally. Sabrina remembered their last night together. Anna really loved Aaron even though she only knew him for a few weeks before they entered into marriage. Anna and Sabrina discussed their dreams that evening, how many children they wanted, and how they would always be close with one another.

"Sabrina, do you ever wonder about the future?" Anna asked.

"It is hard for me to even think about the future. I always feel like I need to look over my shoulder," Sabrina answered.

"Sabrina, there are no guarantees, but it is very unlikely that you will ever be recognized, especially after all this time," Anna replied. "Look at America. It is the beginning of the twentieth century, and the country is flourishing. I just love these times. Father is busy, and we are all doing well. I am getting married, and you will probably be next."

"How can you just marry a stranger?" Sabrina asked.

"Aaron is no stranger. We have spent many hours speaking to one another. Someday you will meet someone, and you will just know it is the real thing. You'll see," Anna exclaimed.

The wedding was perfect. Anna looked beautiful in her white

gown. Sabrina was her maid of honor. Their brothers were attendants. It was so nice to experience a day where everyone was happy and exuberant. For those several hours, Sabrina was able to forget about her family in Russia and what had become of them.

Sabrina now had a room all for herself. From time to time, she needed to share the room when other family or an acquaintance would arrive in New York. Anna tried to keep in touch, but between attending to her husband, maintaining a home, and seeking employment, she was kept quite busy.

"Sabrina?" Mother called. "We will be sitting for photographs tomorrow. I would like you to wear your new formal dress for the occasion."

"But, Mother, do you feel it is a good idea for there to be a photograph of me?" Sabrina asked.

Mother replied, "Sabrina, it has been more than a year, and that is what people are doing. I would like to have a photograph of the family and each of you as well. It is my belief it will give more credibility to your position in our family."

Sabrina had a foreboding about a photograph, but she reluctantly went along with Mother's wishes. When the family arrived at the photo studio, Sabrina appeared very different from the others. Her poise, posture, and beauty were in marked contrast to most of the other people who had sat for photographs. Sabrina's long gown flattered her figure. Her hair was styled up in a bun, exposing her long, slender neck. The photographer took notice of Sabrina and commented on her appearance. His assistant, a young Russian immigrant, was captivated by her beauty and grace. The young Russian glanced at Sabrina, and when their eyes met, he nodded.

Sabrina did not know that there was another family preparing for photographs. The older woman took one glance at Sabrina and knew that she would be the perfect match for her eldest son. As fate would have it, the photographer was not ready. Both families had to wait in the reception area. They began to speak to one another. Sabrina was introduced to the woman's son, a handsome man with a mustache. As he began to approach Sabrina, her heart began to beat faster and faster. The older woman said, "This is my eldest son, Martin."

Sabrina's mother said, "And this is our youngest child, Sabrina."

Martin and Sabrina's eyes met. Sabrina was speechless.

"I am so pleased to meet you, Sabrina," Martin said.

Sabrina never felt this way before; this man took her breath away. In the other room, the young Russian observed what was taking place. He entered the room and announced that the photographer would be with them shortly. Sabrina turned to him, smiled, and noticed his presence. Martin thanked the young Russian. As he exited the room, Sabrina thought of how similar he looked to the guards at court. Sabrina blushed.

"Is everything all right?" Martin asked.

"Oh, yes," Sabrina responded. "It is just a little warm in here."

The photographer entered the reception room and called upon Sabrina's family to enter the studio.

Martin's mother spoke to Sabrina's mother. "Perhaps we can meet for tea next week?"

"That would be nice. We will look forward to hearing from you," Sabrina's mother responded.

Mother did not waste any time. After the photo session, she informally spoke to a number of people and found out that this family had emigrated from England. Furthermore, Martin's mother knew Queen Victoria. The particulars about their relationship were vague. Her family was well educated. She married a physician at fourteen. Martin was the older of two children. He was a relatively shy and reserved. He served in the United States Army during World War I. Martin was recently discharged from the military. However, the specifics were not forthcoming. He now worked in an office.

Mother was excited to report the information to Sabrina. It amazed Sabrina how the families were interconnected. *Is this fate—or is it somehow predestined to keep the bloodline intact?*

"Sabrina, what will you be wearing to tea?" Mother asked.

"I am not certain," Sabrina replied.

"Your Sabbath dress that your aunt just finished might be a good choice," Mother suggested.

"I will see how it fits," Sabrina responded.

"Would you like some help?" Mother asked.

"I believe I am all right except for the row of buttons on the back. I will have you assist me after I try it on. Thank you, Mother, for your offer. Mom, how about you?"

"I will be wearing my black dress with the collar," Mother answered.

Sabrina emerged from her room in a dark navy blue dress. It was a good choice for her pale peach skin. Her large eyes and curly black hair further enhanced her beauty.

Her mom brushed her hair and placed it in a bun above her head. "Sabrina, I would like you to wear these earrings. They were my mother's." She took out a small velvet pouch from her dressing table and inside was a pair of pearl earrings.

Tears appeared in Sabrina's eyes. It had been a long time since she had worn jewelry. Her biological mother had given Sabrina her last pair of earrings.

Placing her hand on Sabrina's shoulder, Mother said, "It will be all right, Sabrina." Mother helped Sabrina put them on.

"They are beautiful. Thank you," Sabrina responded.

"You look stunning, Sabrina. Martin is going to be in awe. It is such a nice day. Why don't we walk to Martin's house rather than taking a trolley?"

As they left the house, the young Russian from the photo studio surprised Sabrina. He nodded to her as she passed.

"Who was that, Sabrina?" Mother asked.

"It was the young assistant from the studio," Sabrina answered.

Mother replied, "I wonder what he is doing on this side of town."

As they continued to walk, they met family and friends along the way. People commented on how beautiful Sabrina appeared.

"Perhaps it was not a good idea to walk the several blocks," Mother commented. All along the way, they needed to stop and speak to people. They were going to be late if they didn't hurry along. Mom made apologies and explained they were invited to tea as they made their way down the street. "Ah, here we are, Sabrina," Mother said.

There in the distance was a brick and stone dwelling with a white picket fence. As they walked up the stairs to the front door, Sabrina became increasingly nervous.

Mother noticed her distress. "Don't worry, dear. Everything will be all right."

Several minutes after they knocked at the door, it opened. A short old woman opened the door. She wore a black dress, oxford shoes, and a black cardigan sweater. Her short salt-and-pepper hair was in marked contrast to her stoic black garments.

"Come in, come in," she said. They were led through a vestibule and center hallway to dining room. On the table were a white-laced tablecloth, napkins, china, silverware, and several plates of cookies and cake.

Mother looking at the spread and said, "You should not have fussed."

Martin's mother replied, "It was no bother. I just threw some things together. Thank you for joining us for tea."

At that moment, Martin entered the room. Sabrina did not realize he entered the room until his mother commented on his arrival. He was six feet tall with dark brown eyes. He sported an impeccably trimmed mustache. His broad shoulders tapered to his waist. He wore a dark suit, white shirt, and tie. He glanced at Sabrina, and they stared at each other for a few moments.

Martin slowly approached Sabrina. He reached out for Mother's hand. "Thank you for joining us with your beautiful daughter." He turned to Sabrina, and she felt her body quiver. "Sabrina, it is nice to see you again." He walked to Mother's side, pulled out her chair, and motioned for her to sit. Martin then did the same for Sabrina and his mother. Then he sat across the table from Sabrina.

The conversation at the table continued for several hours. The time went by quickly.

Mom stated, "Sabrina and I need to be going."

"I shall call you a car," Martin offered.

"That would be nice," Sabrina's mother responded.

"Sabrina?" Martin continued, "Would you like to go for a walk next week?"

"That would be nice," Sabrina replied.

Martin retorted, "I will certainly be in touch."

Sabrina looked at him, smiled, and replied, "I shall look forward to that."

The ride home was one filled with conversation. Her mom could not stop speaking about the afternoon.

Sabrina tried to listen, but Martin consumed her thoughts. She wondered when she would hear from him again. She was hopeful that he would call soon. She was very taken by him. As they approached their home, she had a flash in her mind of the young Russian. Why could she not get the image of that man out of her mind?

That night, Sabrina did not sleep. She tossed and turned and thought about her future. It was several days before she received a note from Martin.

> *My Dearest Sabrina:*
> *I would like to call on you tomorrow.*
> *Until then,*
> *Martin*

Sabrina was nervous the entire morning while she waited for Martin. When the doorbell rang, she was standing on the landing of the stairwell. Her mom opened the door, and to her surprise, it was the young Russian. He was carrying an envelope. He introduced himself and informed Mom that he was from the studio. He gazed up the stairwell and his eyes met Sabrina's. Mother tried to distract the Russian, but he was steadfast in his resolve.

Mother said, "I will look at the photographs and contact the photographer by the end of the week. Thank you." She shut the door.

"Sabrina, what is going on with that lad?" Mother asked. "He seems to have been smitten by you."

"I have never spoken to him."

Before the conversation could continue, the doorbell rang. Mom thought it was the young Russian. She opened the door, and it was Martin. The look on her face must have startled Martin.

"Did I interrupt anything?" he asked.

"Oh, no, Martin. We were just having a discussion. Please come in."

"Perhaps later," Martin replied. "The weather is perfect for a walk, and I am looking so forward to speaking with your daughter."

Sabrina felt it best to leave the house and take Martin's cue. He reached out for her hand, and they walked down the path to the street. "The park is just a few blocks away," she said.

"That sounds good, Sabrina," Martin replied.

Sabrina was happy about her first official date. However, she could not get the image of the young Russian out of her mind. Martin was shy, and the conversation was somewhat labored. As they continued their walk, they each became more relaxed and exchanged stories. They walked around a small pond. They both admired the beauty of the setting. Two swans were crossing the pond.

"Sabrina, you are from Russia? What was it like to grow up there?"

Sabrina was stunned by his question. *How can I possibly answer it without knowing details of my family? What if Martin's mother did research about her family? She could not make up any story without revealing that she was lying.* She thought for several moments and then continued the discussion.

"Tell me, Martin, what were the circumstances by which your mother met Queen Victoria?"

"My mother has never been very specific about the details that have surrounded that event. Whenever someone asks her, she changes the subject. However, she does speak very highly of the queen. I feel so bad for the imperial family—to make them prisoners in their own country. I wonder what their plans for them will be."

Sabrina's eyes welled up with tears.

"Sabrina, I was not aware that would upset you. I apologize for my insensitivity."

"Oh, Martin, it is nothing that you said. I was thinking of my brother Jake."

"I can understand that. It must be hard to lose a brother. Would you like to talk about it?"

Sabrina thought that Martin was so sensitive and caring. Sabrina felt his warmth and concern. He was a special man. There were not many men who would take the time to show empathy. At that moment, she felt a special connection to him. It would grow and blossom as their relationship continued.

"I was born in America, and my views might be influenced by what I have been taught and experienced," Martin said.

"Aren't we all affected that way, Martin? It is hard to separate fact from fiction. The Bolsheviks have spread many false rumors about the imperial family." Sabrina realized after she denounced the Bolsheviks that she had crossed a line. How would she have known that information, especially being born to poverty? "On our voyage to America, I spoke to someone who worked in the palace about these things."

"Sabrina, will you be continuing your education?" Martin asked.

"I am afraid not. At this time, I need to work. How about you?" she asked.

"I have a good job, and there is room for advancement. I am hoping that I will be given the opportunity to move up in the company. I really enjoy what I am doing," Martin exclaimed.

Sabrina and Martin approached a wooden bench and decided to sit. "Sabrina, would you like Italian ices?"

"That would be nice, Martin." Sabrina had no idea what ices were.

"What flavor?" he asked.

Sabrina gazed into Martin's eyes and said, "Why don't you surprise me?"

As Martin walked away, Sabrina noticed the young Russian in the distance. *What is he doing in the park?* When she glanced again, he was gone. Sabrina thought that perhaps she was imagining his presence and soon forgot about what she thought she had imagined.

Martin returned with the ices. It was refreshing. Sabrina followed Martin's lead and slowly caressed the ices with her tongue. "Thank you, Martin. I appreciate your kindness."

There was not a cloud in the sky. The flowers were in bloom, and their moment together was perfect.

"My family traveled to America for better opportunities; however, my mother misses England. Rarely a day goes by that she does not mention it." Martin was very attracted to Sabrina. As she continued to eat the ices, Martin became aroused. He felt an intensity building inside of him and became embarrassed.

Sabrina was not aware of what was happening, and Martin tried to conceal his excitement by crossing his legs. Sabrina caught a glance at Martin's thigh prior to his crossing his legs and looked away. She turned to Martin and said, "It is getting late, Martin. We should probably be going home. My mother will worry."

"I will walk you home," he said.

"Martin, it is really not necessary," she replied.

"No, Sabrina. I want to." He reached for her hand.

As she touched his hand, she felt the warmth of his body travel through hers. She gasped. Sensitive to her reaction, he asked, "Is everything all right?"

Sabrina looked into his eyes and smiled. "Yes, Martin. Everything is just perfect."

When they reached her home, Martin requested another date. She was delighted and accepted his offer.

CHAPTER TEN

The Young Russian

S abrina continued to meet with Martin on a regular basis. Their mothers were busy talking to one another and exchanging information. Sabrina felt pressured by the situation but did not say anything to anyone but Anna. Anna's advice was to just let things naturally develop. "As long as you care about him, that is all that is important," Anna advised.

"Sabrina?" Mother called. "Can you do me a favor and go to the store to buy me flour? I am running out, and I need it to bake bread for Shabbos. You may also want to purchase your hair dye. You will be due for a treatment in the near future."

Sabrina enjoyed walking to the store. She usually met a number of friends, and it was always good to be outside in the fresh air. As she left the house, she felt as though she was being watched from afar. She looked across the street and then down a few blocks. In the distance, she saw a dark-haired fellow wearing a cap. He looked familiar, but she did not think much of the situation. As she crossed the street, she realized that the young man with the cap was approaching her. He was a handsome lad with a boyish face. She recognized him as the photo assistant. They met face-to-face and stopped.

"Hello, Sabrina," he said.

"You remembered my name?" she replied.

"It is hard to forget a beautiful name that is accompanied by a beautiful face," he replied, gazing at her eyes and smiling.

Sabrina blushed. "Thank you, kind sir. I don't believe we were ever introduced."

"I am Alexander. Do you remember we first met at the photo studio? You were there with your family."

Sabrina was surprised by his outward manner. She looked at him for a moment. He was a tall, muscular man whose form-fitting clothes accentuated his physique. He was tanned, and his beard was neatly trimmed. *He so resembles one of the palace's guards.* Sabrina remembered her association with the guard. Most of them would not dare to interact with the imperial family.

Olga used to flirt with several of them. One day, Papa was walking down the corridor and observed Olga speaking to the guard. He later asked her about the interaction. When he found out that it was nothing more than a social event, the guard was never seen again at the palace.

Alexander spoke Russian, and it had been a long time since she was able to converse with someone outside of her family in her native tongue.

"I have seen you around our neighborhood several times, Alexander," Sabrina stated.

Alexander looked up at Sabrina and replied, "Yes. I have wanted to meet you."

Sabrina asked, "Why is that?"

Alexander replied, "I have been interested in speaking to you since you had your sitting at the studio." He wet his lips with his tongue. "It is very warm out today, and I am thirsty. Would you like to stop for a drink?"

Without even thinking about what he had asked, Sabrina said, "Yes, I would like that."

"I know of a nice café several blocks from here where we can sit and get acquainted."

Forgetting her purpose, she said, "That will be fine."

They walked and chatted. It was a rather long distance, but they eventually came upon a small cafe and went in and sat at a table. A waiter came over to the table, and Alexander spoke to him in Russian, ordering two drinks.

Sabrina innocently assumed that a Russian owned the shop. "He speaks Russian," she commented.

"Yes. The shops in this area of town are owned and operated primarily by Russian immigrants. Where in Russia are you from?" he asked.

Sabrina was so absorbed by the conversation that she impulsively responded. Sabrina had been used to giving the name of the town in which her family was from in Russia.

Recognizing the name, Alexander said, "That is a very rural area. Your dialect and accent sounds like you are from another part of Russia."

Sabrina felt very uncomfortable by the question and quickly changed the subject. "Do you frequent this shop often?"

"I know the owner. His family is from an area of Russia near where the revolution began." Alexander looked steadfastly into her eyes.

Chills ran up and down Sabrina's spine.

"Sabrina, are you all right? You look as though you just saw a ghost." He placed his hand upon hers. Although this was a rather forward action for a first encounter, she was spellbound and did not move her hand away. Sabrina felt a warm sensation fill her body.

Alexander kept his hand on hers for several moments. His knee touched Sabrina's, and she instantly moved back. "Excuse me, Sabrina. These tables are rather small."

Flustered and becoming overwhelmed, Sabrina said, "It is getting late, Alexander. My mother asked me to purchase flour, and she will worry about what is taking me so long. We should go."

"Will I get to see you again?"

"I do not know," she said, standing up.

The young Russian remained seated for a moment and looked up at Sabrina. "I really would like to speak to you. Could we meet for a little while tomorrow?"

Sabrina was very attracted to Alexander, but there was something that she felt was not right. She wondered if she was just nervous and anxious as a means to distance herself from someone she could really want to know. He was so different from Martin. He was so outward and charming. He was so muscular, and she was excited whenever she looked at him. His hand was so comforting, and it felt so soothing to her.

Sabrina looked into Alexander's eyes and said, "How would tomorrow be? At the river near the factory they are building?"

Alexander stood up, smiled, and said, "You made my day, Sabrina. I shall look forward to seeing you at the river." He walked over to Sabrina.

She felt the warmth of his body as he stood next to her. She felt a warm sensation that sent chills down her body.

He asked, "Could I accompany you to the shop?"

Sabrina wanted to, but she knew better and declined his offer.

"Until tomorrow," he said. They both walked out of the café and continued on their way.

The young Russian captivated Sabrina. She reflected on their interaction. *I must have seemed like an idiot when he asked me questions about my past. Why couldn't I share with him who I am and where I am from? He is an immigrant just like I am. He has no hidden agenda. He just wanted to get to know me better. He is so cute, and I like the way his shirt and pants fit. His body is so perfect. I could make out the outline of his buttocks. It is not right for me to be thinking about him in this manner. A woman of my background and position should have different thoughts. What would Mama say? He is just a commoner who works in a photo studio. Why am I meeting with him tomorrow? I do want to be with him again, but what if he kisses me? This is too much for me. I will just buy the flour and help mother bake. I just cannot think about this anymore. It will drive me crazy.*

Sabrina arrived home, took off her coat, and went into the kitchen.

"Sabrina, I was starting to worry about you. It has been several hours since you left."

"Mother, it was so beautiful out. I thought I would take a long walk," Sabrina replied. Sabrina was conflicted as to whether she should share with Mother the rendezvous with the young Russian. She knew that Mother did not like the fellow and preferred Martin. She decided that it would be best not to say anything this afternoon. They both busied themselves with the dinner preparation.

The next day, Sabrina got dressed and went downstairs for breakfast. Mother was already up and doing household chores. When Sabrina walked into the kitchen, Mother said, "Sabrina, you are up so early, would you like me to fry you a few eggs? I just brought some in from the chicken coop."

"No, Mother, I am not too hungry, I am just going to have tea and toast," she answered.

"Ah, Sabrina, you must be in love. Anyone I know?" Mother smiled.

"Oh, Mother, stop pushing. If it happens, it will happen in due time," Sabrina replied.

"What do you mean *if*?"

Sabrina thought it best to ignore Mother's comments. She was getting frustrated and did not want to be upset when she met with Alexander. "Mother, has Martin's mother called you lately?" She knew if she asked a question about Martin or his family, Mother would stop prying.

"As a matter of fact, she has. We will be going out shopping some time next week. I was going to ask if you would like to accompany us." Mother replied.

Sabrina looked up at Mother. "That sounds nice." She walked over to the sink, washed her plates, and placed them on the drain to dry. "I am going out for a walk. I want to take advantage of the beautiful weather."

Mother, feeling satisfied with Sabrina's invitation to go shopping, replied, "Enjoy your walk. I will see you later."

Sabrina left her house and was excited about her rendezvous with Alexander. She wondered what they would talk about today. Her desire to know about him was strong, and perhaps she would question him about his life in Russia and why and when he came to America.

As she approached the construction site, she saw a man sitting on a bench. It was a little too far away to make out who he was. Sabrina heard the sound of a tugboat on the river. A flock of seagulls flew overhead. The area was desolate except for the workmen in the area.

As she passed several, they looked up at her and nodded. Sabrina wondered if it was a bad idea to be walking unescorted in this area. She began to become anxious, especially with all the workers in the area. What would she do if someone approached her? Should she turn back? Her uneasiness was escalating; her hands began to tremble, and the man on the bench stood up. She realized it was Alexander, and he began to walk toward her.

"Oh, thank heaven it is you, Alexander. This was probably not the best place for us to meet. I was beginning to feel scared and uncomfortable with all of the workers around here." Alexander reached out to give her a hug. "Sabrina, I am here now, and you have nothing to worry about." She felt his muscular arms around her waist and the warmth of his body next to hers. He smelled good, and his dark hair, which hung to his shoulders, hit Sabrina's face as a gust of wind stirred.

Sabrina stepped back, giggling. "Your hair tickles," Sabrina said.

"Oh, I am sorry for that, Sabrina. I will just put it up." Alexander took a piece of cloth out of his pocket, placed his hands on the sides of his head, pulled his hair back, and tied it with the piece of cloth. He then took his cap out of his pocket and placed it on his head. "That should be better. Let's go sit on the bench."

As they walked over to the bench, Sabrina noticed that Alexander adjusted himself and looked away. Alexander realized what he had done and smiled. He became overly aroused during the hug and needed to reposition himself. He automatically did so without noticing that Sabrina was watching him. Alexander felt it best not to say anything. "So what did you say about the town you came from in Russia?"

"Interesting you asked about that," Sabrina said. "When I was walking over here today, I was going to ask you the very same question."

He took her hand in his and placed it on his thigh. "Well, I am from St. Petersburg. My father was a guard in the imperial army." She looked down and realized that his tight pants exposed the outline of his penis. She moved her hand and nodded. "Father was stationed at the palace."

I wonder if he ever came into contact with his father. If he did, we may have met some years ago. Once again, she had a horrible feeling.

"My uncle was a member of the Bolshevik Party."

It gets more intriguing with every word.

"Father did not want me to have to go to war. He made arrangements through my uncle's connections for me to come to America."

Sabrina thought it was reasonable, but she wanted to know more. She said, "Alexander, why did you come all this way? Couldn't you have traveled to another country much closer to Russia and your family?"

He replied, "I did what they told me to do." Alexander moved closer to Sabrina and said, "Sabrina, I brought you something." He reached inside his pocket and pulled out a piece of chocolate. "I thought you would like to taste this. My friend gave it to me."

She held out her hand. Alexander placed a piece of chocolate in it and closed it. Sabrina started to move her hand to her mouth.

Alexander reached over and gave her kiss. "Now, Sabrina, tell me which one tastes better."

Sabrina blushed and placed the chocolate in her mouth. As she did, she noticed two men in suits standing next to a building. She said, "Alexander, this place makes me feel uncomfortable. I know you will think that I am crazy, but I feel people are staring at me."

"Sabrina, I took some time off from work to meet with you today. I need to go back. Could we meet tomorrow at a place of my choosing? I promise you will feel a lot more comfortable. There is a park not far from your home. Could we meet by the pond?"

In spite of his disclosures, Sabrina wanted to meet with Alexander again. There was something within her that wanted to see him. She replied, "I will try to meet you in the afternoon."

"That will be wonderful, Sabrina. Let me walk you back to your neighborhood."

"That will not be necessary," she insisted.

"I enjoy being with you and prefer not to leave you yet," Alexander said as he stood up.

They walked together and spoke about their native land. Sabrina tried to be vague, but Alexander was asking questions that necessitated more answers than she was willing to give.

He realized she was holding back, and he wanted to know more about her. Alexander looked into her eyes and said, "There is a mystique about you, Sabrina, and I intend to find out what that might be."

As they crossed the street, Sabrina motioned to Alexander and said, "Until tomorrow then."

Alexander replied, "I will be counting the minutes until we speak again."

Sabrina purchased some flowers and then returned home. Father was waiting for her at the door.

"Dad, you are home early tonight," she declared.

"No, Sabrina. It took you a long time to return from your walk. What held you up?"

Sabrina, realizing that she was out for the second day in a row, felt it best to tell the truth in spite of the consequences. "I met someone."

"Oh," Father said.

"Yes—that young lad from the photo studio. Yesterday we walked for a while and then shared a table and a cool drink. Today we met at the new construction site by the river."

"Sabrina, how do you know this fellow?"

"I really don't. Actually we were never formally introduced."

"What was he doing in this part of town?"

"He told me he has wanted to meet me," Sabrina replied.

Father appeared puzzled. "Mom said he dropped off the photo prints several weeks ago."

"Yes, but I was going out with Martin that day, and we did not speak." Sabrina asked Father why he was so interested in knowing about the Russian lad.

Father realized that if he continued the conversation, Sabrina might become more apprehensive with what she would share. "I was just worried about your whereabouts," Father said.

"Is there a problem?" Sabrina asked.

"No, no problem. You know how your mother worries about you."

Sabrina did not know why her father pursued the questioning if it was her mother who was anxious about the delay in her return.

That evening, Sabrina could not sleep. She thought of the young Russian. She could not get him out of her mind. The smell of his body, his warmth, and his trim and muscular physique excited her. She felt a warm sensation building inside of her. She was attracted to Martin, but there was something different about Alexander. She had not felt such intense feelings since that day on the ship. She recalled the men she had observed. The Russian attracted her. How could she feel this way when she was dating another man? What would her family say if they knew that she was going to meet him again tomorrow? She placed her hand on her thigh and moved it toward her. Sabrina imagined his warm body on top of hers and placed her finger inside herself. She gently stroked herself, and within a few moments, she felt the rapture of her private thoughts of the Russian.

When Alexander left Sabrina, he was very confused. He was falling in love with a woman who had a strong resemblance to Anastasia, the Grand Duchess of Russia. If Sabrina is the grand duchess, she will need to be taken care of like the other members of the imperial family. That would be the order by his high command. How would he come to terms with the issue? If the high command ever found out that he had a relationship with this woman, he would be arrested and at the very least sent to Siberia. How could he disgrace his family? Alexander could not let his heart control his decision. He knew that he must speak to his uncle.

"Nicholas, I met with that girl today I have been mentioning to you. There is something very unusual about her."

"Alexander, you say that about every beautiful woman you meet," his uncle replied.

"No. She says she is from a province in Russia, yet she speaks as though she is from St. Petersburg. She is not like the other women I have met. She is poised and refined. If you look at her photograph, there is a major resemblance to—"

"Alexander, your imagination is remarkable. You know the imperial family is on house arrest. Your father is one of the soldiers guarding them. I am certain that with all the guards surrounding the imperial family, they would know if one of the grand duchesses was missing."

"But what if—"

"There are no buts or ifs. How would a young girl wind up in America? A Jew, no less. You know how the Romanovs felt about the Jews. That was probably the only similarity the Bolsheviks and Romanovs had in common. Didn't you tell me she was buying flour to

bake bread for the Sabbath? That is enough, Alexander. Anyway, John
and I followed you today and although we were not close, it appeared
as though you want more than a casual relationship with this woman.
It is time for us to go. I would suggest you not drink any more vodka."

Alexander tried earnestly to speak, "I—"

"I don't want to hear anymore, and if I were you, I would not say
anything to anyone else. When are you seeing her again?"

"Tomorrow at the park," Alexander responded.

"John and I will be at the park tomorrow, but I am warning you
that if this is one of your fabricated stories like the one that almost got
us in trouble with the authorities last year, I will send you back to your
father in Russia. You should be spending your time recruiting people
for the party. Keep it in your pants."

Alexander realized there was no sense trying to convince him.

Sabrina consumed Alexander's waking hours. He could not stop
thinking about their conversation. *Why was she so hesitant about what
she was saying? It must have been purposeful. Why would she not
disclose more about her past? It seemed that all she wanted to discuss
was the voyage to America. Why did she get so upset when I mentioned
the imperial family, especially if she was from another province in
Russia? I wonder if I should say something to the party leaders in
Brooklyn. If she was ... no she can't be ... she likes me ... how I can
betray her?* His body became tense. *Perhaps Uncle Nicholas is right.
I will wait until tomorrow. He has met the grand duchess and will
be able to tell me for certain who this woman is. I am certain if I am
right, this woman will be taken back to Russia. If I am wrong, they
will admonish me, but I will be able to pursue her.*

That evening, he could not control his thoughts. As he imagined
Sabrina, he became increasingly more aroused. Alexander fantasized
about her. He imagined her undressed, her breasts, her warm body,
and her wanting him. He reached under his nightshirt and felt himself
on fire. He was excited and markedly aroused. He released himself and
fell calmly to sleep.

The next day, Sabrina arose and went to the window. There was
a gentle breeze that blew through her window. Her breasts pressed
against her nightgown as she glanced at a robin building a nest in

the neighbor's tree. She heard Mother call, quickly dressed, and went downstairs for breakfast.

"Good morning, Sabrina. You are looking well today. Have you heard from Martin?" Martin was the furthest thing from Sabrina's mind. However, she said, "We spoke at synagogue on Saturday, and we plan on meeting tomorrow."

"How about today?" Mother asked.

"I thought I would take a walk," Sabrina replied.

"Do you have any plans with any of your friends?"

Knowing where Mother was going and becoming increasingly more impatient, Sabrina said, "No. I have not spoken to any of my friends since last week."

"When you go out, could you purchase some sugar for dinner?"

"I do not think I will be going out this morning. I want to wash and treat my hair," Sabrina replied.

"The afternoon is all right. And please be careful. Things are not always what they appear to be."

"Thank you, Mother," Sabrina replied.

Sabrina looked through her closet for something to wear that Alexander would like. She washed her hair and brushed it.

Mother said, "Sabrina, you are spending a lot of time this morning fixing your hair. Did you hear from Martin?"

Sabrina knew Mother was aware that she had not heard from Martin and was trying to find out if she was meeting the Russian. However, Sabrina did not mention the Russian because she knew Mother would not be too happy, especially after her conversation with Father yesterday afternoon.

After lunch, Sabrina told Mother that she was taking a walk to the park. On her way home, she would purchase the sugar. Sabrina hurried out the door and walked to the park. As she approached the park, she met one of her friends. Leah was a talker, and Sabrina was not interested in having a long conversation. She tried several times to end the conversation, but was not successful. Finally Sabrina stated, "Leah, it was so nice meeting you today. Perhaps we can have lunch later in the week."

"That would be nice, Sabrina. Did you hear about Sarah?"

"I need to go—until later in the week then." Sabrina did not care about how Leah reacted to her sudden departure, but she did not want to keep Alexander waiting.

As she approached the water, Sabrina saw Alexander in the distance; however, he was not alone. There were several other men in the immediate area. In fact, they appeared to be similar to the men in suits she observed the prior day standing.

Alexander was speaking to one of them, and the other was standing to the side. Her instinct told her that something did not appear right. Why were these two men with Alexander? Wasn't the plan for them to meet alone? Had they spotted her yet? She did not think so. There were too many obstacles in the path, and they appeared quite involved in the discussion.

She slowly backed away from the situation and walked home. She passed Leah, but in spite of Leah's attempt to stop and talk, she continued walking. Her heart was pounding, and she wanted to arrive home as quickly as possible.

Anna walked into her parent's house.

"Anna, what a welcome surprise. I did not know you were going to be on this side of Brooklyn today. What brings you here?" Mother asked.

"I have some news for you and Father," she said.

"Is everything all right?" Mother replied.

"Yes, I just came from the doctor's office."

Before Anna was able to continue, Father burst into the room. He appeared extremely upset and distressed. "Ruth, I need to speak to you. It is urgent. Anna, please excuse me. There is something critical that I need to share with Mother."

"Should I leave?" Anna asked.

"No, that is not necessary. Where is Sabrina?" Father asked.

"I believe she is in the park," Mother responded.

Father said, "We need to find her as soon as possible. She may be in danger."

"What do you mean?" his wife asked.

"There is no time for a lengthy conversation. You will just have to trust me. We all need to leave immediately and try to find her. Which park?"

His wife said, "I believe the one with the pond. I think she may be meeting someone."

"Could it be the Russian lad again?" he asked.

"I am sorry to say yes. I told her to—"

"Not now, please. Did she tell you she was meeting him?"

"No, I just think she is going there to meet him," she replied.

"Enough then. Let's leave immediately to find her. If she is speaking to him, tell her she must come home immediately. Do not accept *later*. Her life and the family are at risk. We will speak later."

They took different routes to the park. However, none of them were able to locate Sabrina. They walked around and circled the area for an hour.

Anna was the first to arrive home. She began to cry. *Where can she be? Where are Mom and Dad?*

In the park, Nicholas said. "I told you, Alexander, that she would not show. Where is this Russian girl?"

"Nicholas, I do not know where she is, but I am certain she will be here," Alexander replied.

"Alexander, John is growing very impatient. He does not have time to take walks in the park. If this woman does not show, he is going to think that you contrived the whole story."

"That's them," a husky voice said. "Pick them up and bring them to the designated place. Be quick and without incident. There are too many people around today." Within seconds, three men surrounded Alexander and his companions.

John said, "What is happening?"

"Do not ask any questions. Just follow me."

John had no choice. He felt a pistol at his side and knew that any move to the contrary would result in his demise.

The others followed. They walked for several blocks to a deserted house.

When they entered the building, Alexander said, "If it is money you are after, we do not have much."

"It is not your money. You are a danger to this country. We have reason to believe you are Bolsheviks and are planning against the government."

"What leads you to that opinion?" Alexander asked.

The man in the raincoat pointed to the three men and ordered them to give him their wallets. The three men looked at the man and did not move. "I want to see those wallets now." He took the pistol from his pocket.

John looked up and asked, "Are you government agents?"

Once again the men ignored his question and demanded their wallets.

Two of the men reluctantly gave the man their wallets.

The third Russian man said, "I was not prepared for your interrogation and do not have my wallet."

Nicholas stared at John and shook his head.

The man with the husky voice turned to John, drew his pistol, and said, "I want all of you to empty your pockets. Do not make any comments. Just do as I say."

His associates stood in back of the three men with their pistols drawn.

He motioned to one of the men to frisk each of the men.

John turned to the man and was about to say something.

The man stuck the pistol against John's ribs and said, "Not a word. You must be having problems with your memory. Now step back." He opened the wallets and examined their contents. "Just as we thought. You have entered the country with a purpose. It is not going to happen on my shift. How dare you think you can spread your filthy Bolshevik beliefs here? This is a country of the free. We do not want the likes of you."

The men looked at him with disgust, and John spit in his face. "You are a filthy pig. Go to hell with your democracy."

The officer glared back at him and pistol-whipped his face. "Take that, you Bolshevik ass. Tie their hands and cover their faces."

Alexander grabbed a chair and threw it at one of the men. "You fucking bastards."

The other two men tried to escape.

A shot was fired, and John fell to the ground. His leg was wounded.

Alexander was fighting fiercely with one of the men. He punched the officer in the face and then his gut. The officer dropped his gun.

He tried to pick it up, but Alexander kicked the gun to the other side of the room. Alexander jumped on the officer. They began to wrestle. Alexander picked up a broken bottle, but the officer knocked it out of his hand. Alexander reached inside his boot, drew a knife, and stabbed the officer in the leg. The officer cried out.

On the other side of the room, Nicholas was being handcuffed. He broke loose from the officer and kicked him in the scrotum.

The officer fell to the floor and yelled, "Fuck you."

Nicholas kicked the officer.

The officer stood up, reached inside his coat, took out a pistol, and shot Nicholas in the face. A part of his skull blew off and hit John.

John wiped the blood from his face and then put his hands above his head.

The officer behind John struck him with full force to his head with the pistol. John was instantly knocked unconscious and fell to the ground.

A shot was fired to Alexander's midsection. Alexander screamed in pain. Alexander looked down. His stomach was bleeding profusely. That did not stop him from throwing one more punch. Another shot was fired from across the room. The bullet pierced his heart, and Alexander collapsed.

The officer motioned with his hand. The other officer placed his gun to John's temple and pulled the trigger. It was over.

The man in the raincoat said, "Take their pulses. This one is still alive."

Alexander opened his eyes and looked around.

John and Nicholas were each in a pool of blood. Alexander made eye contact with one of his captives. "I guess I must have been correct with my assumption—"

A muffled shot silenced him.

"Men, I cannot stop the bleeding from my leg."

Another officer ran over and tied his belt around the man's leg. "We must get help."

The officer's eyes rolled back.

"It is too late."

"I want the bodies of these Bolsheviks removed and discarded this evening. Search their apartments and remove all papers. I do not want any trace."

"Contact the officer's family and make the necessary arrangements for the funeral. I will write the report that his pistol went off accidentally in the line of duty."

"Yes, sir."

❧

When Father got home, he said, "Anna, I guess you did not have any luck."

"No!" she replied.

Within minutes, Ruth entered the door. She was in a near panic. "Tell me what is happening. I cannot take it anymore."

Father replied, "I was at work, and I overheard several of the men talking. I did not think much of what they were saying until one of them mentioned a Russian girl and a photograph. He said he had a friend who was employed at a photo studio, and this afternoon he was meeting him in the park and showing him both the photo and the girl. Upon hearing this, I called my contact at immigration. He instructed me to leave work, find Sabrina, and bring her home. He indicated that he would take care of the details."

"What do you mean?" she asked.

Lowering his voice, he said, "He did not say anything more."

"Where could Sabrina and the young Russian be?" Mother asked.

"I do not know," he replied.

"What should we do?"

He glanced at Anna and looked down at the floor, shaking his head. "I cannot do anything else without causing suspicion."

At that moment, the door opened. The three of them were stunned when Sabrina walked in.

"Where have you been?"

"I went to the park."

Mother said, "We were all just at the park and did not see you."

"I had to leave in a hurry," Sabrina answered.

"What do you mean?" Father asked.

Sabrina began to realize that something was wrong. She softly said, "I was supposed to meet someone there."

"Yes," Mother said.

Sabrina continued, "When I arrived, I did not feel comfortable. The person I was supposed to meet was with other men. I became scared and left." Raising her eyebrow and looking at Father, she asked, "Why do you ask?"

"Sabrina, you realize that your safety is our greatest concern? I realize you want your privacy, but that is not possible due to your position in life. Your instincts were correct. Your young Russian friend was part of a Russian network with close ties to the Bolsheviks."

"Father, don't you think you are overreacting?"

"You placed yourself and the rest of us at great danger. Think back, Sabrina, to your meeting with this lad. I do not need to know what you discussed, but his intentions were not honorable," Father explained.

Sabrina reflected on their meeting and began to cry. *He seemed so sincere. How stupid was I to trust a stranger? What peril is now going to befall my family?* "Father, what should I do now?"

"You do not need to do anything. If he should ever try to speak to you again, tell him you are not interested. If you see him around this neighborhood, come home as quickly as you can—and tell your mother. If you are too far from the house, go to the nearest shop. Stay there—and have them contact us immediately. Do you understand?"

"Yes, Father," she replied.

"Let this be our last conversation about this matter."

"Yes, Father."

"Now, Anna, there is something you wish to share with us?"

She smiled. "I am pregnant."

"Ah, that is the best news I heard all day. Mazel tov! We need to celebrate," Father stated.

Sabrina was elated, and for a moment, it took her mind off the events of the day.

The telephone rang. Mother took the call. Taking a deep breath and sighing she said, "Sabrina, it is for you. It is Martin."

"Hello. Yes, I am all right. I have been very busy, and it has just been a hectic day." Sabrina caught Anna's eye and pointed to the telephone. Anna acknowledged that it would be all right. "Martin, we have good news. Anna is pregnant. Yes, I would love to see you. Tomorrow will be fine."

On the kitchen table, the newspaper was still rolled up. Sabrina's father took the paper and sat down to read it. His face turned pale as he glanced at the headline. He motioned to his wife to come to his side; she held her hands to her face.

Anna and Sabrina walked over to their side. Before Father could say something, Sabrina read the headline: *The tsar and his entire family assassinated by the Bolsheviks.*

Sabrina cried out. Mother ran to her side. Sabrina burst into tears. She will never see them again!

In the young Russian's apartment, a governmental officer said, "Over here. This must be Alexander's apartment. Check to see if this key opens the door." He slid the key into the lock, and it opened. "Ah good. Let's remove all the identifiable information, including all papers. What is that on the floor? It looks like an envelope that was slipped under the door. Give it to me."

The officer read the correspondence. "Men, listen to this. It is from Alexander's uncle in Russia." He began to read the telegram.

My dearest Alexander,

As you're aware, my brother was a guard in the military and was ordered to the Ipatiev House in Yekaterinburg. He was not told what his orders would be until he arrived. He, amongst other men in his regiment, were sent there to guard the imperial family. We have since been told by another guard who was a friend of his that your father became mesmerized by one of the grand duchesses. He conspired with another woman to meet the grand duchess and have this woman exchange places with her for a while so he could let us have fun with her. On the night of July 16, 1918, the two women changed places by exchanging clothes. They were supposed to have been returned to their respective places. I am sorry to inform you that a series of events took place, and it never occurred. Something went wrong with my brother's rendezvous with the grand duchess, and she must have escaped after she killed him and set the building on fire. Early in the morning the next day, the guards were ordered to shoot the imperial family and their servants. My brother's friend heard one of the grand duchesses call out, "I am not Anastasia." Furthermore, there was only one body in the apartment. We are certain that the grand duchess escaped. We also had word from our high command that our sources in England were told that a woman meeting Anastasia's description was seen boarding a ship to America. It appears that it is reliable information from an official in England. We know that you will want to seek revenge for the death of your father. Please share this information with your uncle and your comrades. Once again, I am sorry to be the bearer of such bad news and am hopeful you will do what needs to be done.

Uncle Peter

The officer stated, "We need to get this telegram to the captain. He will need to address its contents. It is fortunate that we intercepted it before someone else did."

CHAPTER ELEVEN

Reflection

That evening, Sabrina was tired and distressed by the events of the day. She retired early to her room and thought about what had taken place. She thought of her parents and her siblings in Russia and how much she missed them. Her hopes of seeing them again had vanished with their untimely death. *How could the Bolsheviks be so barbaric and not only kill Father but Mother, brother, and sisters?*

For a moment, she realized that her parents downstairs had lost a daughter. She ran downstairs and hugged Mother, stating that she was remiss in not acknowledging that they had probably lost a daughter.

Mother looked at her and said, "Sabrina, it is possible that she may have escaped like you did."

Sabrina knew in her heart that was probably not the case. If that gave her parents some hope, that was all that was important. The family seemed to receive comfort from that option and Sabrina mentioning it. Sabrina hugged her brothers and then called Anna. They arranged to meet the following day so they could speak without the fear of a party line and someone hearing what they were saying.

Sabrina then returned to her room. Over and over again in her mind, she thought about her family and how they were slaughtered.

She was even angrier with Alexander. *How could he be one of them?* How could she have fallen for a man who ultimately was responsible for the deaths of her family members? He probably would have had her killed in the name of the republic.

She wanted to leave the house and kill him. She knew she would never be able to hurt anyone, but her fantasy was real. *He will get his.* Sabrina would never know of his fate, but she often wondered what happened to that young Russian. She found it very interesting that after Father spoke of him, he was never seen again. She felt it best never to ask and didn't.

❦

The Russian Palace—how beautiful was her last dance there. The orchestra played and everyone was so nicely attired. She wore a long, white, beaded lace gown. The seamstress had taken every effort to make sure all the gowns in the family were similar. Her brother wore a white uniform, as did Father. There were fine linens on the tables, silver, crystal glasses, and plates with the imperial seal. The men were all in uniform, and their wives were finely dressed. She danced with Father. It was as if she was floating around the palace floor. It was a time of no worries, no pressure, and no stress—a fairyland of gaiety and laughter. Why couldn't it last forever? Little did she know that it would be her last formal celebration at the palace. Where are those people today? Have they too been slaughtered? It is so hard, she thought.

❦

There was a knock on her door. "Sabrina," Mother said. "May I come in?"

"Certainly. You never have to ask," Sabrina responded.

"What have you been doing?" Mother asked.

Sabrina looked at Mother. Her eyes were reddened, and she said, "Just lying here thinking about the past."

"Yes. I can understand why you would be reflecting at a time like this. I know it must be hard for you. To find out the way you did without any preparation or warning. We are so sorry, Sabrina."

"Mother, it is not your fault. How would anybody have known? Fortunately, I was home and did not hear it in the streets," Sabrina exclaimed.

Mother walked over to Sabrina, bent down, and gave her a hug. "Yes, I guess you are right. It has been a long journey for you. Our family is truly now your family, and we will always be here for you. You are a part of us, and we love you."

Sabrina's eyes began to tear. "I know. It has been so hard to deal with all these changes."

Mother looked at her, paused for a moment, and then said, "When we thought we lost you today, your dad and I were frantic. We just knew that the young Russian was up to no good"

"How could you tell?" Sabrina asked.

"After all of our years in the world, you just sense those things—and you can spot them."

Sabrina reached for Mother's hand. "I never really did understand why Rasputin placed me with a Jewish family."

"Oh, my dear, it was not his idea. Your relatives thought it would be the easiest way for you to escape. They would never expect a member of the imperial family to be living as a Jew."

"What do you mean?" Sabrina asked.

Mother looked at Sabrina with surprise. "You mean you do not know?"

"No, Mother, I do not."

"Well, the Jewish people were not too well liked by the people in power," Mother replied.

"You mean my mama and papa?" Sabrina asked.

"Not your mother. She had your great-grandmother to remind her that everyone should be treated with dignity. However, those close to the tsar felt differently. That is why we wanted to leave Russia. There were the pogroms."

"What were those, Mother?"

"The military would travel to our small towns and cause an uprising, burning our villages, and then we would have to move like gypsies. They needed to blame someone for the problems that were going on in Russia, and they chose us. I am not certain if the tsar and the empress knew exactly what was happening because they were so far removed from the situation. We wanted to come to this country, but it would have been financially impossible for us if it were not for Rasputin. When he saw our daughter, he knew what he had to do."

"But, Mother, wasn't it hard for you to give up your daughter?"

"Of course it was. We did not believe she would ultimately be in danger. Actually we believed that the tsar would leave Russia until the unrest within the country calmed down. At the very least, he would make provisions for his children. I am still quite puzzled why that did not happen. Even his mother was able to escape. Your father believed that generals would take care and protect him. He would not listen to anyone. Your mother was a brave woman to let you go with us."

"What do you mean?" Sabrina asked.

"The empress was the one who ultimately made the decision. She believed that you would leave one at a time and all of you would be reunited some day here in America or England. I know you miss her, and I will never be able to take her place. Remember how you nursed me to health on the ship? You were everything a mother would want in a child. Your mother raised you well. You are a strong woman, and you need to gather that strength. I know you have what it takes to move forward in life. You must keep the family line going."

"For what purpose?" Sabrina responded.

"For the purpose of knowing in your heart that the family's blood was not spilled in vain. You are the offspring of several royal families. Your great-grandmother was England's greatest ruler, your grandmother was the Duchess of Hesse in Germany, and your parents were the last rulers of Russia. Your heritage as a Romanov depends on your survival. It does not matter if you are ruling an empire or not. What matters is who you represent. You will marry and have children. Although they will not know their true heritage, the Lord will know—and from them, great things will ultimately come."

Sabrina stared at Mother.

"Yes, my dear. It is a lot to grasp, but you have the mind and the fortitude to move into the future. Now go to sleep. Tomorrow starts another day—one that will be another memory someday."

Long Island, New York, 1974

His grandmother coughed. "David, could you get me something to drink?"

David was spellbound by his grandmother's disclosures. "Yes, Grandmother. I shall return shortly." He walked quickly, thinking about what she had told him. Now things started to make sense to him: why there were no photographs of her as a young child, why she looked so different from other family members, why she seemed so poised and refined coming from a poor family, and why she was so attached to the ivory brush.

"Thank you, David."

David placed his hand behind her head and gently lifted her so she could drink through the straw.

"Thank you, my dear. Let me continue."

"Grandma, don't you think you should rest?"

"Yes, my child, later, later."

"Grandma, why are you not sharing this with my uncle?"

"David, I do not believe he would be able to understand and would share what I have been telling you with his wife. I am sorry to say I do not trust her. She thinks she is something she is not. Any of this information would be used for the wrong purpose. I know you will keep my confidence. Your upbringing and values are good. Your mother was a giving woman like the women in my family. She would give her last piece of bread to a hungry infant rather than ingest it herself. I know in my heart that you will do the right thing."

Her voice was softer now, and David said, "Please, Grandma, rest—just for a while."

"David, it will be all right. I would like to share more with you."

Brooklyn, New York, 1918

The sun shone through the window, and Sabrina heard the telephone ring.

Mother said, "She had a difficult night and is sleeping."

Sabrina opened her door. "Mom, I am up."

"It is Martin. He said something about a date today?"

Sabrina thought for a moment. She had said when she spoke to Anna that she had made arrangements with Martin.

"I will take the call," Sabrina said.

"Hello, Sabrina," Martin said. "It has been a long time."

"Yes, Martin, it has," Sabrina replied.

"I thought we could go to the park today?"

"I would love to go to the park, but I promised to meet Anna. I guess I became caught up in her news yesterday, but I do want to meet with you too. Could we meet later this afternoon?"

Martin paused, initially feeling disappointed by her date with Anna, but as he heard her offer, he exclaimed, "That would be wonderful, Sabrina. What time did you have in mind?"

She responded, "How is four o'clock?"

"That is great. I will meet you at your home."

"No, Martin. It would probably be better if we met at Anna's. She lives closer to you."

"That will be fine. Until later." Martin felt happy about how receptive Sabrina was to him. He was beginning to think that she might not be interested in him. He had heard talk that Sabrina had been seen in another part of town with another gentleman. Martin just thought it was idle gossip and did not place much emphasis on it. He took a deep breath and went back to what he was doing.

"Well, Sabrina," Mother said, "you handled that with dignity. Good thinking."

"Thank you, Mother." Sabrina smiled. "I really did want to meet with Martin. He is such a nice man, and I could use some of his kindness today."

"I know he will not disappoint you," Mother replied.

Sabrina left for her sister's house shortly after breakfast. She would have midmorning tea with her sister before lunch and Martin's call. Sabrina wanted to speak to her sister about her loss, but she was well aware that she had to be careful about what she shared. If her sister was ever placed in a compromising position, it was best for her not to know specifics about Sabrina. The basics were enough. Sabrina had to respect her parents' wishes. She was not going to repeat the same mistake. Her relationship with Alexander had a major impact on her. Sabrina thought for a moment about how she was captivated by his charm and sex appeal. She realized that she was much too smart to let emotions stand in the way of her safety and well-being. She would never let it happen again. Sabrina would never let another man put her in a position of vulnerability.

Anna greeted Sabrina at the door.

Sabrina walked in and hugged her sister. "Anna, how wonderful you look. No morning sickness?"

"No, Sabrina." She held up two fingers on each hand and said, "Poo poo."

Sabrina stared at her sister.

Anna laughed and said, "It is a custom and superstition to ward off evil spirits for saying something good about yourself."

Sabrina replied, "Oh, I am glad. I thought you were going mad."

They both began to laugh.

Sabrina looked at Anna very seriously and said, "I wanted to speak to you about your sister and what happened to her."

Anna's eyes welled up with tears.

Sabrina said, "You should not know of such things. It is a terrible, terrible thing. I cried all night."

"I appreciate your condolences, but you need to understand it is not your fault. No one would have ever predicted that a child would be at imminent risk. The sad thing is we cannot even sit Shiva because we are unsure of her fate."

Anna said, "I am sorry, Sabrina. I do not necessarily agree with you. If there is even a slight chance of hope, we must pray. Perhaps the good Lord will hear those prayers."

Sabrina nodded. She wanted no further discussion and felt it best to change the topic.

Anna looked at Sabrina and asked, "Would you like some tea?"

"Yes, that would be lovely," Sabrina replied. "Anna, what a beautiful samovar."

Anna looked at Sabrina and walked over to the table. "Mother gave it to me for our wedding." *It looks just like mine*, Sabrina thought. "It is from Russia."

Anna lifted the samovar and started to carry it to the table.

Sabrina arose from her chair and insisted that she take the samovar from Anna.

Anna said, "You treat me like I am not able to do anything. I am only pregnant."

"Anna, I am here—and am more than capable of lending a helping hand."

Anna returned to the kitchen and brought out a plate of freshly baked cookies.

"Those look delicious." Sabrina placed a napkin on her lap and took a small bite of a cookie. "These are exceptional, Anna. I did not realize you were such a good baker."

"Thank you, Sabrina. Coming from you, that is a 'royal' compliment."

They both started to laugh. The visit went by very quickly. They had just finished washing the plates and teacups from lunch when the doorbell rang.

"What time is it?" Sabrina asked.

"It is almost four o'clock."

"I forgot to tell you, Anna. I asked Martin to meet me here at four. I assumed that it would be all right with you. I was supposed to meet him earlier, but I wanted to visit with you."

"Sabrina, it would have been just fine if you put off our visit or even have asked Martin to join us."

Sabrina replied, "I know, but I really needed to speak to you alone. I was concerned about you, and I knew you were looking forward, as I was, to our visit."

Anna leaned over and gave Sabrina a kiss on her cheek. "Thank you, Sabrina. You are a good sister and friend." They embraced.

The doorbell chimed again. Anna looked at her sister and pointed to the front of the house. "Sabrina, you better go to the door or he will think no one is at home."

Sabrina opened the door. Anna looked on from the distance. As soon as she saw Martin, Sabrina's face began to glow.

"Hello, Sabrina. I missed you."

Sabrina stood in silence, stunned.

Martin smiled and said, "Well, can I please come in to your sister's home so I can congratulate the mother-to-be?"

"Of course," Sabrina replied. "Come in. Come in."

Martin wore a dark suit, white shirt, and blue tie. His brown hair was combed back, and his mustache was trimmed to perfection. As he approached Sabrina, she felt a warm sensation travel through her body. Her faced turned bright red.

"Are you all right, Sabrina?" Martin asked.

Embarrassed, Sabrina replied, "Yes, of course. It is just very warm in here."

Anna looked at her sister and said, "Sabrina, would you like me to open the window?" She looked at Sabrina and smiled. Sabrina knew her sister was aware of what she was feeling.

"No, Anna. Martin just wanted to say a few words—and then we will be leaving."

Anna said, "Oh, I see."

Martin looked at Anna. "My dearest Anna. I heard the good news. Congratulations to you and the father-to-be. He must be very excited."

Anna smiled. "He sure is. He has not been able to sleep since I told him, and I believe he is even nauseous in the morning."

"Better him than you I guess," Martin added.

They all laughed.

"Would you like a drink?" Anna asked.

Martin said, "No, Sabrina and I need to go before the sun begins to set."

Sabrina and Martin said their good-byes, and even before the door closed behind them, Anna was on the telephone with Mother.

"Sabrina, I have a surprise for you in my right pocket," Martin exclaimed.

"What is it?"

"It is a book of my favorite poems. I bought it for you. I thought you would enjoy them as much as I have," Martin said.

Sabrina opened the book and leafed through it. "Martin, you are so thoughtful." She grabbed his hand, pulled him closer, and gave him a kiss on the cheek.

Martin began to blush and smile.

"Martin, this is a special moment. You are speechless."

"No, Sabrina. I am just enamored by your beauty. I missed you so much. These poems best express how I feel," Martin said. They looked into each other's eyes, and for a moment, they both stood still.

"Sabrina, there is the trolley. If we do not hurry, we will miss it. Here, give me your hand."

They ran to the trolley and arrived without a second to spare. Partially out of breath, they climbed up the step of the trolley. Martin took out the correct change and handed it to the conductor. They were each breathing heavily. After they sat down, they looked at one another and began to laugh.

"Wherever you are taking me, I hope it was worth the run," Sabrina exclaimed.

"Excuse me, Sabrina? I thought you would be happy with any of my choices."

"Isn't that taking me for granted?" Sabrina responded.

"No, Sabrina. You would be a hard woman to take for granted," Martin said, smiling.

Once again, they began to laugh.

"The next stop is where we are going." He reached over, brushing his sleeve against her chest in order to pull the cord to notify the conductor to stop. They looked at each other but did not utter a word. At that moment, she really wanted to hug him. Sabrina wanted to feel his body close to hers. However, she knew that such a public display of emotion would be inappropriate. Anyway, how could she possibly feel that way? The other day, Alexander captivated her. *Am I losing my mind?*

The trolley stopped in front of a group of shops and cafes. "I thought we could have some coffee."

Sabrina looked up. It was the same café she had gone to with the young Russian. Her heart began to pound, and her face turned red.

"Sabrina, do you feel all right?" Martin asked.

"Yes, I am a little uncomfortable because I do not feel that I have dressed appropriately for today's weather. I am a bit warm from our run. Would you mind if we walked a little before we had something warm to drink? Anna fed me so much that I am so stuffed. A walk would make me feel so much better," she said.

"Your desire is my command, Sabrina," Martin replied.

Sabrina looked at Martin and said, "Let us walk this way." She pointed in the direction the trolley had just come from. She did not want to be seen in this part of town. What would happen if the young Russian or his friends were in the area?

Sabrina grabbed Martin's hand, and they walked toward Anna's house.

Martin thought, *Maybe it was not idle gossip. Is this the section of town that the woman was referring to? Well, it does not matter. She is with me now—and that is all that counts.*

They spoke, laughed, and shared experiences about their families. When they were back in the vicinity of Anna's house, Sabrina saw a quaint café. "I am very thirsty. I would like to have that drink now."

"It is fine with me," Martin replied. The quaint café had small round tables and red-and-white tablecloths. There were small candles on the table, and the waiter was beginning to light them.

"I do not know about you, Sabrina, but that walk built up an appetite for me. Would you like something to eat?"

Sabrina realized that in this neighborhood, the café had to be kosher. *If we were to have drink, it would be one thing, but to eat an entire meal would be another.*

"Sabrina, do not worry. I already examined the menu. This place is kosher. My family and I also respect the dietary rules. My mother would never let me forget it if I took you out to eat in a place that was not kosher."

"Yes, Martin, dinner would be lovely. Why don't you order for me while I use the facilities." Sabrina stood up and started to walk to the restroom.

If Martin was unsure about the dietary laws being practiced by the establishment, he sure knew it when he read the menu. It was written in Hebrew!

Martin ordered dinner for Sabrina and himself. They dined for several hours. Before either of them realized, it was nine o'clock.

"I believe we should skip dessert; it is getting late," Sabrina said.

Martin replied, "Well if we continue speaking, we can order breakfast."

"No, Martin, we need to leave. My parents will send out the police in search for us if I am not home by 9:30." After what happened at the park, Sabrina knew better than to stay out too late.

Martin reached over and took Sabrina's hand. "I will take care of the bill, and we will be off."

As they left the café, Martin waved down a car. "What are you doing, Martin?"

"I thought it best to call for a car so you can be home as soon as possible."

"No, Martin. A trolley will be here in just a few minutes. Look, there is one now." Sabrina pointed.

In less than fifteen minutes, Sabrina was home. Mother was waiting patiently to find out about Sabrina's date.

Sabrina looked into Martin's eyes and said, "Martin, I had such a good time today. Thank you for everything, especially the book of poems. You are a special man." She reached over and kissed him on the cheek again.

Martin turned to Sabrina and said, "I too had a great day. You make me feel special, and I am fortunate to have met you." He took her hand. "You are cold." He gave her a hug and then looked into her eyes. When their eyes met, he moved his head toward her and kissed her.

She felt the warmth of his body next to hers. Sabrina felt protected and safe.

Martin was becoming increasingly more aroused. He felt himself becoming excited and erect. He became embarrassed since his body was in such close proximity to Sabrina's. He waited a moment and then moved back.

Sabrina looked at him and thought about where she was. It was not proper to be in view of the neighbors. That is how women get reputations, and she should not let the moment dictate her actions. She needed to think of the effects of her actions. She thought of her previous encounter and said, "It is getting late."

"Yes, it is," Martin replied.

"Thank you again, Martin. Perhaps we could spend some time together this weekend? Perhaps we can get together after Shabbos."

"That would be nice," Martin replied.

Sabrina opened the door and said, "It has been a lovely evening. Thank you for making my day a special one. Good night."

It was late, and there was a small lamp lit in the parlor. She did not expect anyone to be up, but Mother said, "Sabrina?"

"Yes, Mom. You did not have to wait up for me. You know I would be safe with Martin."

"I know, but after last evening, I wanted to be sure that you were doing all right."

"That is very caring of you, and I appreciate it."

"Now since we are both up, it should not be a total loss. How are you doing?"

"I am doing fine. Anna and I had a nice visit today. She even baked delicious pastries for me. Wasn't that so nice of her?"

"Sabrina, I know about your visit. I was asking about your date with Martin?"

"He is so wonderful and thoughtful. You will not believe this, but he first took me to the café where I had tea with the young Russian."

Mother's expression radically changed.

"Mom, don't alarm yourself. I told him I was not thirsty and that I felt warm and desired to be out in the fresh air for a while. We walked quite a while in the direction of Anna's. We then stopped at the café near her house. It is kosher, and we had dinner. By the time we finished, it was nine o'clock."

"Sabrina, did he kiss you?" Mother winked.

"Mom! Aren't you being a little personal?"

"Yes, but you know me."

"A little too well. And if we did?"

"So was it what you expected?"

"Mother."

"Well then, it is time to have Martin over for Shabbos dinner."

"Aren't you rushing things?" Sabrina looked at Mother with displeasure.

"Well, you have been invited to his house, and I thought it would be a nice gesture to invite him here. Since you two seemed to be enjoying yourselves on the front porch, I thought it might be something you would like."

"Mom, I guess you were doing more than just reading in the other room."

Mother looked up at Sabrina. "We will talk more tomorrow. Have a good night."

"Thank you," Sabrina replied.

Sabrina floated upstairs to her bedroom. It was a very pleasant afternoon and evening for her. Martin was, in fact, a special man. She did not realize his attributes the first few times she had dated him. Sabrina realized he was a quiet and shy man who needed time to get to know her before he felt comfortable enough to interact more openly.

She sat down at the window in her room and looked up at the stars. The bright moon lit the street. She looked out and saw a stray dog knocking over her neighbor's garbage can. Her eyes glanced at the stars and she thought about how much she missed Mother if she was only there to share in her experience this evening and her dreams. *Why did they have to kill my family? What is life all about? One moment you are free and happy—and the next you are sliding into an abyss. I am so afraid. What will happen to me if I am discovered? Will I have the same fate as my family? I have so much to share about my early life, and now I have to bury it all. My adoptive family are very good people and care about me. I am fortunate, but it is not and will never be the same. I will survive. I will not let anyone ever take advantage or hurt me. I must be all I can be. My great-grandmother would want it that way. I will not let my family down!* A tear dripped on her arm. *I will take one day at a time, and with each passing day, I will begin to heal and become stronger. I will. I have to.* She clenched her fist and held it up to the sky.

When Martin arrived home, his mother welcomed Martin. She was waiting at the door and did not even give him a chance to take off his coat.

"Well, I have been waiting."

"I am thankful that you are waiting up, but it was not necessary," Martin said. "I am tired, and I have work tomorrow."

"You are not going to share anything about your evening. At least let me know if you had a good time."

"Mom, I did not have a good time."

"What?"

"Mom, I had a great time." Martin winked at his mother and gave her a big hug and kiss on her cheek. "I am going to sleep. We have time to discuss things when I return home from work tomorrow."

Martin was ecstatic. He ran up to his room. He wanted to call Sabrina, but it was too late. He had never felt that way about another woman. *There is just something different about her. She is so beautiful, intelligent, witty, and refined. I am so thankful I was wearing a coat that extended below my waist. I want to see her again. Will she accept my offer for after Shabbos? What if she does not? I will not let her say no. I will persuade her.*

The next morning, Sabrina went downstairs and smelled the aroma of freshly baked bread and muffins. Mother had already been up for hours.

"Mother, why didn't you wake me to help you? I feel badly."

"Sabrina, you had a late night—and you needed your rest," Mother said.

"Mom, you were up late yourself."

"I know, I know. I do not need much sleep. I will be fine. Here eat. You need your strength. I made you some muffins."

"Sabrina, do you remember what we discussed last evening?"

"Yes, mother. You would like Martin to share Shabbos dinner with us on Friday. But it is already Wednesday. He may be busy."

"If you don't ask, you will never know."

Sabrina looked at the gleam in Mother's eye. She knew that she better make the call or Mother would persist. After all, she would like to see Martin again. She thought about dinner with her family. *Will her brothers scare him away? She knew how shy he could be around people he did not know.* Martin was at work, and she could not interrupt his day with a dinner invitation. *I better wait until he returns.*

Sabrina was anxious when she made the call that evening. She and Martin spoke for almost an hour. When she placed the receiver down, Mother asked, "So can he come for dinner?"

"Oh, Mom. I forgot to ask."

Mother smiled. "That's all right. Just call him back."

Sabrina picked up the telephone and said, "Hi Martin, I forgot to ask you something."

"Yes, Sabrina."

"My family would like to invite you over for Shabbos dinner this Friday. If you are busy, I will understand."

"Sabrina, I gladly accept your gracious invitation for Shabbos dinner this Friday evening. I will be over before sundown. I look forward to meeting the rest of your family. Please thank your family for the invitation. Have a good night. Sabrina?"

"Yes, Martin."

"I hope this does not mean that I have to wait until Friday to speak to you again."

"No, Martin. You don't."

"I will call you tomorrow after work."

"I look forward to that call."

"Good night, Martin,"

"So Sabrina?" Mother said.

Sabrina smiled. "Set another place at the table on Friday night. Martin is coming."

Mother looked at her and replied, "Let's plan the menu."

CHAPTER TWELVE

Till Death Do Us Part

"Martin, you are going to be late for work," his mother shouted.

He walked quickly down the stairs, tripping on the last step. His mother heard a loud, echoing sound.

"Martin, are you all right?"

"Yes, Mother, it was just that last step. Someday I am going to break my leg. I need to try to fix it. It is getting worse."

"Martin, perhaps you are just trying to rush a little too much."

"Thanks, Mom, but you know I am somewhat of a klutz. Too bad I am not as coordinated as Cousin Jacob."

"Martin, you look tired today."

Martin ignored his mother's comments. He knew if he reacted to the conversation, it would continue—and he would certainly be late for work. Anyway, he was not going to let anything upset him this morning. He was still thinking of Sabrina, and he was in a major state of peace and tranquility. He quickly ate the breakfast his mother prepared, thanked her, kissed her on the forehead, and left for work. On his way to the train, he stopped at the cleaners to drop off his suit.

Martin hurried down the street to the train. Martin did not want to be late today. His boss had called a meeting. He arrived at the station at the same time as the train. It was crowded, and there were no seats. He stood, holding the center pole in the car.

The doors closed, and the train gave a quick jerk and began to move. Martin lost his balance, and his back hit the person behind him. Martin said, "Excuse me."

It was Sabrina's father.

"Sir, I did not expect to see you on the train. What a surprise. Good morning."

"Good morning, Martin. I am meeting someone in the city this morning. You are right. I usually do not travel into the city. I hope your family is doing fine."

"Yes, they are," Martin responded. "How are things with you?"

Sabrina's father took a deep breath. "I am busier than ever. And yourself?"

"I am doing fine," Martin replied. "I had a nice time with Sabrina last evening."

The train came to a halting stop. The wheels squeaked.

"Excuse me, Martin? I could not hear you. I need to go. This is my stop. Perhaps we can talk again soon." He exited before Martin could say anything more.

People pushed into the car, and there was little room to move. A person repeatedly coughed, but they had no room to raise their hands to their faces. Martin hated the commute, but it would soon be over.

The train stopped, and Martin charged to the door. It was like basic training moving to the door that early in the morning. People would not give up their spaces in spite of someone needing to get by them.

He took a deep breath upon his exit and walked at a fast pace to his office. *I should have skipped breakfast*, he thought. *It would have given me another ten minutes.*

"Good morning, Martin."

"Good day, Sally."

She smiled and said, "You can go right in to Mr. Shine. He is expecting you."

Mr. Shine looked up as Martin walked into his office. "Martin, please sit down. You look like you just ran a race."

Mr. Shine was in his fifties, partially bald, overweight, and very outspoken. He was an exceptional businessman and had bought the company seven years earlier. At that time, the company had few employees—and the owners had no vision. Mr. Shine seized the opportunity.

Today, the company had two factories and a hundred employees. Martin had managed the office for several months after he received his discharge papers from the military. Mr. Shine had known Martin prior to the time he became an employee. Mr. Shine had been at several family functions through the years. His wife was a distant cousin of Martin's mother. Martin did not realize that he was going to be the only one at the meeting. He assumed that the other office staff would be there as well. There was no indication to Martin that Mr. Shine needed to speak to him alone.

"Ah, Martin, would you like some tea or coffee? I am going to have some tea this morning. Shall I have Sally bring you a cup?"

To say no to a food offer from Mr. Shine would be an insult. "That would be nice," Martin replied.

"Good. Sally, may we please have two teas and some of those lovely cakes Mrs. Green brought in this morning? Mrs. Green is an exceptional baker. Her parents were schooled in Germany."

Martin just wanted to get on with the meeting. *Why does everything have to be centered on food? Can't people say what they have to say and move on?* Martin sighed.

"Martin, just relax. Your secretary is more than capable of getting things started this morning. I have already spoken to her. She is aware we will be tied up for a while."

A while? Martin thought. *What is going on? Am I getting fired?*

"Ah, here is the tea and those cakes. Mmmm. They sure look good. Sally, please close the door. I love the aroma of freshly brewed tea, and I can't wait to set my teeth into these cakes."

Martin had to bite his tongue not to laugh. *This man is getting so aroused by the food. I hope he does not wet his pants.*

"Martin, so how are things going for you here?"

"Mr. Shine, I believe the office is working well and efficiently. It is my opinion that there could be some savings if we consolidated some of the departments."

Mr. Shine slapped Martin on the back. "That is what I like about you, Martin. You are always thinking about efficiency and profitability. Since you arrived here, the company's bottom line has increased significantly. The cookies are good, aren't they?"

"Mr. Shine, I certainly cannot take the credit. We are a group of players, and I am just a single member of that team."

"Thank you, Martin, for your modesty. However, I know how things were operating here before you joined us—and I am aware of where they are now. Take a cookie. They are good. Here, here take this one. Martin, I am opening another factory in Brooklyn—close to where you live—and I would like you to run it for me. There is no one more qualified than you. I can depend on you, and I know if you have any concerns, you will come to me for advice."

Martin bit into the cookie, chewed for a moment, and took a sip of tea. "Thank you for your confidence, Mr. Shine, but I have only been with the company for several months. There are others who have been here longer."

Mr. Shine shoved a piece of cake in his mouth and slurped his tea. "Ah that is good. Mm, my wife needs to get that recipe. Martin, you need to realize your value here. Yes, there are others, but I have chosen you."

Martin looked down. "Thank you for your confidence in me, Mr. Shine."

"Wait a minute, Martin. Not so fast. Would you like a piece of cake with your tea? It is really good."

It is a miracle that I have not gained fifty pounds. I better say yes or I am going to offend him. "Maybe a little piece would be nice."

"A little piece. Have a bigger piece of cake. It is good for you, and you can afford it. Look at me." Mr. Shine pointed to his stomach. He placed a large piece of cake on Martin's plate. "Taste it. It is good."

Martin broke off a piece with his fork and placed it in his mouth. "You are right, Mr. Shine. It is good."

Mr. Shine chewed with his mouth open and looked at Martin. "I would not steer you wrong. Now, as I was saying, the factory will be opening in several months."

Martin thought for a moment. *There has been construction on a building not too far from my home. Evidently, this has been in the works for some time.*

Mr. Shine continued, "The building is located several blocks from your home. We will go over in a little while, and I will give you a tour. Until it is fully open, you will be working here with me. We will be hiring sixty workers and an office staff. I also want you to consolidate several operations of the company, and those will be run out of the new factory site. Martin, I realize this will involve additional responsibility for you, and I am prepared to give you a bonus and a raise. Here." Mr. Shine reached into his top desk drawer. He handed Martin a check for one thousand dollars.

Martin's jaw dropped.

"You can close your mouth now, unless you want more cake. Finish your tea—and then we will be off to Brooklyn."

He walked over to the door, opened it, and said, "Sally, have them drive my car around to the front of the building."

The factory was indeed the building Martin thought it was. He was not aware how much work had been done. The building was nearing completion. Martin was impressed by all the equipment, the spaciousness, and the bright light from the large windows. It was not going to be a sweatshop. Mr. Shine knew how to treat his employees. His motto was: *Lead through example and give back to those who helped you achieve your career aspirations.*

His employees respected him and were loyal. He rarely had anyone leave his employ. In fact, Mr. Shine gave incentives for attendance and production.

"You have planned this well, Mr. Shine," Martin exclaimed.

"Thank you, Martin. Now I will take you to the offices."

They walked to the other side of the building. "Here," Mr. Shine said. "This is where your office will be." Ahead of them was a large office encased with glass walls. Surrounding this office were cubicles separated by glass partitions. "You will be able to keep an eye on everything from your office." Pointing to the far glass wall, Martin could see that he would have a view of the entire factory floor. Mr. Shine walked into the office and pointed outside. "See those buildings several blocks away? We have the first option on all the land to those buildings. Martin, we always have to think of the future. Any questions? How foolish of me. There is a lot here for you to digest. We will talk over lunch. Let's go. There is a nice café down the street."

Wonderful, Martin thought, *another heavy meal.*

"Let's walk. I could use the exercise," Mr. Shine said.

They sat at lunch for several hours and discussed the plans for the new factory. Martin was extremely appreciative and pleased with the offer. Mr. Shine never gave him the opportunity to make a decision. He just assumed a yes. Martin could not wait to tell his parents and Sabrina.

"Martin, I have filled your head with enough today. Since we are so close to your house, why don't you take the next few hours off and head home? I will see you first thing tomorrow morning in my office. Please send my best regards to your parents. Give your mother a hug from me." He took money out of his pocket and put it on the table. "It is time to go. I have another meeting in half an hour."

Martin stood and said, "Thank you for the confidence you have in me. I will not let you down."

"I know you won't. See you in the morning." Mr. Shine shook Martin's hand, turned, and walked away.

Martin made a brisk dash to his house. He opened the door and called to his mother repeatedly.

She came running in from the kitchen. Her apron was stained with food, and her hands were full of flour. "Martin, what is wrong? Why are you home so early?"

"I have some news. I just came from the café."

"Good, I hope?"

"Mr. Shine offered me a new position."

"Call your father. He would love to hear your good news. Martin, please call him. Oh I have to go. I will be right back."

Martin picked up the telephone, "Dr. Stein's office," the receptionist said. "Can I help you?"

"It's Martin. Can I speak to my father?"

"Certainly."

"Dr. Stein, here. Martin, it is you. She should have told me. She just handed me the telephone. I thought it was your mother. Is everything all right?"

"Yes, Dad, I am holding a thousand-dollar bonus check. Mr. Shine offered me a promotion."

"Mazel tov, Martin. I am so proud of you. We will talk later. Thanks for calling."

His dad's reaction was important to Martin. He often wondered if his father was disappointed in him for not pursuing medicine. Martin realized that his dad only wanted the best for him. His dad knew from other families that pressuring a child could result in conflict and failure. Martin's father had learned this vital lesson from his patients and had put this knowledge to good use.

Sabrina called that evening, and she and Martin spoke for several hours. He gladly accepted her invitation for dinner. Over the next several weeks, they were inseparable in spite of Martin's long hours at work.

One evening, Martin made a surprise visit to Sabrina at her home. He did not call prior to arrival.

Sabrina's mother said, "I wonder who that could be at this hour." She called to her husband to open the door.

Sabrina was always worried when the doorbell rang, especially during the evening, in fear of her safety and that of the family.

As Father approached the door, he saw the silhouette of a man. He walked through the vestibule and looked through the window. He opened the door. "Martin, you startled us."

Martin shook his hand and said, "Sir, may I speak to you in private?"

Sabrina's father asked, "Is everything all right?"

"I did not mean to alarm you, but I just returned from work and wanted to speak to you."

"Who's there? It is for me?" Mrs. Sholin asked.

Mr. Sholin shouted, "No, dear. It is for me. I am going into the parlor, and I do not want to be disturbed." Mr. Sholin took Martin into the parlor and closed the door. "What is it, Martin?"

Martin looked down and raised his head, facing Mr. Sholin. "Sir, I would like the honor of asking for your daughter's hand in marriage."

"Martin, you scared me. Is that all! Of course you may, my son. Sabrina's mother and I would be honored to have you as our son-in-law."

Martin looked at Sabrina's father and said, "I am thankful for your support. There is just one thing."

"Yes, Martin."

Martin looked anxiously at Mr. Sholin. "I have not said anything to Sabrina."

"You may want to say something to Sabrina. Isn't your speaking to me putting the cart before the horse?" Mr. Sholin smiled.

"Yes, sir, but I feel it is customary for me to first ask you for your daughter's hand in marriage before I propose to her. I also respect you and would not do anything that you did not support."

"Thank you, Martin. That means a lot to Sabrina's mother and me. I am very pleased with your formality and respecting my wishes. Let's go into the other room. Is Sabrina expecting you?"

"No."

Father thought, *This is going to be a first. I am interested in seeing how Martin is going to proceed.*

"There is just one more thing," Martin said.

"Yes, my son."

"I would like you to make the announcement."

"Are you certain she is going to say yes?"

Martin was taken aback by Mr. Sholin's response. "Well, I am not certain, but there is a reasonable probability."

Mr. Sholin smiled. "Martin, get over here give me a hug. We are not all that formal here. Loosen up a bit. Enjoy this moment—and cherish it."

Martin felt the pressure of the moment start to dissipate. Father's hug was just the right medicine for him. He smiled.

They entered the kitchen together; the family was sitting around the table having tea.

Sabrina's mother said, "Martin, what are you doing here? We were not expecting you—or were we?"

Sabrina shook her head and then looked at Martin. Their eyes met, and everyone in the room looked at them.

"There is something I need to announce." Mr. Sholin said.

Everyone stopped what they were doing and looked at him.

Sabrina could hear the water dripping into the drain. The clock ticked, and the chimes began to ring. At the end of nine chimes, it ended. Everyone waited in silence.

Mr. Sholin looked at his wife.

Mrs. Sholin stated, "Well, we are waiting."

Mr. Sholin looked at his wife and stated, "Martin has just asked me for our daughter's hand in marriage."

Sabrina looked at Martin. Mother began to cry. Her brothers stood up to congratulate Martin.

Sabrina said, "Wait a minute."

Martin looked at her, wondering what she was going to say.

"I was not formally asked." Sabrina turned in the direction of Father and winked.

Without missing a beat, Martin walked over to her, got down on one knee, and reached into his pocket. There was total silence in the kitchen.

Opening his hand and reaching out to Sabrina, he said, "My love for you will be everlasting. You make the days brighter; you bring tranquility and peace to my heart and soul. I would like to pledge my love and spend the rest of my life with you. Will you please accept this ring as a token of this devotion and be my wife?"

Sabrina's eyes began to tear. "I do! I do!"

He slipped the ring on her finger. The family walked into the center of the room and collectively said, "Mazel tov."

Father shouted, "Martin, I will get us some schnapps, and we will drink to your engagement." He grabbed the bottle from the dining room. Mr. Sholin took out four schnapps glasses, poured the liquor, and they toasted the occasion.

After conversing for several hours, Martin and Sabrina walked out to the vestibule.

"Martin, I am so happy—and the ring is beautiful. I was so surprised. You must have spent your whole bonus check."

"You deserve the best, Sabrina. It looks so beautiful on your finger."

"Thank you, Martin." She stood on her toes and gave him a kiss. He smiled. "Until tomorrow."

"I will count the seconds until you return," she said.

Martin was tired, but he decided to walk home. There was a damp chill in the air and a breeze blowing from the north. When he was close to his home, a light rain began to fall. Martin was cold and wet when he hurriedly entered his house. It was late, and everyone was sleeping. Martin took off his clothes and went to bed.

The next morning, he arose and was sweating. He took a shower, combed his hair, and went down for breakfast. It was early, but he wanted to share the news with his parents.

"Martin, are you all right? You seem so tired and pale," his mother said.

"Where is Dad?" Martin asked.

"He will be right in."

"There is something I wanted to say." His father entered the room and looked up at Martin.

"Martin, are you all right? You look a little flushed."

Martin looked at his parents and said, "I wanted to let you know that last night I asked for Sabrina's hand in marriage—and she accepted."

His parents ran over to him and hugged him. "Mazel tov. We are so pleased. Are you sure you are feeling well?" His mother took the back of her hand and felt his forehead. "You feel a little warm."

"No. I am just tired. I got home very late last night."

"Why don't you stay home today? Mr. Shine will understand," his mother suggested.

His dad said, "Perhaps you should stop at my office before you go to work. It is on your way."

"No. I have too much to do. The factory is going to open in less than thirty days. There is too much to do."

"Martin, you are run down, and the flu is quite bad. There are clinics opening up everywhere. Your Aunt Rona almost died from the illness," his father said. "Let me at least take your temperature."

"Father, it is not the flu. I am just tired. I will be just fine. It is Thursday already, and tomorrow I stop work at four o'clock to get ready for Shabbos. Please just let me finish breakfast so I will not be late."

Martin gulped down his breakfast, went to the bathroom, and left the house. On his way to work, he developed a slight cough. *I should have put some lozenges in my pocket.*

When he arrived at work, Mr. Shine was already in his office with a pile of papers on his desk. "Hi, Martin. When you get a chance, I would like to speak to you. No hurry. It can wait, but sometime this morning would be appreciated."

Martin walked over to his desk, reviewed his messages, and then headed down the hallway to Mr. Shine's office.

"Splendid, Martin, please come in. Are you feeling all right? You look flushed. Come over here." Mr. Shine took the back of his hand and felt his forehead. "You have a fever, boy. Go home!"

"But there is too much to do," Martin exclaimed.

"Enough," Mr. Shine replied. "We will just have to get through the day without you. Anyway, I certainly do not want to catch whatever is ailing you. Go. That is a direct order. In fact, wait a minute. Sally!"

"Yes, Mr. Shine," she said.

"Please call a car for Martin. He is going home."

"I can take the train," Martin replied.

"Martin, not another word," Mr. Shine shouted.

When the car arrived in front of Martin's house, his mother was at the front window. When she saw Martin, she rushed out of the house. Martin slowly opened the door and looked up. He was dizzy and sweating profusely.

His mother took one look at him and said, "Here, take my hand. I will help you up."

He strained to reach out. The driver ran to Mrs. Stein to assist her with Martin. They managed to get Martin up to his bed.

"I will be right back," Mrs. Stein said to her son.

His mother thanked the driver and indicated that he could return to work. She rushed down the stairs and tripped on the last step, but she caught her balance. She immediately placed a call to her husband.

"I realize he is in the examining room, but this an emergency. Please call him to the telephone."

"Yes, what is it? I am very busy."

"It is Martin. He came home from work. You must come home immediately."

Hearing the urgency in her voice, he told his staff that he had an emergency and would be back later. When he arrived at the house, there was a distinct odor coming from Martin's room. He knew even before entering that Martin was stricken by the pandemic that was affecting the world. The influenza virus had already killed thousands. The United States would be no exception to the disease's destruction. More would die of the disease than would be killed in World War I; 20 million people perished, including 548,000 in the United States.

He called to his wife, "I am sorry to say that Martin has influenza. He is very ill and needs to go to the hospital. I need to call for an ambulance. Anyone Martin has been in contact with during the last twenty-four hours needs to be notified."

His mother started to rush to Martin's room.

"Stop," he shouted. "You will be endangering yourself and the rest of the family."

Martin's mother began to cry. "I want to take care of him. I cannot let him go to a hospital."

His father looked at his wife and said, "I am sorry, but we do not have the necessary equipment to manage his illness. If he needs emergency care, he will need the hospital. He was very ill as a child, and his lungs are already compromised. I need to call the ambulance."

"This is Dr. Stein. I have a patient with influenza who needs to be admitted. Yes, I realize the situation, but you will need to make an exception. He is my son. Let me speak to Dr. Fine. Hi Bob, this is Steward Stein. My son needs to be admitted immediately. Thank you. I would appreciate that. Thank you."

"An ambulance is on its way. Please do not worry. I will go tell Martin. You wait down here and let me know when the ambulance arrives. It should be less then ten minutes."

Martin's father walked up the flight of stairs. When he entered the room, Martin was on his back. His face was pale, and he was staring at the ceiling. His father walked over to the bed. He looked at Martin and took his pulse. He closed Martin's eyes and placed the sheet over his face. His father began to cry. The disease was too much for Martin's immune system. Martin's early years of ill health had taken a toll, and his body was very vulnerable. His father thought, *I should have never let him leave the house this morning. It was a grave mistake.* He slowly walked downstairs. He entered the kitchen, his head bowed. He looked at his wife.

"What is it?" she demanded.

Her husband shook his head. "It is too late for the ambulance. Martin has passed."

She screamed, "Let me go to him!"

"No, I can't allow that. You will not be permitted upstairs until the necessary precautions can be taken."

Crying hysterically, she tried to get by him.

He stopped her and yelled, "No. Stop!"

She pounded his chest with her fists. Tears were streaming down her cheeks. "No, no, no. This cannot be happening. He just became engaged last evening. No. No. He has his whole life in front of him." She collapsed.

Her husband held her tightly. He carried her to the couch in the living room. He took spirits of ammonia from his pocket and passed them by her nostrils.

She shook her head and opened her eyes. "Tell me this is a bad dream, my love."

"I wish I could, but it is not." He gave her a hug. "I need to make some calls." He called the rabbi, the undertaker, and the children. "Is there anyone else you would like me to contact?"

"Yes, you and the rabbi will need to visit Sabrina to share the unfortunate and terrible news before she hears it from anyone else."

The body was removed from the house. The funeral home was contacted, and the burial was planned.

"Rabbi," Dr. Stein said, "we must leave immediately to call upon Sabrina and her family. You are not aware, but Martin proposed to her last evening."

The rabbi looked at Dr. Stein. "How unfortunate and sad. We must leave without delay. Are you sure your wife will be all right?"

"Yes, the other children have arrived, and I have given her a sedative. She should be fine for a short while."

Sabrina was having a wonderful day, sharing her news with her family and friends. The telephone was busy all morning. She was speaking to Anna when she heard the doorbell ring.

Sabrina's mother called, "Sabrina, I need to see you in the parlor."

"Anna, I need to say good-bye. Mother is calling me, and it sounds very important. I will speak to you later." As she entered the parlor, she saw Mother, Martin's dad, and the rabbi.

Sabrina thought, *Thank heavens it is only the rabbi to congratulate me and discuss the wedding plans.*

There were no congratulations or smiles. No one was speaking. The silence hung over the room like a dark cloud. She felt something was dreadfully amiss. She stood and stared at Dr. Stein. *Every moment of silence is like an eternity. Why isn't anyone speaking? What has happened?*

"Sabrina," Dr. Stein said, "something has happened to Martin. He came home from work today, and I was called to the house. When I arrived, Martin was very ill."

Sabrina felt a major electrifying sensation travel down her body. Her heart began to pound. Something was not right. *What is he trying to tell me?*

"I tried everything I could, but he has—"

She lifted her hands to stop the words.

"Passed."

Sabrina's eyes rolled back, and she fainted, hitting the floor.

Imperial Palace of Livadia 1906

The sun's rays glistened upon the ocean. It was a perfect day in Russia when Papa decided to go swimming. Sabrina rushed back to her room and could not wait a moment to change. Sabrina's sisters would wait for assistance—but not her. Sabrina wanted to be the first down to the sea.

The scent of the water and the melodious sound of the sea as the waves of white foam hit the shore were music to her ears. Papa loved the sea, and one of his favorite pastimes was swimming. This place was their oasis. The warm water and its isolation were a welcome change.

When they were all present, it was time for fun. They raced into the water. Sabrina got caught up in the moment and did not realize the magnitude of the water's undertow. Sabrina felt herself being pulled under. She tried to free herself from its relentless grasp, but she was defenseless against the mighty strength of the water. Water was filling her mouth and nasal passageways. Sabrina could not breathe. The light began to darken, and there was a major jerk to her head. A large hand grasped her long red hair and pulled her up. Sabrina must have lost consciousness for a moment because the next thing she knew, Papa was carrying her to the beach. The servants put a blanket on the sand and Papa gently placed Sabrina down.

"Anastasia, are you all right?" Papa asked.

"Shall we call for the empress?" the servants asked.

"No, that will not be necessary," the tsar replied.

He looked back at Anastasia. "I am so thankful that you are all right. It was a very close call. I thought we had lost you. Thank the Lord that you are all right."

"Thank you, Papa. I am sorry," Anastasia said.

The tsar replied, "Anastasia, it is not your fault. No one could know how rough the water was. I did not realize it until it happened." He covered her with another blanket and gave her a kiss. Anastasia looked up at him and smiled.

The men rushed to Sabrina's side, lifted her, and carried her to the couch. Dr. Stein removed the spirits of ammonia, and it awakened her.

"Where am I? Who are you? Papa? Where's Papa?"

Mother asked if she could have some time alone with Sabrina. She could not take any chances if Sabrina started shouting out names from her past. She knew that Papa was not a name she had called Father. She was calling the tsar.

Sabrina's eyes were glassy and unfocused. She gradually regained her consciousness and composure. "Mother, what is happening?"

"You suffered a major shock and fainted. I am so sorry, Sabrina, about what happened."

"Then it is true?" Sabrina said. She put her head down on Mother's shoulder and cried. There would be no consoling her.

The door opened. "Do you need us? Would you like Dr. Stein to check her for a concussion?"

"No, that will not be necessary. She has gained full consciousness. Please send our regrets to your family and let us know what the funeral arrangements will be."

The men said, "We are very sorry for your loss. We will see you tomorrow."

Sabrina walked over to the men. Her eyes were bloodshot, and tears were streaming down her face. "I appreciate that you took the time to speak to us in person. Thank you." She shook the rabbi's hand and gave Martin's father a hug. She whispered, "I am awfully sorry for our loss. He was a very special man."

He looked at her with tears in his eyes. "Thank you, my dear. You are very special to us as well."

Dr. Stein said, "You should wash or throw out the clothes you were wearing last evening." They both then left the house.

"Sabrina," Mother said.

"Mom, I cannot talk right now. I need to go upstairs and be alone." She slowly walked to her room and closed the door. *Why is this happening to me? Haven't I suffered enough? I could not even enjoy my engagement for twenty-four hours. I loved Martin more than anyone else. Why? Why? Why? I just cannot continue like this. What is there to look forward to?*

Thinking of her birth parents, Sabrina yelled, "Mama? Papa? Please come and take me with you. I need you. I am so very much alone." She fell into a deep sleep.

CHAPTER THIRTEEN

The Dream

The sun rose over the water. It cast its beautiful colored rays upon the ocean. Anastasia looked out from the deck of the family yacht and gazed at the red and orange hues reflected on the calm water. She loved the smell of the sea and the melodic rhythm of the sound of the water thrashing against the sides of the boat. It was very early, and the others had not awakened. She loved to gaze out over the sea. It was so tranquil and peaceful. Anastasia felt happy and content. Today her life was perfect. The entire family was together, and she was aboard her favorite vessel. Perhaps she would be able to jump off the bow and go for a swim. She wondered if Papa would join them.

"Anastasia," Mother called. "What brings you up on deck this early in the morning?"

"I love to watch the sun as it rises over the ocean," Anastasia said.

"I must confess I do too. Do you know when I was about your age, I was on the family yacht en route to see your great-grandmother, Queen Victoria. After Mother died, she became a mother to all of us. Father did not know the first thing about raising us, and grandmamma took us under her wing. She was so loving and caring, but let me tell you, my love, you better do as she said or you were in major trouble.

If there was one person you would not want angry at you, it was Grandmamma."

Anastasia looked at Mother with amazement. She loved to hear stories about her great- grandmamma.

Alexandra continued, "When she was angry, you would hear her voice echoing throughout the palace—and she did not let you forget it either. Once my brother played a trick on her. He placed a frog in her boot. When she went to put it on, she felt something slimy and screamed."

Anastasia began to giggle.

"And when she found out it was a frog, she lined us all up in a row until she found out who did it. We stood there for two hours until my brother told her the truth. We really never did find out the punishment because she took him into a room and shut the door. Several minutes later, she opened it and said, 'This is a private matter, please leave. No eavesdropping.' Knowing your great-grandmamma, she probably had a long talk with my brother and then taught him how to play chess.

"I loved that woman, and marrying your father was the best thing I could have done. I would do it again today, but I missed your great-grandmamma and England so very much. Leaving her was so difficult. Grandmamma always said, 'The monarchy comes first. You have a duty to your country. No matter what might happen, remember that England needs us. Never abandon her.' She also said your heritage is paramount. You may experience adversity in your life, but you must carry on. I have experienced great tragedy in my life, but I know who I am and that I must move forward. There is a plan for us rulers. We should never question it—just make the most of it. You cannot feel sorry for yourself. I did that, and all it did was drown me in self-pity. Never again will I let that happen. Learn from me. Forge ahead just like a ship out to sea.

"Grandmamma was a good lady who lived a long time and taught me many things. I am a very fortunate woman, and someday you will understand her teachings and their value. Remember that your heritage is paramount."

"Ah, good morning. Is anyone else up?" Anastasia's father said.

"No, Papa," Anastasia replied.

"Glad to see the both of you up and about on this beautiful day." The tsar turned to Alexandra and asked, "My love, are you feeling better?"

"Yes, my dearest. I am so thankful and blessed on this fine morning," she responded.

"After breakfast, I would like everyone to dress for a photograph for Mama. I wish to surprise her. Their new white morning dresses and Alexei's sailor uniform will be perfect. I asked the photographer to be ready at eleven hundred hours. I will see you at breakfast in a half hour."

Alexandra walked over to Anastasia and said, "Anastasia, you will need to excuse me. I must take my leave and assist Alexei—or else he will never be ready."

"Yes, Mama. I will see you at breakfast."

"Where are your sisters, Anastasia?" Father asked.

Anastasia, looking at Father replied, "I do not know, Papa. I have been up on deck."

"Here we are." Olga, Maria, and Tatiana hurried to the table.

"Oh, I see you are dressed for the photo. Good, good. Ah, here comes your brother and mother. They too are dressed. Anastasia, you and I can change after breakfast."

"Are you all here?" the photographer asked.

"Yes, we are," the children shouted.

The photographer walked over and said, "I will place you. Emperor, please stand here. I will have the empress sit on this chair. The grand duchesses please stand here. Tsarevich Alexei can stand by his father, and there is one more. Where is Grand Duchess Anastasia?"

"Here I am!" Anastasia announced. "Better late than never."

"Hurry up, Anastasia. I am tired of standing," Maria said.

"Don't worry, Grand Duchess, we will be out of here quickly. You know I am fast." He motioned with his hand and said, "Anastasia, here by your mom."

"All right, everyone, please look over here. That is splendid. One more, just let me change this. There we are. Look here one more time. Alexei turn your head just a little. Great. We are done."

Nicholas faced the children and said, "Thank you. Now, everyone, off to your rooms to change into your swimming clothes. We'll have a swim before lunch."

"But, Nicky, do you think it is a good idea for Alexei? He was just ill," Alexandra asked.

Nicholas said, "He will be fine. It is the hottest part of the day. Please have the servants bring plenty of towels. The last one on the deck is the last one in the water."

Anastasia and Alexei were the first on the deck, followed by Nicholas and then Alexandra, Maria, Tatiana, and Olga. The girls jumped in followed by their papa, and then Alexei ran to the rail. The deck was wet, and he slipped into the rail. His entire left side crashed into the solid railing. He cried out.

Alexandra looked at what was happening from the distance. She ran to her son's side, but it was too late. His leg and head began to swell. She called to his servant to quickly fetch the doctor. The girls and their father were already in the water and were unaware of what was happening. In minutes, the doctor appeared on the deck and carried Alexei to his room.

Alexandra motioned to her husband to return to the deck.

The children followed. They dried and rushed to Alexei's room. The doctor was trying his best. "We need to return to shore. We may need to take him to the hospital."

"Yes, doctor. I will see to it immediately." Nicholas returned to the deck to inform the crew.

Anastasia looked at her brother. *I should have never jumped into the ocean. I should have been watching him. If I was there, I could have stopped him.* "I am a terrible sister," she mumbled.

"Anastasia, I have told you several times that Alexei is not your responsibility."

"Yes, Mama, but he is my responsibility. I am the only one he listens to, and I do not know what I will do if something bad happens to him."

It took several hours to return to port.

Alexei was in substantial pain. The medical care proved to be somewhat helpful, but his leg was still swollen and blue.

The doctor spoke to Nicholas and Alexandra. "Your son is not doing well. I have done all I can do. We will have to wait and see."

Alexandra summoned Rasputin to come immediately to the palace. She sent a courier and several guards to retrieve him. Within several hours, he appeared.

He entered the palace and was immediately brought to the emperor and empress. The empress said, "Rasputin, Alexei had an accident while he was jumping off the royal yacht. His leg is swelling, and the doctor is unable to do any more than he has done. Please help us."

Rasputin walked into the room. "Can I have a few minutes with him alone?"

Nicholas looked at his wife. "Please, my beloved, comply with Rasputin's request."

"Yes, Rasputin. As you please."

"Doctor, please step outside. If I need you, I will call," Rasputin said.

The doctor looked at him and complied with reservation.

The door was closed for an hour, which felt like days. When it opened, Alexei was sitting up and laughing.

"He is going to be all right. Just keep him in bed and keep his foot elevated for a few days," Rasputin said.

The doctor looked at Alexei and then at Rasputin. He walked into his patient's room and sat down.

Alexandra approached Rasputin. "This is not the first time you have come between my son and fatality. I am forever grateful." She took his hand in hers and squeezed it.

Nicholas was horrified by his wife's lack of royal decorum, but he did not say anything.

Rasputin left the palace.

During the next few days, Alexandra and Anastasia kept vigil at Alexei's side. Just as Rasputin said, with each passing day, he improved and became stronger. After a week, he was up and playing again in the courtyard.

Anastasia was getting ready to leave the palace to play with her brother. As she passed a doorway, she overheard one of the guards speaking to the servant. He told the servant that it was only a matter of time before the monarchy would be overthrown by powers within the government. The tsar would be forced to step down and at the very least would be exiled, and there was talk of assassination.

Anastasia, without realizing what she was saying, yelled, "You are wrong."

The guard grabbed her.

She kicked him, and he fell to the ground. Once again, he picked her up.

"Leave me alone. Leave me alone. Mama, Papa, help me. Please leave me alone. Help, help."

⁂

"Sabrina, wake up," Mother called. "Sabrina wake up. You are having a nightmare."

Sabrina opened her eyes. "Where am I?"

"Please, Saul, get your sister a glass of water. You are here in your bedroom in Brooklyn. You were having a bad dream. Here, have some water."

"Sam, wet a towel for me." Her son ran in, and they placed the towel on Sabrina's forehead.

"You are safe now, Sabrina, No one is going to harm you. You are with us," Mother softly said, placing her hand on Sabrina's shoulder.

Sabrina realized she was dreaming. It was so real. Perhaps the whole thing is a nightmare. She looked down at her finger.

"Yes, my dear. That is the truth. You were not dreaming about Martin. He has passed. Tomorrow morning is the funeral. We just received word from his brother."

Yes. Tomorrow is the funeral—and yet another death of a loved one. As Mama said, "In spite of any adversity, you must persevere. Do not ask why, just forge ahead like a ship at sea."

"Are you all right, my dear?" Mrs. Sholin asked.

"Yes, I am. I will be just fine. I would like to be alone again, if you please," Sabrina said.

"Yes, my dear. Have a good night. If you need anything, call us. We are just in the next room." Mother bent down and gave her kiss.

Sam and Saul wished her a good night and left for their room.

It was a dreadful day for Sabrina. Word traveled quickly through the community. The funeral home was overflowing with people. Sabrina wondered if they were there to pay their respects or just because they were curious about the circumstances.

Sabrina sat with the family next to the casket. It took hours for all the people to pay their respects. She was exhausted. She felt badly for the family since they had to repeat the same story so many times. As the last person passed by, Sabrina walked over to the casket. She placed her hand on the casket and said, "My dearest Martin. How I will miss you. You were my dreams. You were my hopes. You were my love. I will never forget you, and someday we will be together again. May you rest in peace." She lowered her head and kissed the casket. A tear rolled down her cheek and dripped onto the pine box. She walked into the chapel and sat down beside her parents.

The service was long, and many people spoke on Martin's behalf. He was liked and respected by many. Mr. Shine spoke eloquently, and most of the workers from the shop were present. The factory closed for the day out of respect for Martin.

As the pallbearers walked the casket out of the chapel and the rabbi said his prayers, Sabrina thought of her own family and their fate. She would never be able to pay homage to them. However, someday—like with Martin—she believed she would be reunited with them.

The cemetery was several miles away. When they arrived, the family gathered at the graveside. An American flag draped the coffin, and there was a military presence. Martin was an officer in the army and would receive a full military burial with a three-shot rifle salute. Sabrina had never experienced an American military burial. After the secular and religious ceremony, the flag was folded and handed to Martin's father.

Tradition required the people to return to the house for food and drink. However, due to the influenza outbreak, the period of Shiva would be held in private. Only at sunrise and sunset would seven additional men be allowed into the house to say the prayer requiring ten men. They would be Martin's father, two brothers, and seven others.

Time has a way of healing the deepest of wounds. Weeks and

months passed, and Sabrina learned to deal with her loss the way she had to deal with all her previous losses. However, she did not leave her home for months.

One day, Mother came to her and said, "Sabrina, I need your help with the shopping. Could you please accompany me to the shops? I hurt my arm this morning, and I do not believe I will be able to carry all of the bundles. Your brothers have already left for work."

"Of course, Mother," Sabrina replied.

"Thank you, Sabrina," Mother said.

CHAPTER FOURTEEN

Turning the Page

I t has often been said that life is like a book. Our experiences write upon the pages. Our journeys takes us on many adventures, and in so doing, the chapters of our existence are created. Another day another page is turned. What may happen is destined, and some wait patiently to see what the next day will bring.

The sun was bright, and it was midday as Sabrina and Mother ventured out to the market. It was not like the days before and would not be like any other day. Sabrina walked slowly down the street. She wore a black dress and a large-brimmed hat with a veil. Although she was with Mother, it was difficult to make out who she was.

"Sabrina, why don't we take the trolley? It will be more private that way. I really do not want to stop and speak to many people today," Mother said.

"Thank you for your understanding, Mother," Sabrina said. "It is comforting to know that you respect my feelings."

"Sabrina, you have been through so much in your short life. The least I can do is be there for you. You need to believe there is a master plan, and in time, you will see what I mean. Oh, here comes the trolley."

Sabrina always enjoyed traveling on the trolley. It reminded her of her rides with Martin. In some ways, she could feel his comforting presence. "Mother, look. There is a sign for Coney Island and Nathan's. Have you and Dad ever been there?"

"No, Sabrina," Mother said. "I heard it is wonderful place to go on a date. They have a carousel, and the beach is supposed to be beautiful. I read in the newspapers that they are building a boardwalk."

"What is a boardwalk, Mother?" Sabrina asked.

"It is a pathway built up over the sand made of wood. It is like a boulevard above the ground. It is going to be by the beach."

Sabrina wondered what it was going to look like. She loved the ocean, and the thought of there being amusements and the beach intrigued her.

"Sabrina, that was quick. We are already here. I love when you accompany me. The time goes by so much more quickly," Mother said.

"Mother, it is nice to be out with you. It has been a long time," Sabrina replied.

Mother looked at Sabrina and said, "I think we will stop at the grocery store first. Sabrina, could you please get me sugar, flour, and a few of those delicious pickles in the barrel. The clerk will assist you. The last time I tried, the pickle juice spilled all over me, and I smelled like a pickle barrel all the way home. Your outfit is too pretty to have the scent of pickles." Mother laughed.

Sabrina looked at Mother and smiled. She then walked slowly over to the pickle barrel. As she approached it, she saw a tall man with an apron tied around his waist. He was facing the other direction, and when she moved closer and was ready to ask for his assistance, he turned around. Less than a foot separated them.

Sabrina was startled and moved back. "Excuse me."

The gentlemen, also surprised by the nature of their stance, said, "Excuse me."

The man looked familiar to Sabrina, but she could not place where she may have seen him before. The gentlemen said, "Aren't you Sabrina?"

Sabrina looked up. *How does he know my name? Isn't he just a little forward in his manner?* "Yes, I am. But how do you know who I am?"

"I apologize if I seem forward. I hope I have not insulted you in any way. My name is Jacob. I am Martin's cousin." His eyes welled up with tears. "I have just returned to the area. My aunt has spoken very highly of you, and there is a picture of you in the parlor. Once again, I apologize if I have offended you."

"No, Jacob, you have not. I just wanted some pickles and was not expecting that kind of a welcome at the pickle barrel." She smiled.

"You have a lovely smile—and now for the pickles." Jacob reached over to a shelf for a jar. His resemblance to Martin was remarkable. They were of the same height and coloring.

As he reached to the pickles, she said, "Jacob, if you don't mind my being forward, what did you mean that you just returned to the area? Where were you?"

He looked up at her and said, "Oh, Sabrina. I thought you knew. I am the cousin who was hurt in combat and was convalescing in Washington."

"I am sorry, Jacob. I did not know. I see it is something that is difficult for you to discuss. Please accept my humble apology. I guess our casual meeting and informal introduction has not gone very well," Sabrina said.

"That is all right, Sabrina. It could have been worse; I could have turned around and knocked you unconscious by mistake. Perhaps we will have the opportunity to meet again," Jacob said, smiling.

Sabrina, taking the bottle of pickles, smiled. "Thank you, Jacob, for your assistance." She approached Mother.

"Sabrina, what took you so long to get the pickles? And where is the flour and the sugar?"

"I was speaking to the clerk. Do you know who he is?" Sabrina asked.

"What do you mean?" Mother asked.

"His name is Jacob. He is Martin's cousin and just returned from being wounded in the war."

"Oh yes," Mother replied. "I think I remember something about that. Yes. Martin's mother did tell me that her nephew was working at a grocery store. Can you imagine him being here?"

"Yes, Mother. By the expression on your face, I can believe that he could be working at the first market you decided to enter this morning."

"Oh, Sabrina. Would your mother ever do something like that? Let's go get the flour and sugar before we both forget."

Sabrina and Mother continued shopping for the rest of the morning. Both women gathered the groceries at a number of the market places. Sabrina's mother had a wealth of information about Jacob.

Jacob and Martin both entered the military together. They were very close growing up and were like brothers. They shared many interesting adventures together. However, after basic training, Jacob was assigned to infantry and was deployed overseas. Martin remained in the States and was first to be discharged.

Jacob was finishing his last tour of duty when he was ordered to fight in the Battle of Belleau Wood in June. He was seriously injured in the battle when he took enemy fire while saving three of his fellow men. He was shipped back to Washington to convalesce in the military hospital. While there, he was decorated with the Purple Heart for his bravery. He does not like to speak about it.

He was very upset about his cousin's death and was not able at the time to travel to his funeral. Jacob was a family man. His mother had an untimely death, and although Jacob lived at another residence, Martin's mother raised him. The boys were inseparable from an early age.

"Sabrina, he would have never introduced himself to just anyone. Your relationship with Martin was probably the foremost thing on his mind. Do not think he was trying to push himself on you."

"Mother, I realized that as soon as he spoke. When he mentioned Martin, he almost cried."

Sabrina's mother placed her hand on Sabrina's shoulder and said, "See? He is extremely torn up by the death of Martin. You both unfortunately have that in common. You are wearing black, and that mourning veil probably contributed to his reaction."

"But Mother," Sabrina said.

"No, Sabrina. I did not mean anything by it. I was just making an observation. People understand that you were engaged the night before, and they certainly understand your feelings. I was not being critical. I just wanted you to better understand his reaction to the situation. The two of them resemble each other, and that probably played a part in your response to him. In any event, from what you told me, both of you handled the situation quite well under the circumstances. We are home. You take those packages. I will carry these. Sabrina, dear, pull the cord. We have so much to do to get ready for Shabbos. Your father is going to be home early, and your brothers like to nibble a little when they arrive home. I better put up the chicken soup."

Sabrina thought about her conversation with Mother. *Jacob has had many losses in his life as well. His mother, his best friend, and facing death himself must have been extremely difficult for him. And here I am feeling sorry for myself. He has persevered. He is not in a room somewhere. No, he is out there working. His faith and his family are there to support him. Just like me, my family and friends are there for me. I must call Anna before Shabbos and tell her what happened today.*

The next morning, Sabrina looked in her closet and decided that she would not wear black. She chose an outfit and a matching hat without a veil. She brushed her hair and looked down at the ivory handle. "I hold you and all you represent close to my heart. You will enable me to move forward in my life. I pray for each of you today and every day, and I know you are at peace. It is my turn to uncover the truths that will be before me and contribute to the world all that I can give." She repeated the words to herself several times in succession.

"Sabrina, you are up early," Mother said.

"Yes. It is a beautiful day, and I wanted to be ready in time for synagogue."

"Sabrina, look at you. You look lovely in that dress. No black?"

"No, Mother, it is time."

"Yes, I believe it is."

"Yes, I believe it is."

As the family approached the Kane Street Synagogue, Rabbi Goldfarb was standing at the entrance. "Good Shabbos," he said. "It is nice to see the Sholins here this morning."

"Good Shabbos, Rabbi. It is a beautiful day," Father said. "We are looking forward to your sermon."

"Yes, yes. Thank you. Thank you. I better go in. You will excuse me, but there are a few things I need to do before the service. Good Shabbos, Mr. Hyman. Thank you, Mrs. Krolnet and Mr. Solemen."

Sabrina never understood why the Orthodox tradition required men and woman to sit in different sections of the synagogue, divided by a partition. *How demeaning,* she thought. *Women are second-class citizens. They cook, clean, and raise the children. Some even work, but in the eyes of the Lord, they are not equal to men. Women could not even vote in New York until last year, and we still don't have that right on a national level. My great-grandmother ruled the greatest empire. I would like to see the men at this synagogue tell Empress Victoria that she could not do something equal or better to men.*

"Sabrina, go move down and sit by the divide. We are first in this row. Give others room to sit," Mother requested.

Sabrina sat next to the partition. She did not understand any of the laws and traditions but was learning quickly. She could read Hebrew thanks to Anna and was beginning to understand much of the service. She was amazed by how some of the women would just sit idly and be more concerned about someone's new dress or a new hat and what was going on around them than taking an active part in the service.

The rabbi walked to the front of the ark that housed the sacred Torah. "Welcome. Good Shabbos to you all. We will all rise and turn to page 111."

Sabrina stood and faced the ark. She looked down at her prayer book and began to chant the first prayer. The service would take three or four, hours depending on how long the rabbi's sermon was. She always enjoyed how the rabbi discussed the week's readings and how they were relevant to the events of the day. She looked up and then to her right. In the distance, she saw Jacob. Their eyes met. He nodded—and so did she. Now she understood why there was a divide. How easily her focus on the prayers waned when she noticed him. She looked down, and after a few moments, she found her place in the prayer book.

Sabrina felt spiritually connected in the sanctuary—more connected than anywhere else other than by the sea when she was with her birth family or Martin. She felt their presence, and it was soothing to her. It was the solace she looked forward to each week. She had learned that whether she was in a Russian Orthodox mosque or a synagogue, she was connected and at peace with herself, family, loved ones, and nature. There was a balance for her, and she felt fortunate to have found it.

CHAPTER FIFTEEN

Jacob

Jacob returned home from work. He was exhausted and just wanted to eat and go to bed. The next day was Shabbos, and he wanted to go to the synagogue. His aunt had called, but he did not want to leave his house again and visit her for Shabbos dinner. His arm and shoulder were bothering him, and he'd had enough for one day.

Jacob had very mixed feelings about meeting Sabrina that morning. She was beautiful and witty, but she had been engaged to his cousin. Jacob felt that he had to distance himself from her. He felt it would not be right for him to have feelings for her. How he missed his cousin. Jacob had been looking forward to coming home and spending time with Martin again.

Wars—why do men declare war? Why can't civilized men live together in harmony and peace? Man is such a strange breed. He has a need to conquer and sometimes destroys what he has built. History is the blueprint to the future. Why haven't men figured it out? War is futile and results in havoc and destruction. It is such an ineffective attempt for power and control. The cost—the financial and the innocent lives lost—don't we have enough fatality with the spread of disease?

"Poor Martin, my beloved cousin." Jacob began to cry. "My partner in wild adventures. I need you more than ever." He closed his eyes.

Battle of Belleau Wood, June 1918

"Lieutenant," a voice called out.

"Yes," Jacob replied.

"It is time. Have your men attack at the signal," his commanding officer ordered.

"Yes, Captain," Jacob replied.

Jacob made the command. The men in formation prepared themselves. There were young men from around the country, barely out of their teens. They were frightened and scared. Each of them had experienced the deafening sounds of gunshots, the smell of gunpowder and burnt flesh, and the ruins of war.

There was a sea of men covering the battlefield. The order was given. The men charged forward with the others. Hundreds hit the ground—many injured or dead.

Jacob called out, "Men, we can do this. Follow me." He was his men's support, their confidence, their strength, but that day would not be a good one. The battlefield was full of slaughter. As the men traversed the field, they stepped over many of their fellow troops.

"Hit the ground, men," he ordered. A loud explosion was heard. Jacob looked up; the exploding mortar hit several of his men. He ordered his men to retreat. Gunshots were increasing in his direction, but he knew he had to save his men. He crawled over several bodies and limbs to the men who were too badly injured to move. He turned his head. "Men, keep your heads down. Keep your heads down." He tried to be heard over the thunderous gunfire. He approached one man, threw him over his shoulder, and carried him back to a safe area. He dropped him to the ground and then went for another and another.

The captain, observing what happened, accompanied him on the second endeavor. Another bomb exploded, and Jacob hit the ground.

The captain also hit the ground. However, he did not move. Jacob crawled to his side and called to him. He did not respond. He turned him over. His eyes were open and fixed. He looked down. Mortar had torn his midsection open, and he was dead.

"Oh no!" Jacob cried out. He continued moving forward into the gunfire. He came upon a man who was moaning and trying to move. His legs were badly injured. He picked him up and heard an echoing sound pierce through his ears. It was a deafening sound and then a sharp penetrating pain in his right shoulder. Jacob continued to run with the injured soldier on his shoulder. He reached the destination and then collapsed.

When he opened his eyes, he was on a cot. For a moment, he did not realize what had happened.

"Soldier, glad to see that you are awake. You are brave man to do what you did," a medic said.

Jacob tried to move. He felt excruciating pain in his shoulder. He cried out.

"Soldier, please do not move. You were shot in the shoulder, and there is a dressing on the wound."

Jacob turned his head and looked. His shoulder had several pieces of gauze on it.

"You are heading back to Washington in the morning. Someone will be here soon to further attend to your injury." Jacob tried to respond, but he passed out.

When Jacob arrived at the Veteran's Hospital in Washington, his shoulder was still in considerable pain. In addition, he had spiked a high fever and soon became unconscious. He stayed in his bed for several days before he gained consciousness. An infection had set into his wound, and it needed to be drained. Medication was required for the infection. When he opened his eyes, he heard some voices approaching.

"Who is this?"

"It is Lieutenant Jacob Meyer, sir."

"Ah, yes. I seem to remember his name. My association with Jacob Astor of course."

"Yes, sir."

"He is on my list, isn't he? Why are we not speaking to him?"

"The men in this area have been unconscious. We thought you wanted to pay your respects."

Jacob turned his head in the direction of the voices.

"He does not appear unconscious to me."

"Yes, Mr. President. We will approach him."

President Woodrow Wilson was standing in front of Jacob. He tried to raise his arm to salute.

"That will not be necessary, Lieutenant Meyer. If anything, I should be saluting you. I am here today to award you a Purple Heart for bravery. I would like to read you something. This Purple Heart is awarded to Lieutenant Jacob Meyer for his bravery at the Battle of Belleau Wood, June 1918. Lieutenant Meyer fought enemy fire and injury and returned three times to retrieve injured men. Due to these courageous efforts, these men have survived. You are a valiant man, and through your efforts and the efforts of many others, this war will soon be coming to an end. On behalf of the United States, I applaud you."

"Thank you, Mr. President," Jacob responded. His eyes were filling with tears.

Placing his hand on Jacob's left shoulder, the president said, "My son, it is a distinguished honor to meet and present you this award. I am hopeful ... may I see the lieutenant's chart please?" The president was handed his chart. He thumbed through it. "Yes, I am glad to say you should recover and I—"

Someone interrupted the president.

"Can we discuss this in a moment? I am in the middle of ... oh, I see. Yes."

"Lieutenant Jacob, the nurse just informed me ... I am sorry to inform you that we just received news that Private Stein has succumbed to the epidemic that is facing this nation. It is yet another war we face, and I hope we soon conquer."

Jacob looked at the president and began cry. "He was like a brother to me."

The president requested a chair and sat down at the side of the bed. He requested that his entourage step back.

"My mother died when I was very young. We grew up together, and his mother helped raise me," Jacob explained.

"Lieutenant Jacob, the least we can do is to have you return as soon as possible to your aunt. Nurse, please summon a doctor here immediately."

"Yes, Mr. President."

A doctor arrived within minutes.

"Yes, Mr. President."

President Wilson looked at the doctor and asked, "Could you please review this chart and let me know when this officer will be ready to travel?"

The doctor looked through the chart, examined Jacob, and replied, "Within a week, Mr. President."

"Lieutenant Meyer, I will see to it that when you are ready to travel that you will receive transport to New York. Your medical treatment can be followed by the military hospital in New York. If you need anything at all, you feel free to contact the White House directly." He called to his staff and requested that they make the necessary arrangements. "Lieutenant Meyer, I am terribly sorry for your loss. Please extend my personal condolences to your family."

"Thank you, Mr. President."

"We need to be moving on." The president looked at the clipboard and said, "I would like to meet with—"

The nurse approached Jacob. "Lieutenant, is there anything I get you?"

"No, Nurse, thank you," Jacob replied.

"Lieutenant, you appear tired. Why don't you try to rest? I am truly sorry about your cousin. When you first arrived, you called out to him several times."

Jacob began to cry. "Thank you for mentioning that to me."

"You are a very strong man, Lieutenant. Many a man would have given up, but you are a fighter. You overcame a major infection."

Jacob looked at the nurse, and his large, brown eyes closed.

The nurse tucked in the sheet, smiled, and walked away.

Brooklyn, New York 1916

"Martin, are you ready yet? We will never get out of here."

"Jacob, I am almost ready. What is your rush?"

"You know I like to go out Saturday evening for a drink."

"I know, but I have to finish what I am doing."

"Can't it wait until later or tomorrow?"

"Jacob, enough already. You will just have to order one less drink tonight."

The two left the house and walked down the street. It was a beautiful summer evening, and the stars shined brightly in the sky. "Martin, look. There is the Big Dipper."

Martin gazed at the stars and said, "There is the North Star."

"Where will it take us? Perhaps to the café to meet the women of our dreams."

"Jacob, is that all you think about?"

"Why not? It can't hurt you. You remember what your father told us. Go out, have some fun. You are only young once."

"Jacob, I bet he did not say that in front of my mother."

"Martin, loosen up. It is Saturday night."

The café was crowded as it usually was on a Saturday evening.

"Hey guys," a face in crowd said. "It is about time you arrived. Let me buy you the first drink."

Martin and Jacob had many drinks that evening. It was nearly 12:30 when Martin said, "Jacob, we should go before they carry us out."

Jacob replied, "Not even one more, Cousin."

"Jacob, I am surprised you are still standing."

Jacob spilled the remaining part of his drink all over himself.

Martin took his handkerchief from his pocket. "Here, Jacob, you need this."

Jacob wiped off his face and shirt and placed the handkerchief in his pocket. "Thanks, Cousin."

"Let's go. All right, all right. You are a real party stopper." Even with assistance, Jacob still managed to knock into several people on the way out of the café.

"Oh, Martin, let's sing a little."

"Jacob, we will wake up the neighborhood."

"You are not going to even let me serenade you? Come on. Come on." Jacob started to tickle Martin.

"Stop it. Stop it. Jacob, you are relentless."

"Okay then." Martin pushed Jacob away.

Jacob pushed back, and within seconds, they were wrestling on the ground.

"Guys, guys. Get up. You are making another spectacle of yourselves."

Another voice said, "So why should this Saturday night be different than any other Saturday night? Remember last week? Martin gave Jacob a black eye, and the week before, Jacob dumped a pitcher of beer onto Martin's head. Hey you two, enough. Get up. You take Martin, and I will get Jacob." With a little coaxing, each stood up—but not before Jacob threw up on the road.

"Oh not again," Martin said.

Jacob said, "And last week, it was okay when you left your donation on the street."

"Jacob, we were not supposed to mention that again. I really had to go."

The guys standing around started to laugh.

At 1:30, Martin and Jacob arrived at Jacob's house. They stumbled upstairs and fell into bed.

"Jacob, are you ready?" Martin asked. "We have to report to the army recruiting station for our physicals."

"Yes, I am ready," Jacob said. "I think this is a day we will both remember."

As they approached the recruiting station, there were men waiting in line out the door. "What are they doing in there?"

One of the other men in line said, "My brother told me it is a full physical, even a rectal."

Martin asked, "You mean they—"

The man said, "Yes."

"What in the world are they checking for?" Martin asked.

"Who knows?" Maybe hemorrhoids—or they are just examining every crevasse in the body."

"Well, we can look at it as one asshole to another. Better his finger than mine," Jacob replied.

The line moved quickly, and within a short period of time, they were inside while their paperwork was processed.

"Strip down to your underwear. Get into a straight line."

An elderly, gray-haired doctor with a stained, white coat entered the room. He started at the beginning of the line. "Stick out your tongue." He looked at the fellow's nose, ears, and eyes. This was followed by listening to his heart. The doctor went down the line and then walked to the front of the line. "Okay, gentlemen, drop your underwear."

Jacob whispered, "Here comes the best part."

"Real funny," Martin said.

The doctor examined each man's testicles and penis.

Martin leaned over to Jacob and whispered, "I guess not all men are created equal."

When the doctor completed the examination of the genitals, he walked to the front of the line. "Gentlemen, I saved the best for last. Turn around, bend down, and spread your cheeks."

The men moaned.

"What are guys moaning about," the doctor exclaimed. "I have to look at and examine each of you." As the doctor moved down the line, the men groaned.

Jacob and Martin were quite anxious, and Martin would be the first victim. Martin grunted.

"Oh, son," the doctor said. "That wasn't that bad."

Of course not, Martin thought. *No one is sticking his finger up your ass.*

Jacob smiled at the doctor's comments, and before he knew it, he was the next victim. He called out, "Oh no," Martin said. "Would you like another round? I am sure the doctor would comply with your request."

"No, thank you, Martin. I think you would appreciate the doctor's other hand better than me. Perhaps he could use two fingers the next time?" Jacob responded.

All the way home, Martin and Jacob discussed the physical. It would be a day neither of them would soon forget.

Martin said, "We are leaving tomorrow for basic training. Do you really want to go?"

Jacob looked into his cousin's eyes. "Not especially, but we need to protect this country. The war is raging on, and many people are being killed. Perhaps with our intervention, it will end sooner. I know we will be back soon and we will be going to the café. You owe me the first drink when we return."

"That's a bet, Cousin. Let's shake on it."

"Jacob, wake up. Wake up."

Jacob mumbled, "Is it time already, Martin? I need just a few more minutes. It is my last sleep here for a long time."

Brooklyn, 1918

"Jacob. Jacob?" his father said. "You must have been dreaming. You were calling out to your cousin."

"Father, I guess I fell asleep after my shower."

"Jacob, we are due at your aunt's house within the hour. Go get dressed."

"I believe she called, and I told her I was too tired."

"Nonsense. We have to eat anyway, and they may need us for the minyan. It would be terrible if they did not have ten men."

Jacob thought the likelihood of that happening was remote.

"You also know that your aunt looks forward to us being with them at the table."

Jacob's father was starting to make him feel guilty. *The least I can do is be there for her. She has been there for me for so many years, but I am so tired.*

"Jacob, come. It will only take you a few minutes."

"All right, Father. Enough. I will get dressed," Jacob replied.

CHAPTER SIXTEEN

The Carousel

When the service ended, the congregants walked to the back of the synagogue. There was a table set with bread, wine, and various Sabbath delicacies. Here, they greeted one another and discussed the topics of the day.

Sabrina and her family usually left shortly after they broke bread and drank some wine. Today was different; as Sabrina began to walk over to Father, a voice said, "Good Shabbos, Sabrina."

"Jacob, good Shabbos to you. How have you been doing?"

"All right. I am just a little tired."

"Are they working you hard at the grocery?"

"Not too bad. It is a beautiful day today. Why don't we step outside for a while? It is so crowded in here."

"That will be nice."

From a distance, Sabina's mother and Jacob's aunt looked at each other and smiled.

Sabrina and Jacob walked outside. The sun soared in the radiant blue, cloudless sky. The gentle breeze felt refreshing to Sabrina. A flock of birds flew overhead.

"So tell me, Jacob, what has it been like returning home after being overseas?"

"It is an experience. I miss my cousin a great deal." Tears started to form in his eyes.

"I know you do. I never knew how close the two of you were."

"You mean Martin never discussed me?" Jacob asked.

"Of course he did, but we never shared too much about your relationship."

"We were like brothers and did everything together growing up. We got into so much mischief along the way." Jacob began to smile.

"It is nice that you have those fond memories. That will comfort you during this time of loss. I too have many pleasant memories, and I cherish them."

"Yes, the two of us have our memories of Martin that fill our emptiness due to his untimely death."

They both looked at each other and began to cry. When they saw each other's reactions, they smiled.

She grabbed his hand. "Jacob, it will be all right. You need to believe me. The pain will dissipate over time, but we will each carry him close to our hearts."

"There you are, Sabrina. We wondered what happened to you," Mother said.

"Are you ready, Mother?"

"Yes."

"Jacob, we are leaving. It was nice speaking to you. Good-bye."

"Sabrina?" Jacob asked. "Are you doing anything tomorrow?"

Sabrina looked at Mother. She was shaking her head.

Before Sabrina could answer, Jacob said, "Well then, how does one o'clock sound to you?"

Sabrina responded. "It sounds just fine."

That afternoon, Sabrina had mixed feelings again about her encounter with Jacob. He was a nice fellow, but she felt as though she was being unfaithful to Martin.

Mother approached when Sabrina was passing through the kitchen with a pitcher of water. "Sabrina, you seem preoccupied. Is there anything bothering you?"

"No, Mother. I was just thinking."

"Yes, we sometimes think too much. Don't we? Tell me what is going on."

"Well, Mother. Every time I speak to Jacob, I feel uncomfortable."

"Uncomfortable?"

"Yes, like I am cheating on Martin."

"Cheating on Martin?"

"Yes, like he would be disappointed in me."

"My love, Martin was a beautiful person. He was good to you, his family, and us. You know we felt so pleased when he proposed to you. If you married, we would have welcomed him into our family like a son. But, Sabrina, that was. His untimely death shattered your dreams that you had with him. We cannot bring him back, and our memories of him are what are left to comfort us. Sabrina, you are young, and when you are ready, you will need to move on with your life. Martin loved you and would want the best for you. I know we have discussed this before, but it would be helpful for you to hear what I am saying. I believe you are listening, but you have not processed what I have said. I understand it is difficult for you, but you are cheating yourself— not being dishonest to Martin. There is a reason for everything, and perhaps you and Martin were just not meant to be."

Sabrina was crying. "I hear what you are saying, but it does not take that hurt and void away."

Mother looked at Sabrina and said, "It was not to take it away. I was letting you know that it is okay to feel again. I know you are frightened; so many people you have loved have abandoned you. My dear, come here. You need a hug."

❧

Jacob walked home with his father. "Son, you are very quiet. Was that Sabrina you were speaking to before?"

"Yes, Father. That is who I am thinking about."

"You are thinking about Sabrina?"

"No, Martin," Jacob said.

"Martin?" his father replied.

"Yes, Martin. Sabrina was engaged to Martin. I feel I am dishonoring his name every time I speak to Sabrina."

"Son, answer me. I understand that you are uneasy, but how do you really feel like when you are together? Are you not letting yourself experience the moment?"

Jacob looked up at his father with tears in his eyes and asked, "Father, what do you mean?"

"When your mother died, I was very hurt and alone. I buried my feelings for many years. It was so hard for me, especially when I was around other women. One day, I realized that if I had feelings for another woman, it was all right. Your mother would want the best for you and me, and if that meant another woman in our lives, then so be it."

"But, Dad, why didn't you remarry? You are still alone."

"The right person has not come along yet. When and if she does, I am ready. Jacob, do not miss the opportunity because you are blocked by emotion. You have been through so much in the past year. It is understandable that you have pushed your feelings down so far. It has been very painful for you to experience what you did. You may not realize this, but you have been upset by the events in your life. I understand that. I am here for you, and I will always be here for you."

"Thank you, Dad. Your comments mean so much." Jacob turned to his father and embraced him.

"Jacob, you are a very sensitive person—and you always have been. Let yourself feel again, and let fate take its course."

❧

"Sabrina, it is almost one o'clock," Mother said.

"Mother, I will be down in a few minutes. He will have to wait a minute." Sabrina was so nervous. It was as though she was going out on her first date.

"Sabrina, someone's at the door," Mother yelled from the kitchen. "Will you please answer it?"

The doorbell rang again. *He is going to leave.* "Mother, didn't you hear the doorbell?"

"What?"

"Oh nothing."

Mother dried her hands with a dishtowel and walked over to the door.

"Jacob, it is so nice to see you again. Did you have any trouble finding the house?"

"No, Mrs. Sholin. My aunt gave great directions." Jacob looked up and saw Sabrina at the head of the stairs. His attention was solely on her. After several moments, he said, "Excuse me, Mrs. Sholin. You asked about my aunt?"

"No Jacob. That is all right." Sabrina's mother smiled.

"Here I am, Jacob. Sorry I was not ready."

"I understand, Sabrina. You were worth waiting for."

Sabrina started to descend the stairs slowly. "Are you sure, Jacob?"

"Have a good time," Sabrina's mother said.

"Thank you, Mrs. Sholin."

"Thank you, Mom."

"Jacob, what do you have planned for us today?" Sabrina asked.

"Me? I thought you would have planned something."

Sabrina stared at him.

"Sabrina, I am only kidding. Follow me." Jacob walked for several blocks, and then he began to walk toward the train entrance.

"Where are you taking me?" Sabrina asked.

"It is not for me to say," Jacob replied.

"I am not accustomed to following men to unknown destinations." Sabrina stopped walking and looked up at Jacob.

"Oh, Sabrina. I wanted to surprise you. You took the fun out of my plan."

"Jacob, please respect my wishes. This is our first time out together."

"You are safe with me. I thought you would like to see the carousel at Coney Island."

Sabrina smiled.

Jacob laughed and said, "Then let us be off."

The two of them talked all the way to Coney Island. When they arrived at the stop, they quickly exited through the doors.

From the platform, Sabrina was able to see the ocean. The water was shimmering, and the waves were crashing onto the white sand. Sabrina saw a huge multicolored carousel and felt an excitement she had not felt for months.

Jacob looked at her and was delighted by her reaction.

As they descended the steel beam stairwell from the platform and approached the sandy beach, Sabrina said, "Can we approach the water? It is so beautiful."

"Sabrina, your shoes?"

"That's all right. I will manage. If I need to, I will take them off."

"Sabrina, let's go. I feel it would be a good idea if I held on to you."

The air was getting cooler, and it blew against their faces. Sabrina's cheeks were turning bright red.

"Sabrina, are you sure you want to continue? You look cold."

"Oh, Jacob. I would not miss this opportunity for anything." She gazed at the water and the whitecaps thrashing against the beach. Seagulls were singing melodic melodies, and the muted sounds of people in the distance could be heard. Out upon the horizon, ships were bringing cargo to shore. The smell of the salted sea brought back so many memories for Sabrina. She was mesmerized by the moment.

Russia, 1912

"Your Majesty, the *Standart* is ready. Would you like to set out to sea?" the first mate asked.

The tsar replied, "Yes, I believe we are all here. Anastasia, come stand by your father's side. I know you love to watch."

"Yes, Papa. I will be right down." She hurried down the steps from the upper deck.

"Anastasia, no need to rush. The steps might be wet. I would not want you to fall."

She rushed over to Father. The bow of the imperial yacht was the best place to stand. It sliced through the sea, and the water parted for the massive ship.

The wind blew strongly, and the tsar held Anastasia so she would not be caught in its path and be blown away. She imagined herself standing on the front end of the bow, welcoming the sea. The scent of the sea, the movement, the parting water, the wind gusts, and standing with Father's arm around her waist made the moment splendid. Anastasia took in a deep breath. She thought, *What freedom and what peace.*

Coney Island, Brooklyn, New York 1918

"Sabrina, are you all right?" Jacob was staring into her glazed eyes. "Sabrina?"

She turned toward him. "Jacob. I am fine. I was captured by the moment."

"I did not realize your family were sea goers."

"Oh no, Martin—I am so sorry, Jacob."

He appeared stunned by the name of his cousin. Tears welled up in his eyes.

She reached out and grabbed his hand. "I do not know what has gotten into me. Please accept my humble apology. I would never hurt you."

"Sabrina, I guess things happen. I can certainly understand you calling out my cousin's name. It did diminish this special moment we are spending together."

"It wasn't meant to. I was very fond of him, as I know you were. Perhaps he is here with both of us now. Perhaps we can get comfort from that." She pulled him close and gave him a kiss on the cheek.

"Thank you for saying that, Sabrina," Jacob said.

Sabrina felt it best to continue her explanation. "Jacob, I can never forget our voyage here, and being here today reminds me of that adventure."

Jacob was aware that her brother had died on that voyage, but he felt it best not to ask any questions.

"Can we sit a while?" Sabrina asked.

"Here," Jacob said, taking off his coat and placing it on the fine sand.

"Jacob, you will catch a chill."

"Not while I am with you, Sabrina."

She looked up and smiled.

They looked out at the water and discussed their various experiences. The wind started to pick up, and the sand started whirling.

"Sabrina, I think we ought to be going. I wanted to walk over to Surf Avenue. I have another surprise for you."

"I have enough sand in my shoes for another beach."

"Lean on my shoulder to empty your shoes. I will help balance you."

"Jacob, there is a bench just down a little. Let's sit there. I am clumsy, and I do not want to fall. I can just see both of us tumbling over one another."

They walked over to Surf Avenue.

"The buildings are so colorful. What is the Roller Rink?" Sabrina asked.

"That is my surprise, Sabrina. Let's go in," Jacob replied.

Sabrina looked at the men and woman skating around in the rink. Music was drowning out the sounds of the skates and the people's talking and laughter.

"You expect me to do that?" Sabrina pointed to the people in the rink.

"Yes, I will show you. Do not worry. Martin and I used to come here all the time," Jacob replied.

"But, Jacob, I—"

"Come on. Come over here." He walked to the counter. "What size do you wear?"

"Jacob, do you think it is proper?"

"Sabrina, just give it a chance. I will stand next to you and hold onto you," he said.

Sabrina slipped on the skating shoes.

"Here, Sabrina, let me give you a hand with the lacing of your skates." Jacob kneeled down and laced her skates. He looked up and observed Sabrina looking at him.

"Jacob, I hope there are no other surprises in your pocket." She laughed.

"There you go. You are all ready. Just give me a minute." Jacob placed his skates on and exclaimed, "There. Are we ready?" He stood up and reached for her hand.

"You really want me to do this and make a fool of myself? Are you sure you want me to do this?"

"Sabrina, you are a natural." They stepped onto the rink. He placed his arm around her waist. She felt her body tremble and closed her eyes.

"You are doing just fine. Sabrina, open your eyes. You are going to skate into someone."

She heard the music of her beloved Sergei Vasilievich Rachmaninoff. Sabrina had not heard his music since she was dancing with her papa in the palace. She felt so comforted, protected, and safe with Jacob's arm around her waist.

"Can't you see where you are going?" a man shouted. "Are you two blind?"

"Calm down," Jacob said. "We are sorry. We did not intend to get in your way."

"You should be sorry." The man skated to the other side of the rink.

Sabrina started to lose her balance. She fell toward Jacob.

He grabbed her and helped her regain her balance.

Sabrina felt his strength and his solid muscle mass under his garments. She felt her face flush.

"Sabrina, it will be fine. Nothing is going to happen to you while I am at your side. As far as that rude guy, I have previously had altercations with him. It has been years ago, but he has been terrorizing this rink for years. Martin and I have already stood up to him. If I need to, I will do it again."

Sabrina looked at him in amazement. *He is not really afraid of anyone. I could just see him in action.*

"Sabrina, this is not too bad, is it?"

"Jacob, with you at my side, of course not—but I do not believe I am going to make this a profession."

They both laughed.

"It is time to go, Sabrina. I hate to pull you away from the skating."

"That is fine, Jacob. I just need to sacrifice for you. Just this once."

"Thank you, Sabrina. I knew I could count on you." Hand in hand, they walked off the rink, replaced the skates with their shoes, and walked outside.

The wind had quieted down, but there was a chill in the air. The afternoon was beginning to part. As they walked down the bench-lined street, they saw several people on a bench.

As they got closer, Sabrina noticed an impeccably dressed elderly lady. She wore a hat with a veil so it was difficult to make out her face. The woman called out to Sabrina in Russian. "Come here. Come here, my *malenkaya*."

How could she possibly call me that?

Jacob stopped and looked at the woman.

"Come here," the old woman said.

A woman sitting beside her said, "Do not mind her. She calls out to everyone. My mother used to live in Russia. She was a distant relative to the tsar and visited the court several times."

Sabrina froze. She could not move. She felt an explosion of anxiety within her. "Jacob, let us go. I am getting cold and tired, and I want to be home before nightfall."

"Sabrina, I am interested in what she has to say. We cannot be disrespectful. It will only take a moment."

"Jacob, don't you care that I am cold?"

"Sabrina, here is my coat." He approached the old lady.

The old lady looked at Sabrina. "Don't you recognize me?"

"No. Should I?"

"You look so much like a little girl I once knew. Here." She lifted her veil.

Could it be? Yes. It was her distant cousin. She wanted to run over, give her hug, and ask a thousand questions. "No. I am sorry madam, but I never met you before."

"My grandmother is getting old and can barely see, but she still insists on trying to identify people from the old country."

"Jacob, we ought to be going. Here is your coat. Good day, madam."

The old woman said, "If you please, could you give me the honor of an introduction?"

Sabrina was extremely hesitant, but Jacob wanted to comply with the old woman's request. "Certainly, this is Sabrina Sholin from Brooklyn. I am Jacob Meyer from Brooklyn."

"Excuse us, madam, but I am cold and am expected at home. I do not want to worry my mother. Good day." She turned and walked away.

Jacob said good-bye to the older woman and her granddaughter. "Sabrina, we were so rude. What was your rush?"

"I just was not very comfortable. There was something about her that made me unsettled. Jacob, I would have preferred for you to take my lead."

"I did not realize that you were so uncomfortable. I am sorry."

"Let us hurry," Sabrina said.

They sat in silence for most of the train ride home. Sabrina was concerned that her identity might have been compromised by Jacob's kindness.

"Sabrina, you appear so pale and frightened."

"Jacob, I am just tired. It has been a long day."

"Are you still annoyed by my stopping to speak to the old lady?"

"No, Jacob, that is my issue—not yours. I will need to work it through, but I need to on my own."

"Sabrina, thank you for insisting on going to the beach. It was absolutely breathtaking."

"You are welcome, Jacob. It was lovely."

When they arrived at Sabrina's home, she whispered, "Jacob, I am very tired or else I would ask you in. Thank you for a lovely day." She reached over and gave him a kiss on his forehead.

When Sabrina entered the house, her parents and brothers were in the kitchen. When she entered the kitchen, Mother said, "Sabrina, you look as though you saw a ghost. What happened?"

Sabrina told her family what had happened and her desire to walk away, and there was a knock on the door.

"Who could that be? Sabrina, you stay here. Let me go to the door." Mother walked over and peered out through the curtains. She saw an elderly woman, a young woman, and two men dressed in black suits. She motioned to Sabrina to go upstairs and then walked over to her husband and quickly explained the situation.

"You stall them. I need to make a call," Mr. Sholin said.

Sabrina's mother walked back to the door and opened it. "Hello?"

One of the men said, "Is this the residence of Sabrina Sholin?"

"Why do you ask?"

"We have reason to believe that your daughter has another identity."

"Excuse me?"

"Yes, this woman here feels that she knows that woman and has insisted that she is Grand Duchess Anastasia."

"Let us not have this discussion out here. Please come in and wait in the parlor. I will get my daughter so we can straighten this out. May I ask who you are?"

When they entered the vestibule, one of the men took out his wallet, opened it, and showed Mrs. Sholin a card. "We are from immigration, and we investigate claims of illegals."

"There is nothing about my daughter being an illegal immigrant. We all came over to this country together, and I can assure you that all of our paperwork is in order."

The man said, "Where is your daughter?"

"Oh, she is just upstairs. I will send my son to get her. Samuel, please go get your sister and tell Sabrina there are some people in the parlor who would like to meet her."

"May I ask this other gentleman for some identification?"

"Yes you may." He reached for his wallet. "I do not have my wallet. I guess I left it at home."

"Please be seated." The older lady sat on the arm of the chair. Her granddaughter quickly repositioned her.

Mother said, "I guess she has trouble with her vision?"

"Yes, she does," the granddaughter said.

"Samuel, where is Sabrina?"

"She is taking a shower."

"You will have to excuse me, gentlemen. My daughter just arrived home from being out all day and is taking a shower. If you would like to meet her, it will be a long while—or you can come back another day."

The man said, "We are in no rush. We will wait."

Mr. Sholin walked into the room. "I am Sabrina's father. Can I help you?"

"There is no need to. We are just waiting to speak to Sabrina."

"I overheard from the other room that you had some question about immigration?"

"Yes, we are from immigration."

"Then I am sure you will not mind what I have done since I find your intrusion into my home a little unorthodox."

The old woman looked at Mr. Sholin.

"We are in America now, and we have the right to our privacy. Someone does not have the right to make false accusations, especially when they cannot see very well. It is strange to me that a visually impaired lady has the right to implicate an innocent girl who is on a date with her boyfriend and bring people from immigration to the house."

"Sir, you do not understand. We are just making an inquiry."

"That is not what you said before. Ah, here they are. You will excuse me. There is someone at the door." Mr. Sholin walked slowly over to the door.

Sabrina said, "Saul, what is going on downstairs? Go halfway down the stairs to listen and report back to me."

"Hello, sir. You called?" a man in uniform asked.

"Yes, these men say that they are from immigration."

The man in uniform looked at the men. "I do not recognize you. May I see some identification?"

"They said they forgot their wallets, " Mrs. Sholin said.

"Then what is that bulge in his inside pockets?"

The men reached inside their coats.

"I would not do that." The man in uniform put his hand inside his jacket. He walked over to the man and reached inside his pocket and pulled out a black wallet. "Is this the wallet you left at home? Mr. Sholin, open the front door and let my men into the house. Mr. and Mrs. Sholin, you did the right thing to call us. Will you please excuse us now?"

Two police officers entered the house. "Men, cuff these two—and take them away. Now ladies, what is your involvement with these men? Do you realize they were impersonating immigration officers, which is against the law?"

The old woman stood. "I was just trying to get some answers."

The man looked at the old woman and said, "I can tell you without any doubt that you have made a grave mistake. You are in the home of Mr. and Mrs. Sholin. They have five children. I know these people, and I can assure you of their identity. I was personally present when they arrived. Who do you think this Sabrina is? Who is your cousin?"

"My cousin?" the old woman asked. "She was a grand duchess in Russia."

"Madam, I can assure you—and this is no disrespect to the Sholins—that Sabrina is no grand duchess. I realize you would like to believe she is, but that will not bring her back. I am sorry for your loss. In addition, I strongly suggest that if you have any questions about anyone who has emigrated here from Russia that you believe is a member of the imperial family that you contact me directly. I would want to know so I could contact my superiors immediately. Placing your confidence in imposters is the wrong way of going about it. Do you understand?"

"Yes sir," the old woman said.

"Any further interference with the law will result in your deportation. Now be on your way—and remember, if you need to contact me in the future, here is my card."

The old woman and her granddaughter left the house.

The other two men left in one of the police cars.

"You will need to let Sabrina know that she must be careful. I do appreciate your call."

"Who were those men?" Mr. Sholin asked.

"They were members of the Bolshevik Party. They will not bother you or your family anymore."

"Thank you, sir."

The two men would not be bothering anyone anymore. They vanished into the night. In addition, several other men were also detained that evening and brought into custody. The rumor was that they were deported.

CHAPTER SEVENTEEN

The Spoils of War

"Sabrina, I cannot believe it. You are ready on time. Congratulations."

"I love your sarcasm, Jacob."

"Where are we going?"

"Sabrina, do you think you will ever trust my judgment again? You are always asking me where we are going. I thought we would go to my house. I want to speak to my father, and I have not had a chance this morning because he left for work."

"That would be nice. I have not seen him for several weeks," Sabrina said. "I am looking forward to going."

It was a windy day. The sand and dirt were swept up by the wind.

"My eye," Sabrina said.

"What is the matter, Sabrina?"

"Something went into my eye," Sabrina replied.

"Come with me, Sabrina," Jacob walked over to an alleyway where there was more shelter. "Here, let me look. Oh, yes, I can see a cinder in there."

Her eye began to tear.

"Great, Sabrina. Your tears flushed it out. Your eye should feel better in a few moments. I think we should take a trolley."

"Good idea," Sabrina replied.

As they were seated on the trolley, it started to rain. There was a torrential downpour that flooded the streets.

"Sabrina, it is a good thing we found shelter on the trolley," Jacob said.

"Well I could always use a shower. It did not look like rain. I have no umbrella."

"We will be near a café when we reach my house. We can have some coffee and wait until it lets up," Jacob suggested.

The rain miraculously stopped when they arrived at their destination.

Jacob stepped off the trolley and reached out for Sabrina.

She lost her balance and fell forward into Jacob's arms.

Sabrina was stunned, but she was thankful for Jacob's quick reaction to her clumsiness. She gazed into his eyes. "My hero," she said as she regained her balance and composure. She kissed him on the cheek.

The conductor looked on and smiled.

They walked hand in hand to his house.

"Good," Jacob said. "My father is home, and we will be able to speak."

"Welcome, children," Mr. Meyer said as Jacob opened the door.

"Dad, I need to speak to you," Jacob said.

His father looked at Jacob and said, "What is your hurry? We will have plenty of time. I am not going anywhere. Why don't both of you go into the parlor and put on the radio. I will make some tea."

"Thank you, Mr. Meyer. That will be nice," Sabrina said.

"I am so tired," Jacob said. "It was a long day at work. The shipment was delivered, and I had to unpack it. I think I will just take off my shoes and lean back on the chair."

"The music is lovely," Sabrina said.

Jacob fell into a deep sleep.

Battle of Belleau Wood, June 1918

"Men, it is time."

"Yes, Lieutenant," they responded.

"Proceed at the signal," he ordered.

"Yes, sir."

"Are everyone's gas masks in place?"

"Yes, sir."

"There is a lot of mud on these fields. Remember to keep your heads down."

Gunfire was pervasive throughout the area. The smell of gunpowder saturated the air. The field was covered with men, many of whom had already met their fate. The reddish-brown mud was stained with the blood of unfortunate soldiers.

Men were moaning and orders were being yelled. There were troops and several regiments that had already been deployed.

What is the purpose of all of this? Jacob thought. *All in the name of power. Why did the Kaiser think he would prevail—and at what price for humanity? Hundreds of thousands of men have been lost. We need to put an end to this.* "Men, we will prevail," he shouted above the gunfire. "Let us go."

His men forged forward. Many were starting to fall.

An explosion.

"Oh no," he yelled. "Oh no!"

❧

"Jacob!" Sabrina yelled out. "Wake up. Wake up."

"Stop! Stop!" Jacob called out. *I am coming ... you can count on me. Don't despair.*

"Jacob! Jacob!" Sabrina shouted.

"Sabrina, is everything all right?" Mr. Meyer yelled.

"Mr. Meyer, Jacob is having a nightmare."

"Sabrina, he has been having the same dream for months. Try to speak to him. Maybe he will speak to you. I have tried, but he will not share anything with me. He is very troubled. He needs you. See what you can do." Jacob's father left the parlor and returned to the kitchen.

"Jacob!" She shook him.

Jacob slowly opened his eyes. He was bewildered and in a daze.

"Jacob, I was frightened. I have been calling to you for five minutes."

Jacob looked into Sabrina's eyes, "I am sorry for scaring you." His eyes began to tear.

"Are you all right, Jacob? We have all had things happen to us that have been very disturbing. I am glad that I was here to share it with you."

Jacob looked at her with bewilderment.

She walked over to him and placed his head on her stomach, cradling his head with her arms.

Jacob began to sob. "It was horrible. You cannot believe all the blood that was shed. My men—I trained with them, broke bread with them, and shared our life experiences and dreams. I had a responsibility to them. I let them down."

Sabrina took his hand and gently moved her fingers through his hair. "Yes, Jacob."

"I could have done more. I let them down. If I had not gotten shot, I could have saved more of them. The captain was right in front of me. Why couldn't I have saved him?"

"Could have what, Jacob?'

"There was nothing I could do. He is gone, and he left a family. War, war, war—it is not fair. Not fair, I tell you! The deafening sound of the gunfire—I cannot take it anymore." Jacob placed his hands over his ears. "Stop! Stop! Stop!"

"Jacob," Sabrina whispered. "You are safe. You are with me here in Brooklyn. You will be all right."

Jacob looked at her. Tears were streaming down his face.

Sabrina looked into his eyes and placed her hand on his. "Jacob, we are here in Brooklyn together, right?"

He stared back at her and nodded.

Mr. Meyer was standing in the hallway and observing what was happening. He was crying. He held a cup of tea.

Sabrina walked back several steps. "Jacob it will be all right." She reached out to Mr. Meyer for the cup of tea.

He handed it to her and then returned to the hallway. "Jacob, have some tea. It will make you feel better."

Mr. Meyer was astonished that Sabrina was able to deal with the situation. Her understanding and perseverance captivated Mr. Meyer. She was a strong woman, and he was proud of her courage and emotional strength.

"Jacob, please look at me." Jacob turned his head toward Sabrina. "That's right. Look at me. How is the tea?"

"It is good," Jacob said, staring into Sabrina's eyes.

"Sabrina, thank you. I am feeling better. I must have had a spell."

"You just had a dream and a flashback. You will be fine. It is understandable what you are going through. You suffered a major trauma that was further complicated by your injury. Just as the scar appears on your shoulder to remind you of the gunshot wound, there is also one on your heart for those who lost their lives in the line of duty. In time, the scars will fade, but there will always be some mark that will remind you of what happened. Each day, you will become a little stronger. Someday you will have the strength to overcome this trauma, but there will always be some trace in your consciousness to remind you of the tragedy. I have faith in you and know you will overcome the obstacles. Jacob, repeat after me, 'I will get stronger. I will overcome. I will persevere.'"

"I will get stronger. I will overcome. I will persevere."

"There, Jacob, you said it—and it will come to pass," Sabrina whispered.

Jacob nodded.

Sabrina reached over and gave him a kiss.

"Thank you, Sabrina. I love you. I am very tired." He fell fast asleep.

"Sabrina?" Mr. Meyer said. "Thank you."

"Mr. Meyer, there is no need to thank me. I love your son, and I believe in him. He will resolve these horrible issues. It is not unusual for men to experience these things when they return from battle. My father used to tell me stories of soldiers all the time."

"Sabrina, I did not realize that your father was in the military."

"Oh, did I say my father. It must have been one of the men on the ship when we sailed from Europe. I guess I am tired myself and am not thinking too clearly. Jacob will probably sleep through the night. I ought to be going. If you need me tonight, please feel free to call me."

"Sabrina, let me accompany you home."

"It will not be necessary. You need to be here tonight if Jacob wakes up."

"Then I will not take no for an answer. Let me at least walk you to the trolley. I will call your home, and your brother can meet you. I will explain to them what happened."

"No. There is no need to share with anyone what happened. Just tell them that Jacob was very tired and fell asleep, and I thought it was best to come home. Emphasize that I did not wish to wake him. I will call tomorrow to see how he is doing."

Sabrina and Jacob's father walked to the trolley stop.

Mr. Meyer said, "Sabrina, you did an exceptional job tonight, and I appreciate it. I do not know what I would have done if you were not here. This was not the first time this happened, and it appears that with each occurrence, the episodes are worse."

"Mr. Meyer, Jacob will be all right. It may take some time, but he will be fine. Time has a way of healing—no matter how deep the wounds are."

CHAPTER EIGHTEEN

The Wedding

S abrina wrote in her diary:

> *A time to share, a time to care, a time to desire, a time
> to be scared, a time to overcome, a time to persevere.
> This is another close call. Am I just desperately destined
> for disaster? When will I overcome these odds and be
> the person I need to be?*

She awoke to sunshine and the telephone ringing.

"Sabrina?" Mother called upstairs. "It is Jacob. Do you want to speak to him or should I have him call you back?"

"I will be right down."

"Sabrina, hello. I was not sure if you would ever speak to me again."

"I told you I was just as tired as you."

"Let me make it up to you. Lunch?"

"That will be great. I will meet you at the market."

"About twelve-thirty?" Jacob asked.

"Good, until later," Sabrina replied.

"Mom, I am going to the market to meet Jacob for lunch. Do you need me to do some shopping?"

"That would be nice, Sabrina. I will make a list."

Sabrina could not wait to see Jacob. She rode the trolley and walked through some shops on her way to the market. She arrived just in time.

"Sabrina, you look wonderful. You still have some color on your face from yesterday." Jacob moved his hand from behind his back and handed Sabrina a rose. "Something beautiful to someone who is just as beautiful."

"Thank you, Jacob. You are so thoughtful."

Jacob picked up a large brown bag.

"What is that?" Sabrina asked.

"That is our lunch. I made us some sandwiches. I thought we would walk down to the water's edge for a picnic."

"Jacob, that sounds wonderful."

They walked several blocks until they reached a stone wall that overlooked the harbor.

Jacob placed a blanket down and said, "Let's sit here so we can look out over the water." He motioned to Sabrina to sit and took two sandwiches, several pickles, and two sodas out of the bag.

"Jacob, these are wonderful. I should bring you home."

"I would like that." Jacob smiled. "So what did you do last night, Sabrina?"

"Oh, I just spoke to my parents, had a light bite, and then retired very early. All of that skating the other day wore me out. I enjoyed every minute with you, Jacob. I am sorry I got so upset about the old lady. I like speaking to people, but she scared me. There was just something ominous and forward about her."

"Sabrina, it is over, and we are now in this wonderful moment together. I love looking at you and the backdrop. It is like a painting … a masterpiece."

Jacob's shirt had several buttons that were unfastened. His chest hairs were protruding from the shirt. Sabrina stared at his shirt. Jacob looked down.

"I guess I was in a rush, and I fastened two of the buttons." Jacob had one of his legs folded beneath him, and the other was resting upon the wall.

Sabrina placed her hand on his thigh. "You are right, Jacob. This is a wonderful moment."

Jacob felt a warm surge inside his body. The warmth of her hand on his thigh was extremely exciting. He was becoming embarrassed. He moved his leg down and placed a napkin over his lap. "I almost forgot the napkins. You will think I have no manners."

"Thank you, Jacob," Sabrina said, turning her attention to a ship in the harbor.

"It is almost time to go. We need to pack up. What will you be doing this afternoon?"

"Since I am by the market, I plan on shopping for my mother."

Jacob could not wait to return to the market and put on his apron. He did not know how he was going to stand up and not be embarrassed by the bulge protruding from his pants. Jacob needed to divert his attention to calm things down. "Sabrina, look at the barge." He grabbed her hand and they walked to the market. When they arrived, Jacob quickly put on his apron.

"Thank you for lunch, Jacob." Sabrina gave him a big hug and understood why he was in such a rush to put on his apron. She felt a bulge through his apron and her own garments. *What a well-built powerful man he must be.* "See you later."

Sabrina was happy and finally at peace. She had not felt that way about a man since Martin. She had come to terms with her feelings about Martin and was ready to forge forward. It was apparent that Jacob cared about her as well. She could not wait until she could see and speak to him again.

"Sabrina, is that you?"

"Yes, Mother."

"Do you need a hand? Here, Sabrina, let me take some of those packages. You look like you are beaming. Good to see how happy you are. It has been a long time. Oh, I forgot. Jacob called. He wishes to see you after work. He said seven o'clock—unless he hears from you. Otherwise, he will see you after he goes home and showers."

Jacob arrived at seven.

"Jacob, have you eaten?" Mrs. Sholin asked.

"No, Mrs. Sholin."

"Pull up a chair. We were just going to eat. There is plenty."

"Thank you, Mrs. Sholin, but I wanted to take Sabrina out."

"No, Jacob. Why should you spend money? There is enough to eat here. Sabrina went food shopping today. Come, come in. Join us. I will not take no for an answer."

The whole family was in the kitchen and welcomed Jacob.

Sabrina entered the kitchen, "Jacob, I guess my mother won you over."

Jacob looked at Sabrina. His face was flushed. He dropped to the floor. Everyone's eyes were on Jacob.

Sabrina asked, "Jacob, what are you doing?"

"I wanted to do this at the café, but I guess this will be as good a place." He faced her with one knee on the ground. "No, Sabrina, I am not trying to tie your skates. Ever since I met you, my life has not been the same. You are beautiful, and you bring something to our relationship that makes me want to sing. I have never felt this way before, and I want you to be my wife."

There was dead silence. He reached into his pocket and smiled. "It is not this one." He reached into his other pocket, lifted a ring, and placed it on Sabrina's finger. "Sabrina, I am like your mother and will not take no for an answer."

Sabrina started crying. "I am glad you will not take no for an answer. Mother, we have a wedding to plan."

The family rejoiced at dinner. Samuel hugged Jacob and brought out some wine. Saul and Sidney punched Jacob on shoulder and said, "You will make a fine brother."

Anna looked at Jacob and said, "You should be as happy as I am. I just felt the baby kick. Here. Can you feel that? Someday, the Lord willing, you will too."

Sabrina's father lifted his glass. "Congratulations—and Anna, from your mouth to the Lord's ears."

Sabrina smiled.

The next several weeks were busy. The wedding planning for Jacob's aunt would be somewhat difficult because of the loss of her son.

The wedding list was mounting in number. The Sholins seemed to know everyone in the community. The guest list approached 350. After conferring with Rabbi Jacob, the wedding date was set for January 1919.

Not truly understanding the traditions, Sabrina had to rely on Mother. However, when Mother indicated that she would have to go to the *mikveh*, Sabrina expressed concern.

"Sabrina, it is something that woman do prior to their marriage. It is a cleansing."

"But, Mother, I already go every month after menstruation."

"Yes, my dear, but this is a special time," Mother replied.

"Mom, this is becoming more intriguing as our conversation continues."

"Well, Sabrina, perhaps I should have said something sooner."

"Mother, enough is enough."

"Sabrina, you are Jewish."

"Yes, how can I forget? This ought to be another unforgettable day."

"We will talk more as the day approaches."

"Jacob, you are finally here. I need to get out of here. My mother is driving me crazy."

"Sabrina, did you say driving you?"

"Very funny, Jacob."

"I thought we could go to the park. Dress warm because it is cold outside."

"The park sounds great. Anything to get out of this house!"

It was cold as Jacob and Sabrina strolled down the street to the park. There was a breeze, and from time to time, there was a snow flurry. There was a slight layer of snow on the ground, but the park was a beautiful sight. There were children ice-skating on a small pond, and several people sat on the park benches. As they approached one, they saw an older woman and a younger girl.

Oh no, Jacob thought, *it isn't?*

It was not.

Jacob pointed there is an empty bench. They sat down.

"Look, Jacob. A squirrel is running up the tree. There in the tree is a hole. He is so cute." She put her hand under his coat and on his leg. "You are so warm, Jacob."

"It is your influence, Sabrina." He felt himself becoming aroused.

Sabrina's hand brushed against his leg. "Oh," she yelled, pulling her hand out from beneath his coat. "Excuse me, Jacob."

"That is all right. Things to come," he said with a smile.

"Jacob, you are embarrassing me."

"Embarrassing you? How do you think I feel? Every time you are near me—"

"Perhaps I should stay away."

"Not on your life, Sabrina. I welcome the opportunity. It makes me feel alive and full of energy. I just can't wait until I can fully express it."

"Jacob, aren't you interested in how I feel?"

"Of course I am, Sabrina."

"Good, you will need to wait to find out."

"Sabrina, you are never lost for words."

"Look at the children. They are so cute. I love children. I remember taking care of my brother."

Jacob looked at her. "You mean brothers, don't you?"

"Of course, Jacob. I was not really very good at taking care of them all at the same time. I did better one at a time. Someday I hope to have your children, Jacob."

"That will be nice. I love children too."

"It is cold out here. Without foliage, the trees cannot protect us from the frigid air of winter. We ought to be going," Jacob said.

The pandemic was easing, and people did not mind going into crowds. The rabbi felt that the worst would be over by January. Most of the responses to the invitations were yes.

Mother decided not to mention the wedding in the newspaper. She did not want to draw any additional attention to Sabrina. Precautions would always be taken.

The week prior to the wedding, Mrs. Sholin accompanied Sabrina to the *mikveh*.

Sabrina was not looking forward to the experience. As ritual dictated, Sabrina would need to disrobe and submerge herself in a pool of running water. A prayer would be said, and she would be pure for her husband-to-be.

After the ritual, which Sabrina thought was very much like christening a child, she returned to her dressing room. Mother waited in the outside hallway. While Sabrina was dressing, she heard several voices in the next room. There was a small aperture in the wall, and she decided to look through it. Two older women were completely undressed. They were facing one another. They slowly approached one another, and Sabrina turned away. The situation repulsed Sabrina. She quickly finished dressing and reunited with Mother.

"That was not too bad, was it?"

"No, Mother, but—"

"I am not very fond of the process myself," Mother confessed.

Sabrina thought, *I could understand that.*

On the Saturday of the wedding, Jacob and his father were given honors at the synagogue. They were called up to the ark to read from the Holy Torah. Jacob was very happy, and his father was proud of his son. He never thought that he would have recovered from the emotional scarring of the war. Sabrina was just the right woman for him. She would know how to handle his minor setbacks, and Jacob would be a splendid match for her.

The congregation and the community were thrilled about the union. They felt that Jacob and Sabrina had experienced tremendous misfortune and deserved to have pleasure in their lives.

A light snow fell that morning, and they needed to wear boots to the ceremony. Sabrina was gorgeous. Her wedding gown was made of Irish lace and the finest silk. Her hair was set in a braided bun and adorned with pearls that matched the inlay of her gown. Sabrina was nervous, and Mother and Father were able to feel her body trembling as they accompanied her down the aisle.

Jacob stood in his black hat and suit with his father next to him. He was so proud and pleased. He was looking forward to this new adventure in his life with his wife at his side.

As Sabrina walked slowly, she looked up and her eyes met his. In spite of all the people in attendance, at that moment, it was just the two of them.

The rabbi officiated, and the prayers were said. The bride and groom encircled one another seven times, exchanged their vows, drank wine, placed the gold rings on each other's fingers, and with one forceful forward movement, they crushed a glass wrapped in a white linen cloth under Jacob's shoe. The ceremony was over. All in attendance would now meet the new Mr. and Mrs. Jacob Meyer.

But first, Sabrina and Jacob would be escorted to a room where they would spend time together to consummate the marriage. Jacob and Sabrina entered the small room. Jacob gently closed the door behind them.

The room was dimly lit by candlelight. On a table on one side of the room, there was a bottle of wine, two glasses, a round piece of bread, and several small cakes. White linen napkins were scattered on the table. Across from the table, a large couch was covered with a white sheet, several pillows, and a blanket. There were also two chairs in the room. In the corner, there was a closet and several hangers. Another door led to a private bathroom.

Sabrina looked at Jacob. She was frightened and did not know what to say.

Jacob turned to her. "You are so beautiful, especially by candlelight." He walked over and hugged her. He felt her body trembling. "It will be all right." He gave her a kiss.

She felt his large hands and muscular arms around her. Sabrina felt a warm surge traveling through her body. She placed her arms around his shoulders and looked into his eyes. "I love you, Jacob. You make me feel so safe and secure. Please promise that you will never leave me."

"Sabrina, I am not going anywhere. My place is with you now and forever."

She stood on her toes and passionately kissed him.

He felt his body react. He reached behind her and started to unbutton her dress. "Sabrina, how many buttons are there? I already counted thirty."

She laughed and said, "Keep going. I believe there are fifty."

Jacob replied, "Was there a run on buttons? It is a good thing our trousers aren't fastened this way. We would never make it to the bathroom."

They both laughed.

"Jacob, now that you have finished, let me hang it up."

He walked over to the closet.

She turned and kissed him. Sabrina began to unbutton his shirt.

Jacob removed his cufflinks and unfastened his trousers.

She took off her corset and bra. She stood before him. Her breasts were firm and well formed.

Jacob was extremely aroused. He kissed her and carried her tenderly to the couch. He removed his undergarments and stood before her.

She looked at him and was curious about what she saw. The only nude male she had been so close to was her brother when she was younger. He used to run around the palace, frolicking to the delight of his sisters. He appeared so different. His penis was not cut. Jacob was well developed. His penis was circumcised, and the head was emerging.

She reached out and caressed him with cupped hands.

Jacob kissed her breasts and massaged her nipples with his tongue.

Sabrina rubbed her hands across Jacob's brawny chest.

Jacob continued down Sabrina's ivory white body. His warm tongue caressed her clitoris.

She moaned with delight. Faster and faster, his tongue moved. Sabrina felt her body quiver and then several spontaneous contractions. She was losing control and was in pure rapture. She yelled, "More. More!"

Jacob took his hand and felt her. She was moist, hot, and ready. He entered her slowly and gently.

She cried out.

"Did I hurt you?" he asked.

"That is all right." She felt him deep inside of her. Sabrina felt his massive, warm body on top of her. She kissed him. Their bodies became one. They were moving in unison, and with each thrust, she felt an intense pleasure building within. And then she felt herself repeatedly contracting and a flow of molten fluid shooting inside of her. She wanted it to go on forever, but it was soon over.

They were in perfect harmony and sexual bliss. Jacob kissed Sabrina and then placed his head between her breasts. They both fell asleep.

They were awakened by loud music.

"Jacob, we need to go to the wedding."

"I would rather stay here with you."

She looked down. Jacob was becoming aroused. "I know, but they are expecting us."

"All right, Sabrina. Anyway, it will take a half hour to button you up. I will be right back. I have to go to the bathroom."

"Look, Jacob, there is blood on the sheet. I am so embarrassed."

"Don't be. It is supposed to be that way when you are a virgin."

"What do you mean?"

"Sabrina, hasn't anyone ever told you? You have a piece of skin called a hymen. When a man enters you for the first time, it breaks, which produces blood."

Sabrina ran to the bathroom.

"Sabrina, I really need to go."

"I will not be long."

Within half an hour, they rejoined the celebration. They were escorted to chairs. Each chair was raised, and the guests danced the traditional hora.

Nine months later, their first child was born.

❧

"David," Grandma said, "that was your mother."

CHAPTER NINETEEN

The Ivory Brush

Long Island, 1974

It was an unusually warm day for October. Colorful trees adorned either side of the parkway. There was not a cloud in the sky, and David was looking forward to the visit with his grandmother.

Over the past several months, she had welcomed him and shared her stories of the past. His grandmother's eyes lit up when she saw him. She was determined to impart her tale until its conclusion.

David wished his mother could be a part of this experience, but she had passed years earlier. His grandmother had not been the same since her untimely death.

Jacob had passed this past March, and Grandmother's condition had been deteriorating since then. David lived alone and had been attending a nearby university. He would be receiving his master's degree in May.

As he pulled into his uncle's driveway, he felt a sudden discomfort. He walked over to the front door and rang the doorbell. His aunt answered the door.

"I am glad it is you. Your grandmother has been asking for you all morning. She is driving me crazy."

David looked up at his aunt. "Is everything all right?"

"Yes, yes. It is just that I have so much to do."

Yes, she is so busy with clothes shopping, going to the beauty parlor, and going out for lunch with her friends. I do not know why she makes my grandmother feel she is an imposition on her. If it were not for my uncle—who wants her to be here—I would take my grandmother to my apartment. My uncle believes anything his wife tells him. He wasn't even present for his own father's death. His wife took him out shopping for a new couch. "Yes, Aunt Delores. I can see you have a lot to do. I will be spending several hours with Grandma. Why don't you go out? Just let me know what medication she needs."

"If it is not a problem for you. I was going to wait until the visiting nurse arrives later this afternoon, but if you feel you can handle the situation, I guess it will be all right."

"I am certain."

"I do not know what you talk to her about. She hardly says anything to me."

Why would anyone want to talk to you? I have never met anyone as self-serving as you. I did not realize the type of person you were until I visited my grandmother.

"She is upstairs. I know you can find your way. I will be leaving soon."

"Aunt Delores, what about the medication I asked you about?"

"That's right. At noon, give her one of each of these." She pointed to the medicine bottles.

"When will you be back? I have class at four o'clock."

"I shall return, David. I shall return." And with that, she left.

"Grandma, how are you today?"

"Much better now that your aunt has left. Let us not waste any time speaking about her. She is not worth it."

"Yes, Grandma. I know."

"It does not take much to figure her out. Not too smart, you know."

"Yes, Grandma."

"David, you are very kind to visit me. Your mother and I were very close. She rarely let a day go by without calling me. When she died, a part of me went with her. And then your grandfather—he was my life. You are so much like him. Grandpa Jacob never knew about me. I could never tell him. I was always afraid that his life would be in danger as long as I was still living. Now it does not matter. I am an old lady, and I do not have much time left. Telling you my story makes me feel like I am sharing it with Jacob. I know he is spiritually connected to me David, and he is here with us right now. David, do you ever feel your mother is with you?"

"Grandma, it is funny you should ask. I thought I was unusual and was afraid to say anything because people would tell me I was delusional."

"Those are shallow people who do not understand the spiritual dimension. Rasputin used to tell us that if we believe, we will feel—and not to be afraid of what we feel. Many things have been written about him and his mystique. Most are rubbish and conjecture. Just like all that has been written about me. I was so fortunate when Anna Anderson came forward. It took the pressure off of me. I felt safer that the focus was on her. People need to be out of their minds to trust the Russians and their research. They have not been known to be the most honorable of people, especially if they have underlying agendas. The truth is what lives on.

"Jacob and I had a good life. We had two children, four grandchildren, and one great-grandchild. I have been blessed to be a great-grandmother. I know how my great-grandmother must have felt. I am thankful for her because, without her foresight, you and I would not be having this conversation today.

"Life is unpredictable. It takes us on adventures. Some are exciting, and some end in tragedy. Together, they make up life's journey. You will someday meet someone and have a family. David, you do not have to rush it. Just let it come to you. You have been blessed with a rich heritage. Hold it close to your heart."

"I have something for you. Did you wear a jacket today?"

"Yes, Grandma."

"Where is it?"

"Over there." David pointed to the chair.

"Please bring it to me."

"I am home. Are you still here, David?" Aunt Delores yelled from downstairs.

"Yes, Aunt Delores."

"How is she doing?"

"Good!"

"That's right. Put your coat here on the bed. Go to the top drawer. There in the corner under my nightgown—feel for it as you did so many years ago. Do you have it?" Grandma asked.

"I think so, Grandma. Is it the brush?"

"Yes, yes. Take it out. Ah, the ivory brush. Put it in your pocket. It is something I want you to have."

"But, Grandma, don't you need the brush?"

"David, does it look like I will be going out anytime soon—and I have another."

"What are you two doing?" Aunt Delores barged into the bedroom with two shopping bags.

"Nothing," Sabrina said.

"David, what did she give you?"

"Leave him alone, Dolores."

"David, I asked you a question. Now answer me." She walked over to the bed, placed her hand in the jacket pocket, and took out the brush.

"So much for privacy in this house," Sabrina said.

His aunt looked at the old, worn brush.

"Did you think it was the family jewels?" Sabrina asked.

"Sabrina, if you were going to give something to David, couldn't you find something a little more meaningful than his tattered old brush?"

"Aunt Dolores, the brush is beautiful, and it's a perfect gift for me." He looked at his grandmother and winked.

"Sabrina, he is just going to throw it out anyway."

"Aunt Dolores, could you leave us alone for a little while longer please."

His aunt walked outside of the room and stood in hearing reach of the room.

"There is so much to be learned from the world in which we live. I grew up at a time when people still used horses and carriages for transportation. The car and the airplane were still in their infancy. There was no television, and telephones were newly upon the scene. Medicine was not developed, and many a man died in battle. There were few remedies to assist them with injuries or illnesses. More people died from the pandemic in 1918 than on the battlefield. Many children did not live through infancy.

"I lost a grandmother, an aunt, several cousins, and a great-grandfather to disease or illness. Today we think we have come a long way, but the perils that existed in my early years—in spite of all our advances—still remain. Famine, poverty, disease, and war still plague this world.

"The most deadly is man's greed and lust for power. History has not taught us very much, and man continues on his desperate path for power. Perhaps in your generation, a special person will decide not to conform to the status quo, march to the beat of what is in the best interest of humanity, and break out of this dark cloud that has surrounded us for so long."

David looked at his grandmother and realized she would have had a profound effect if her destiny had led her to position of power. If she had married her cousin Eddy, his untimely death would have resulted in her child becoming the heir to the throne of England. How history could have changed. "Grandma, you are a wise woman, and I love you."

"It has nothing to do with wisdom. It is a matter of common sense, experience, and respect for yourself and others. People need to find a spiritual connection with the world and become humble servants to humanity. If we give to others, it will come back to us multifold because a good deed to others brings positive energy to the world. Faith and spirituality brings us to a special place of peace and tranquility in knowing that our limited time on this planet has provided for others. If we practiced these beliefs, people would be able to benefit from the ultimate positive forces that surround them."

David felt a sudden calm traveling down his body. They were sharing a special moment that would endure forever. It was just a few minutes in a spectrum of infinite time. He reached down and gave his grandmother a hug.

"Thank you, David. That felt so good. There will be days when you will be able to feel the spiritual energy that you do today. Do not fear what you may see in the future. Some of us have a destiny. It is a blessing and a burden to endure. As I have shared with you before, Rasputin used to say, 'Embrace it—but do not let it control you.' We cannot change what has been destined even if we know it is yet to come. It is a power that is best kept unsaid and only used for good. There is no need to discuss it any further, but I know you have been selected—as well others from your line."

"Grandma, I will be leaving. I will call you tomorrow."

"Thank you for coming to visit me. Take care of yourself. I will see you around."

David gave his grandmother a hug and a kiss.

She looked up at him. "David?" she whispered. "What you are feeling right now is all right."

"I love you, Grandma."

"I love you, David."

That was the last time David would see or speak to his grandmother. She died that night.

The next morning, David looked out his bedroom window at the beautiful pond. There was a white swan. It looked elegant but alone.

From from the sky, another swan appeared and landed next to the first. They intertwined their long beautiful necks, separated, and flew off toward the horizon. They would no longer be alone. Their time had come, and they were off to their next adventure.